SNAKES AND SHADOWS

SNAKES AND SHADOWS

PENNY AND BOOTS™ BOOK ONE

AMY HOPKINS

MICHAEL ANDERLE

DISRUPTIVE IMAGINATION

LMBPN Publishing
PMB 196, 2540 South Maryland Pkwy
Las Vegas, NV 89109

First US edition, October 2019
eBook ISBN: 978-1-64202-533-0
Print ISBN: 978-1-64202-534-7

SNAKES AND SHADOWS TEAM

Thanks to our Beta Readers:
Mary Morris, Larry Omans, Kelly O'Donnell, Nicole
Emens, Erika Everest
Thanks to the JIT Readers

Dave Hicks
Jackey Hankard-Brodie
Jeff Goode
Jeff Eaton
Deb Mader
Misty Roa
Angel LaVey

If I've missed anyone, please let me know!

Editor
SkyHunter Editing Team

This one's for you, Michael. You told me to write what I know. You told me to write my soul. Well, here she is. I hope she's as funny, sharp and kind as you envisioned her. I know she's more than I expected her to be!

— Amy

To Family, Friends and
Those Who Love
to Read.
May We All Enjoy Grace
to Live the Life We Are
Called.

— Michael

CHAPTER ONE

B oots wasn't an ordinary snake. Mrs. Chu, however, didn't know that.

"You tell that scaly thing that if she ever turns up at my restaurant with a rodent, I'll—"

"I'll tell her, Mrs. Chu." Penny peered into the hotbox of the Chinese takeaway shop, but none of the plastic bags looked like hers. Boots dangled over Penny's shoulder, almost tumbling off as she tried to get closer to the hot glass. "Am I too early?"

"Your dinner is out back. Extra dumplings, ok? Keep your energy up. And two Cokes, I know you like that rubbish." Mrs. Chu vanished from the servery window and reappeared at the door to the kitchen. She stopped to give a regretful sigh and patted her own plump stomach. "You certainly aren't getting fat from it. You will one day, though!" Regret turned to glee, and she cackled happily.

Penny took the heavy plastic bag full of square containers, two cans of Coke balanced on top as promised.

"Thanks, Mrs. Chu." She turned to go but looked back when Mrs. Chu called her name.

Serious now, the old woman wagged her finger. "That man was here asking for you again. And your snake, too! You stay away from him. Men like that mean trouble."

Stifling a squirm of unease, Penny nodded. "Thanks for the heads up, Mrs. Chu. I'll keep an eye out."

Mrs. Chu meant well. The problem was, Penny didn't know quite what to do about it. She knew the stranger had asked about her at the Takeaway shop before, and the pub. She'd never seen the guy in person, and she had no idea what he could possibly want with her.

Mrs. Chu and Dave, the publican, had both agreed the mysterious stranger was tall, curly-haired, and dressed like a "city boy." He spoke like a Yank and was polite but formal. Dave swore the guy was a government spy.

Larrabee wasn't exactly a bustling town, but with a population of three thousand and growing, the days when everyone knew everyone were long since gone.

Still, what does he want with me? Penny wondered.

She yanked open the passenger door of her car and carefully put her dinner in so it wouldn't slide around. Once she was belted in behind the wheel, she started the car. Then she sat for a minute.

"Dammit." She was out of beer at home. The liquor store's lights twinkled invitingly, a beacon of happiness at the far end of the string of shops. "Screw it. It's hot as Hades out here. I need a drink."

"Stay here, Boots." She killed the engine and pulled herself out of the car, smiling when the tinkling bell above the liquor shop's door announced her presence. "Hey, Dave. Got a six-pack in there for me?"

Dave grinned and gave her a wave as he finished stacking some wine bottles into a display rack. "I'll grab one for you, mate."

"Thanks!" A few minutes and some idle pleasantries later, Penny was the proud owner of a six-pack of beer, although her purse was a few dollars lighter for it.

She stepped outside and squinted, blinded for a moment by the glaring sun.

As Penny turned to her car, she heard someone kicking up a stink.

"You legless bloody skink. I'll show 'em!"

The local drunk's slurred growl sent Penny's heart plummeting to her shoes. "I'll catch ya and stick ya in a box! Then they'll bloody see you're not normal!"

"Oh, shit." As her eyes adjusted, Penny evaluated her options: dash in and drop the beer, or take a moment to set it down carefully.

Deciding Boots could fend for herself for a moment if need be, Penny took the second option.

"Hey, Jerry. What's up?" she called, trying to buy herself a moment as she dropped her possessions safely on a nearby bench.

"It's that fuckin' snake! I told ya, I told all of ya! It's not right!" He pointed at the eight-foot-long rainbow serpent that had wrapped itself around Penny's side mirror. "All rainbow-like and smart. She's got it in for me, that snake."

"She's just a snake, Jerry," Penny soothed. "Nothing special about her. I see a bottle of Bundy in your hand, though, and it's looking pretty empty."

"I'm not drunk!" Outraged at the prospect, Jerry drew himself up. Or he tried to. He teetered and tripped toward the car, then flinched away from Boots hard enough to send him flying in the other direction when she coiled up, ready to strike.

"Jerry? You're *definitely* drunk." Penny approached, holding her hands out to try to calm him. She stepped carefully, knowing rum turned Jerry into an asshole, and that the town's insistence that he was a crazy old fart had given him a vendetta against Boots.

Penny didn't know what the deal was with the glittering multicolored serpent, but she had her theories.

Boots had appeared around the same time as sightings of supernatural beings had started to go crazy.

Videos online were getting millions of hits, although, from the comments left on them, it seemed only a small percentage of people could see what Penny could. Creatures from myth. Living, breathing legends.

That had been three months ago.

As far as Penny knew, she was the only person in Larrabee who could see Boots in her real form. The others in town would call her a tree snake, saying the "pretty green thing" made a lovely pet.

Jerry saw her real form too, but only when he was utterly shitfaced. Penny would have felt bad for him, but Jerry was a racist piece of shit who had harassed Mrs. Chu for years.

"I'm not inberiated...inibriabered... I'm not *drunk!*" Jerry's outrage had turned to desperation. He stumbled back to his feet and pointed at Boots again. "I can see it! A big-assed fucking rainbow sna— FUCK!"

Irritated with the pointing finger, Boots had done what any threatened snake would do. She bit.

Jerry screamed and jerked his hand back, but Boots had a solid grip on the digit. "*FUCK! GET IT OFF!*"

Penny jumped in just as Jerry slammed his fist at Boots' head. He missed, punching the door of the Land Rover instead.

Penny yelled, "Hey! That's my fucking *car!*"

Boots let go, then reared back and hissed, mouth wide to strike again.

"Don't you even think about it!" Penny snapped, turning a warning finger on Boots.

Jerry saw the gesture and lunged at her. His fat, sweaty hands clutched Penny's shirt. "You bitch! You know! You know it's something weird, don't you?"

"Oh, for fuck's sake," Penny muttered. She really didn't want to fight Jerry. In his current state, that wouldn't be fair at all.

She pushed his hands away, but he swung another punch, clipping her ear.

It stung. The bright pain wiped all of Penny's reluctance away, and she let her reflexes take over. Her fists had been itching to swing since the mention of her friendly neighborhood stalker.

Penny tightened her grip on Jerry's wrist. Instead of pushing it away, she pulled it toward her as she twisted . A little dip of her foot, some careful weight distribution, and Jerry was flat on his back, gasping for air.

"You all right, Pen?"

Penny looked over her shoulder to see Dave leaning on

the doorframe of the bottle shop. "Thanks for the help," she said, grimacing.

"You looked like you had it under control. How are you feeling, Jer?" Dave clomped over slowly and hauled the other man up by his elbow. "Remember what I told you? Any more trouble and I cut you off. That right there was trouble, my friend."

Jerry groaned. "It wasn't my fault!" he muttered. Having the wind knocked out of him seemed to have done the trick. He let Dave guide him inside, muttering about aliens that looked like snakes.

Dave already had his phone out to call the local constabulary. "I'll get Pete to drive him home. You take care now, Penny." In a town this size, driving the local drunks home was classed as exciting, so Pete likely wouldn't mind the task.

Penny nodded, feeling tired after the unexpected confrontation. "Thanks, Dave. Maybe next time he'll think twice before downing a bottle of rum before sunset."

The late afternoon sun beat on the dusty road, bathing the old white Land Rover in shades of pink and orange. Penny jerked the driver's side door open, grabbed a water bottle, and twisted off the top. "Come on, Boots. Let's get outta here before Jerry wakes up and decides to turn you into a handbag.

"Boots glared at the bottle, unmoving. Penny jiggled it. "Do you want me to leave you here?"

With an irritated hiss, Boots unfurled her long body and stretched her head up to the water. Penny tilted the bottle just far enough that it touched the lip. Boots touched her nose to it, and in a quick, sinuous motion, she slid into the tiny bottle, shrinking her body so she fit comfortably inside.

Penny nodded in satisfaction. "You didn't have to be so difficult about it, you know."

The rainbow serpent flicked out her tongue, then bared her long fangs before sliding into the warm car with a soft hiss.

"I know they usually think you're just a dumb pet, but a few beers and they suddenly get all open-minded and shit. Then *my* dinner goes cold while some drunk idiot tries to kick the shit out of both of us. Does that sound fair to you?"

Boots curled into a tight coil and hid her face beneath a loop of her long body. No matter what she looked like, Penny knew she was smarter than the average snake. In fact, she'd bet her meager life savings on the fact that Boots understood what she said, at least most of the time.

"Fine, don't speak to me. I'm not sharing my dinner if you sulk, though." Penny turned to exit the car but quickly felt something press against her knee. Moments later, the snake had twisted her way over to drape herself across Penny's lap. "Yeah, I thought so," she muttered, her hand reaching down to scratch the top of the snake's head.

When Penny pulled to a stop in her driveway, she placed a hand on the bag of Chinese food. "Still hot, at least." She pushed Boots off her lap and reached for the beer on the floor in front of the passenger seat.

Someone slapped the car roof above her head. Penny jumped and whirled around, half-expecting to see that Jerry had followed her home.

"Penny Hingston?" The man leaned down to peer in the window, tipping his dark glasses down to look over the top of them. His pressed suit looked uncomfortable in the heat, and his tightly curled hair was streaked with gray.

She pulled back from the window, one eye squinting at the guy. "I didn't do it, but I want a lawyer anyway." She raised her hands defensively. "I wasn't drink-driving, I swear. See? Still closed." She hefted the beers, ready to swing them into the guy's face if she needed to.

The man chuckled. "I'm not a cop. I have something to give you, is all."

His thick American drawl made her blink. Penny had traveled around Australia for a year before coming back home to apply for university. She'd met her fair share of Yanks. She just hadn't expected to do so in the backwater town she had grown up in.

He slid an envelope through the crack at the top of the window—she never closed them all the way because of the baking heat, but maybe that was a habit she'd drop from now on. The letter fluttered onto her lap.

"That all?" Penny eyed the letter as if it were a snake.

The man nodded. He turned as if to go, then wheeled back. "That's a Rainbow, right? Where'd you find her?" He jutted his chin toward Boots.

Penny couldn't help but lift her brows in surprise. In these parts, it was rare to find someone who could recognize the serpent. She rested a hand on Boots protectively. "Down by the creek."

"She's a nice specimen." The man nodded once, then strode off.

Penny sat in her car and watched as he opened the door of a black Cadillac. She didn't move until he drove away, leaving a cloud of dust behind him.

"Well, Boots, let's see what this letter has to say." Penny snatched the letter up and put it between her teeth, using her hands to pile up the rest of her stuff as she headed toward her front door. Once inside, she put her bags down and tore the letter open.

Attn: Penny Hingston.

We are pleased to offer you a scholarship to the March-Blaisey Academy of Historical Re-Emergence.

This scholarship will not only fund your first semester at the school, but provide free room and board, and eight thousand dollars to mitigate relocation and living expenses.

Our new campuses offer state-of-the-art equipment and respected industry specialists as your teachers. Upon graduation, you will have guaranteed employment options with the US government, who will reimburse any remaining tuition after three years of service. Alternatively, you will have the option to move into the private sector with advanced academic credentials and world-class qualifications.

Classes will begin on September 9th. Please arrive at least three days early to secure your dorm room and address any outstanding paperwork.

If you have any questions about this unique opportunity, please contact your handler for more information.

Regards,

Jessica March

Dean of March-Blaisey Academy of Historical Re-Emergence.

"A scholarship? Huh. I sure as hell didn't apply for *that*." Penny flipped it over, then picked the envelope up to examine it.

A brightly colored pamphlet slipped out, showing a luxurious stone building on the front. On the other side, amongst the tiny white text, an image of a group of students caught her eye. They were practicing archery, bows drawn and pointed at something off the page.

Full access to our unique combination of new and old technology, researched and designed to effectively combat the threat of mythological invasion.

"'Mythological invasion?'" Penny muttered. "Guess they finally figured out how to make a buck off of it."

Penny had only loosely followed the information online. Though she had Boots, Penny didn't particularly want to be branded as "one of those crazies." Lately, politicians had been releasing statements confirming that something was going on, although no one seemed to want to state exactly what it was.

A hard knock at her door made Penny jump again. *Get a grip, girl!* She opened it, realizing too late she probably shouldn't have, to find a pair of sunglasses staring back at her.

"Surprise, surprise." She eyed the street, wondering if anyone had noticed his return. "I know you've been asking around about me. What do you want?"

"Sorry." He shrugged. "Didn't mean to scare you. Just figured you might have some questions. Most do."

Could this day get any weirder? "Who does?" Penny folded her arms and scowled.

The man didn't seem perturbed. He leaned a shoulder against the wall and pulled out a cigarette, putting it between his lips unlit while he answered. "The applicants. Or in your case, recruits. I've been watching you, Penny Hingston."

"Oh, That doesn't make you sound like a stalker *at all*. What the fuck is going on?" Penny plucked the lighter away as soon as it appeared. "And no smoking on my goddamn verandah."

Pulsing muscles wrapped around Penny's leg, working their way up until the reassuring pressure of a snake's head rested on her shoulder. A forked tongue tickled her ear. Boots was a curious little thing, and protective.

The man sighed and put away the cigarette. "I'm Special Agent Stuart Crenel, Federal Bureau of Investigation." He stuck out his hand, and Penny reluctantly shook it. "The letter I gave you is bullshit. Some suit in an office wrote it up, but it doesn't *explain* anything."

Penny eyed him for a moment. "I assume that's *your* job, then?" she asked.

Crenel nodded. "You're aware of the sudden increase in sightings of mythological creatures?"

"You mean the apocalypse?" Penny asked dryly.

"Is that what they're calling it this week?" Crenel shrugged. "Whatever you want to name it, the American government has finally recognized the threat it presents. The world is changing, Miss Hingston, and we need people who can keep up."

Slack-jawed, Penny stared at him for a moment, finally stepping aside to let the agent in. "I'm going to need a drink, aren't I?"

By the time Penny had opened her second beer, she was beginning to understand. The school was a response to the appearance of the strange creatures. Students would learn to study, protect, and even fight the beings from myth and legend, and work to keep the public safe.

"So, the FBI started this school to...what, exactly?" Penny asked, trying to sort out her thoughts.

Agent Crenel winced. "It's...not a FBI school. Not yet. We do have a training organization to assemble a team to deal with this, but it's not enough—we need more people." He eyed Penny appreciatively. "You would have made the cut for that if I'd found you a week earlier."

"So, why are you involved?" Penny watched him closely, sure a hint of color had touched his cheeks at the question.

"As a favor for Jessica—Dean March. I'm helping her get this Academy up and running, and my bureau has convinced her to let me act as a liaison. I'm trying to convince Jessica to sign a formal agreement with the Bureau. She hasn't folded yet, but she will." His confident smirk suggested he believed his words. "We need the Academy, but they need us too."

"Tell me more about the classes," Penny demanded.

"Well, they'll teach you to identify the creatures first. Each one so far has been based on a myth or story that's been around for a helluva long time, so we have info and details about them." Crenel pursed his lips.

"Like Boots. She's a rainbow serpent, I know that much. An old Dreamtime story." Penny stroked the snake, who'd looked up at the mention of the Dreamtime.

Crenel nodded. "Right, so those myths can tell us what we're dealing with. Not all the Mythers are bad. There are at least a half-dozen leprechauns hanging around in Irish bars at last count, and for the most part, they just drink a lot of booze and mouth off a little."

"Next question." She tipped the bottle up and took a couple of swallows while she assembled her thoughts. "Why *me?* I'm not exactly fresh out of high school. Don't you think if I'd wanted to go to uni, I'd be there already?"

"Eventually, we want to expand the Academy internationally. Having an Aussie kid graduate with this first batch of students would help that goal." He was already swirling the last drops of his third drink around the bottom of the bottle. "It's not exactly easy to attract applicants when the very nature of the course offerings is… Well, this unusual. We're hand-selecting students, some young, some a little older. Otherwise, there's too much risk of drawing the wrong kinds of people."

"And I'm the right kind, huh?" Penny saw Crenel eyeing the last beer, and quickly cracked it open to take a gulp before he could ask for it. "I don't know who you think I am, mate, but this?" Penny tapped the brochure. "This isn't me."

Crenel leaned over to hold his hand in front of Boots'

nose. "She's an incredible creature," he murmured. Boots nuzzled his wrist and darted her tongue out to lick the condensation from his now-empty beer bottle. His eyes met Penny's. "I've seen the two of you together. You don't think they'll come for her eventually? This is your chance to keep her safe, and to make the world better for Boots and others like her."

Penny scowled. "Guilt trips don't work, bud. *No one* is coming for Boots. I wouldn't let them. Besides, she wouldn't hurt a fly."

Crenel raised an eyebrow and Penny flushed, realizing that as a F-B-freaking-I agent, he probably already knew about Jerry's sore finger.

"Not unprovoked, anyway," she amended.

"It wasn't a threat, Hingston." Crenel looked down the neck of his bottle, then set it on the table. "It's God's honest truth. I've seen creatures like Boots, who don't mean us any harm. The people who make the rules, though? They just see a bunch of scared constituents who are gonna vote for the politician with the biggest weapon against them."

"And what, the Academy will stop that happening?" Penny gave a skeptical snort.

"The Academy will give the public reassurance that if something big does go down, we're ready. As a student, you—and Boots—will have a certain level of protection if laws come down prohibiting the existence of Mythers." He leaned forward, serious. "It's not a game, Penny. We will teach you to fight. To kill, if need be. Not all the Mythers are bad...but not all of them are good, either."

"You're preparing for something." Penny downed the

last of her drink, wishing she had something a little harder. "What is it?"

"We *don't know* what else is coming." Crenel pulled a phone out of his pocket and typed something in. After a moment, he placed it flat on the table and slid it over to her. "That was just last week."

Penny scanned the online article on Crenel's phone. It said a group at a New Jersey rave had somehow captured a Chupacabra, which had subsequently escaped and killed and mutilated the animals at a local shelter.

"God. That's gruesome." Penny passed the phone back and pressed a hand to her swirling stomach. "Lucky I didn't eat before—oh *shit*, I forgot about dinner!"

She darted to the door, grabbed the now-lukewarm bag of Chinese, and dumped it on the table. She fished out the containers and tipped the food into bowls.

"I don't suppose you've got enough for two?" Crenel asked.

Penny snorted. "How'd I know you were gonna ask that?"

She grabbed a couple of forks and threw ice into two glasses for the Cokes, a plan brewing in her mind.

The money would come in handy. And the protection a student—even a *former* student—would receive could help guard Boots. She'd have the chance to learn more about her new friend, and have inside information about what was coming in case Boots needed her protection.

Sign up, learn what I can and get the hell outta dodge. If all else failed, there was a place she could go, an old miner's shack deep in the bush that was all but forgotten. Penny could keep Boots safe there, as long as she knew what she was keeping her safe *from.*

Once dinner was plated up, she sat back down at the table and stuffed a bit of lemon chicken in her mouth. *Still warm, at least.* "Tell you what," she said, muffled by the mouthful of food she was still chewing. "I'll give you one semester. Just one. If you can convince me it's worth staying, I will."

CHAPTER TWO

Six weeks, two plane flights, and a couple of annoying phone calls later, Penny stood nervously outside the open doorway of her first class.

She rubbed her eyes, wishing that a passport holdup hadn't delayed her arrival until the evening before. Jet lag and not enough sleep had left her ill-prepared for her first day at a new school on the other side of the world.

In America.

"Best get on with it," Penny muttered. She put her head down and walked into the room, briefly nodding at the scatter of students who had already taken their desks. *It's just for four months,* she reminded herself. *After that, I'll never see these people again.*

The students were quite the mix. A girl in flowing boho cotton dress sat beside a blonde girl wearing a revealing red blouse. The rebels, two boys and a girl with various piercings and tattoos, sat on top of their desks in the middle of the room.

She spotted the jock—a dark-skinned young man with

a varsity jacket and a smug grin—and the smart kid, who was already typing on his MacBook with one hand, his other tapping calculations on his phone.

Penny slid behind a desk in the back row, quickly setting up her pens and notepad. She glanced over as someone took the spot next to her.

"Hey. You got a pen?" The guy gave her a hopeful grin, gesturing at his empty desk. He pushed black hair out of his eyes and waited expectantly. "And...maybe some paper, too?"

Penny frowned. "Dude. Do I look like a stationery shop?"

The guy stared back for a minute, then nodded. "Kinda."

Penny glanced at the fat, rainbow pencil case on her desk beside three carefully stacked notebooks and an open planner. "You've got a point. Here—but if you lose it, I'll come after you with the vengeance of a thousand drop bears. What's your name?"

"Cisco." He took the offered notebook and matching pen, chuckling as he did. "I love pink!"

She made a face. "Damn, here I thought hot pink stationery would be less likely to be stolen," Penny shook her head before laughing with him. "I'm Penny."

"You sound like you're a long way from home?" Cisco flipped the book open and scrawled the date at the top of a new page.

"Yeah. I just—"

"Welcome, students!" Clicking heels punctuated the words as a woman marched into the room, her face puckered into a disapproving look as she looked down her nose at the class. Or along her nose, at least. Even with her modest heels, she was barely taller than the seated students. "I am Professor Madera. I expect you are all ready to begin?"

The professor's eyes roamed over the students before she snorted at the resounding silence she got in reply. "I'll assume that is a yes." She turned and wrote her name at the top of the board, her tight, gray bun bobbing as she worked.

"Welcome to the March-Blaisey Academy of Historical Re-Emergence."

Madera folded her hands in front of her. "You, and your colleagues who should be commencing their first class this afternoon hold the honor of being the first students to—"

Movement caught Penny's eye, and she turned toward the door.

"Sorry! Sorry, I'll just sneak in here. Whoops! Sorry!" A blonde girl appeared at the door and began picking her way past tightly-packed desks.

She stumbled twice before finally plonking herself down at a desk in front of Penny.

"Nice of you to join us." Professor Madera didn't turn around. "In this class, I expect punctuality and silent attention. We are here to study the history of recent events. Yes, it is history, however recent." Madera finished writing the class topic—*Complete History of Mythological Invasion*—on the board, then turned to pick up a stack of papers.

"Gonna be a short class, then." The voice from the front set off a snigger of laughter through the class.

"Ohhh," Cisco whispered just loud enough for Penny to hear. "That guy is gonna get his *ass* handed to him."

"If your knowledge of the subject is complete, please, enlighten us." Madera stalked over to the offending student and tossed her chalk on his desk. "Mister…"

"Clive. My name's Clive." Clive shrank in his seat, apparently reluctant to capitalize on the attention he'd gained.

"Well, Clive, seeing as you're so much taller than me, you can write the timeline. Start at the top of the board. I want all two-hundred and twenty-seven incidents listed in order of occurrence, interspersed with the evolution of theories that predominated at the time. Oh, and please include the increasing levels of involvement of government agencies." Madera folded her arms and tapped her foot, waiting for her student to comply.

"Uhh…" Clive stood and shuffled to the whiteboard. After a few seconds of hesitation, he wrote *2017* at the top of the board.

"Clive, you haven't left enough room for the previous year." Madera spoke calmly but didn't make any move to relieve the red-faced student's embarrassment.

Clive slumped. "I have no idea what I'm doing. I know the first sighting that went viral was in 2017, but…" He shrugged to indicate his ignorance.

Madera motioned for him to resume his seat. "The first corroborated sighting of a mythological creature was, in fact, a year prior to the broadcast of the Times Square event. It occurred on the ninth of September." She paused, then barked, "If you aren't writing this down, you'd better hope your memory is accurate enough to recall this information during the exams."

Penny quickly opened her notebook, smoothing the

fresh page and scrawling the current date. She jotted the heading Timeline, and under it, the date Madera had mentioned.

Someone tapped her elbow, and she looked up. Cisco jutted his chin at the girl who'd come in late.

"Oh, my God, kill me now!" she muttered, pawing through a tasseled handbag. "I *swear* I put a pen in here!"

Penny stifled a sigh. *Stationery shop, indeed.* She leaned forward and tapped the girl's back with the tip of a pen. The girl jerked her head around, then grabbed it with a groan of relief. "Thanks!" she whispered. "You saved my ass!"

The rest of the class went smoothly. Penny furiously scribbled notes about what was believed to be "Incident Zero," the appearance of a leprechaun at a Boston bar. At first believed to be a promotional event, no one had reported it—at least, no one sober enough to be believed. It wasn't until a video surfaced eight months later, well after the video of a six-foot-tall rabbit crapping foil-covered chocolates in Manhattan went viral, that the bar owner finally denied all knowledge of the small green man encouraging patrons to drink themselves to oblivion.

"And why do you think this particular being was conjured in this place?" Madera asked.

The boho girl in the front row raised her hand, bracelets jingling. "Someone held a seance?"

"Your name, please?" Madera asked.

"Kathy."

Madera shook her head. "In this particular case, it seems to have been a spontaneous appearance. The advertising material or the bar all used the leprechaun's image. It was on their promotional material, and they often had costumed mascots in the bar during sporting events. We believe that the event coincided with the video."

She scanned the class, but no one interrupted.

"The video reached peak virality during a televised local football match. While the sports fans were cheering for their favorite team, four hundred thousand people watched a video." She waited.

"You mean the *Ultimate Truth* video?" The nerdy kid looked up, then ducked his head when he realized all eyes were on him.

"Yes...Trevor?" Madera guessed. The boy nodded. "As those who watched said the words *'Belief makes truth, and faith makes reality,'* a Lucky Charms commercial aired. The bar's mascot, who had been drinking, began to jokingly threaten a class-action suit on behalf of 'underpaid leprechauns' and entered into the persona of an angry mythological creature."

"So, the mascot turned into a real leprechaun?" Clive asked.

Madera shook her head. "He was attacked by one. The visitor tackled the mascot to the ground, yelling that impersonation was a breach of his rights, and proceeded to beat his victim over the head with a tiny cauldron."

"How did we never hear about this?" another classmate asked.

"The patrons were drunk. It was assumed to be a promotional stunt, and they lapped it up. When the bar's records were later subpoenaed over the incident, it was revealed they exceeded normal alcohol sales that night by nine hundred percent." Madera folded her hands neatly in front of her, glancing quickly at Cisco. "What am I missing?"

"The bar owner bribed the mascot to avoid charges," he explained. "And kept his mouth shut, blaming booze on any claims of something unusual going on."

Penny kept scribbling notes, ignoring the cramp in her hand. On the floor at her feet, her bag wriggled briefly. She jumped, glanced around, then nudged it with her toe. The bag stilled.

When the lesson was over and class had been dismissed, Penny quickly packed up her things.

"Can I keep the book for today?" Cisco asked. "I'll copy my notes tonight and hand it back tomorrow."

"You can keep the book," Penny told him. "You were right—I'm a walking supply shop. I've got enough to spare you one."

Cisco grinned. "Pink notebook." He waved it. "It'll be my thing!"

As they exited the classroom, the blonde girl snagged Penny's elbow, walking with them to the next class. "Penny, right? I'm Amelia. Thank you so much for the loaner!" She spoke quickly, barely taking a breath. "I can't *believe* I was late on my first day! I overslept; my new roommate got in at midnight. That was ok, except halfway through the night she started hissing! I didn't get a wink of sleep. I thought she was gonna bite me!"

"Hissing?" Cisco raised a skeptical eyebrow. "Did she smuggle a cat in?"

Penny felt the heat rise in her cheeks. "Um, actually, it wasn't a cat." She gave Amelia an awkward wave. "Hi, roomie."

"Oh." Amelia sidled away while Cisco covered his mouth in a sudden fit of coughing.

"You won't tell?" Penny glanced around.

The hallway was mostly empty. The other students had gone into the next class. Penny leaned over and unzipped her bag and drew out a thermos. A sleepy reptilian head poked out, tongue tasting the air as the snake emerged from the container.

Cisco leaned in for a look. He gave a low whistle of appreciation. "Hey, pretty girl. Or is it a boy?"

"Girl, unless you want a new piercing," Penny confirmed.

Disturbed, Boots raised her head out of the bag. She saw her admirers and stretched, showing off the rainbow pattern on her scales.

"Great. I live with a snake charmer." Amelia didn't seem too upset with the development, though. She carefully reached in to stroke Boots' scales. "Wow. Smooth as butter!"

Footsteps approached, and Penny shoved Boots back down.

"I know it's against the rules," she whispered, eyeing them both. "But I tried to leave her behind, I swear! She stowed away, and I didn't realize until I was at the airport."

Mara—the girl in the red top—passed them, giving her curly blonde hair a flip. Penny watched her go, feeling a stab of envy at the girl's swinging hips, wrapped in jeans so tight you couldn't fit a credit card between the cloth and her skin.

"How'd you get her through Customs?" Amelia asked. "They check for Mythers now."

Penny shrugged. "She's good at hiding."

Cisco gently nudged them along the hallway. "We're gonna be late. And just so you know, the rule against having pets on campus? Doesn't apply to stuff like that." He winked. "You're safe."

Penny blew out a giant breath. "Really? Damn, Boots will hate me if she finds out I stuffed her in a thermos for no reason."

Cisco halted mid-stride, then shook his head and continued walking. "There's so much to unpack in that statement that it'll have to wait until after class."

Penny and Amelia followed Cisco down a winding staircase to the basement level of the academy building. Released from confinement, Boots had slithered off to explore.

"This class is going to run past lunchtime, and I missed breakfast," Amelia complained. "I'm already starving!" She hit the bottom step with a thump, then rubbed her stomach for emphasis.

"What's down here?" Penny looked around, taking in the deep brown of oak-paneled walls and the many doorways leading from the small landing.

"Training rooms, mostly." Cisco shrugged, unimpressed. He pushed open the nearest door and stepped back, holding it wide for the girls.

Penny let Amelia go in first, giving Cisco a timid smile as she passed him a moment later. It was Amelia's low gasp of awe that brought her attention to the room ahead. When she looked up, she almost tripped.

"Big, isn't it?" Cisco's sly grin suggested he'd expected the girl's reaction.

Although the high ceilings and decorative wainscoting matched the rest of the Academy, the scope of the room was like nothing upstairs. "It's as big as my house!" Penny said.

She wasn't exaggerating. Penny guessed the room must be close to half the footprint of the entire building. The staunch pillars interspersed through the room certainly suggested it was big enough to warrant the extra structural integrity.

"That's what *she* said." Already over her surprise, Amelia smirked and sauntered away.

Penny waited until Cisco closed the door. "I didn't miss a day of classes, right?"

Cisco shook his head. "No, today's the first day. Why?"

"I just wondered how you know so much about this place." Penny wasn't sure what she had expected. Maybe that he'd seen it on a brochure or got a tour when he arrived. She certainly *didn't* expect Cisco to blush, mumble an excuse, and walk off. "Curious," she murmured.

"Over here!" Amelia waved Penny over to where she stood huddled in a corner with Clive and another student —a brawny, heavily-freckled guy with flaming red hair. Penny made her way over and introduced herself.

"I'm Red. And before you ask, yes, that's me real name." The boy grinned sheepishly, letting his thick Irish accent explain.

"So, what's with the giant classroom?" Clive asked, letting his eyes roam the space.

Penny shrugged. "The timetable says it's defense class. Maybe they use this for practical lessons?"

"Practical?" Amelia winced. "Maybe I should have paid more attention to the dress code."

Glancing down, Penny compared Amelia's pointed heels to her own utilitarian boots. "Yeah. They did mention something about wearing flats, didn't they?"

"Those boots could even kick *my* ass." Clive chuckled. "What are they for, kickboxing kangaroos?"

"Don't be ridiculous." Penny scoffed. "You try and kick a 'roo, and you'll end up in a hospital. *These* are for fighting crocs."

"Good morning, class!" A man strode in, carrying a cardboard box large enough to obscure his face. He dropped it by the door with a thud. "Welcome to defense class. Suit up." He gestured to the box beside him.

Cisco was closest to it, so he walked over and peeked inside, then drew out a pair of padded sticks. "You want me to hand them out, Professor Jones?"

Huh. So, Cisco had not only been down in the training room before, but he also knew the professor.

"Go ahead, Cisco." The professor clasped his hands behind his back and wandered toward the middle of the room, curious eyes following him. He looked military, Penny decided. If his close-cut hair, confident stride, and tough build weren't enough, he had a pair of dog tags swinging from his neck.

Despite this, he seemed to view the students with a sliver of discomfort. "I'll be right back."

Penny took a pair of sticks from Cisco. "Up close and personal with the professors, too?" she whispered.

Cisco winced and quickly moved to the next student without answering.

"What's gotten into *him*?" Amelia asked from beside her.

Penny shrugged. Any answer she might have given was interrupted by the return of Professor Jones. He held another box, this one small enough to fit under one arm as he pushed the heavy door shut and latched it. The box was made of wood and padlocked shut.

"Are we all armed and ready?" Jones asked.

Penny could have sworn the box moved. Jones's biceps flexed as he gripped it tighter.

"Well?" Jones barked, clearly not used to being ignored.

A smatter of "Yes, sirs" only made him scowl harder.

"Listen up! When I ask, you answer. None of this lolly-gagging. Now...ARE WE ARMED AND READY?"

The professor's bellow made more than one student jump, and Penny saw Clive give a sneaky salute out of the corner of her eye. The "Yes, sir!" chorus was louder this time.

It seemed to sate the professor's temper. He nodded once, then set the smaller box on the ground and drew a key from his pocket. He crouched with his back to the class.

"Right! Ready...and... GO!" Jones dove to one side, and the lid of the box flew open. For a moment, there was silence.

"Go where?" someone called.

"AAAAIIIIEEEEEEEEEE!!!" Something small and red flew out of the box and headed toward the nearest student,

Kathy. It hit her in the solar plexus, and she let out a loud "*Oof!*" as she doubled over.

Chaos erupted. Someone screamed, and another yelled for help as Penny lost sight of the...whatever it was as students ducked and dodged, trying to get out of the way before they were targeted.

"Back up," she snapped at Amelia. "Against the wall."

Taking her own advice, she slipped back to press against the wall behind her, padded sticks gripped with white knuckles.

"There!" Amelia thrust one of her weapons toward the middle of the room, where a tiny creature in a tall red hat was attached to a girl's head, yanking out clumps of her blonde hair as she squealed. "Is that... *No way.*"

"It can't be," Penny murmured. Then again, she'd said that when she found Boots, too. *It can't be a Rainbow Serpent,* she'd assured herself then. Still, this? "There is *no way* we're being attacked by a freaking garden gnome!"

As if her words had called it, the gnome paused for a brief moment. Its tiny glittering blue eyes met hers.

"Oh *shit!*" Penny readied one of the sticks.

The gnome screeched, then leaped like a rabbit onto the heads of students, darting between flailing sticks.

Penny widened her stance, winding up like a softball batter. The gnome took one last flying jump—right into Penny's two-handed strike. Rather than shoot back across the room, though, the gnome gripped the makeshift bat, holding on with tiny hands, booted feet, and a clamped jaw.

"Ahh!" Amelia shrieked and slammed one of her sticks

down on Penny's. Whether by accident or design, she caught the creature on the head.

With the sound of breaking china, the gnome shattered. Sharp ceramic pieces scattered along the floor, showing no sign that they had been alive and moving just moments before.

Penny turned wild eyes toward the professor, who looked just as stricken.

"What. *The fuck.* Was that?" she demanded. America might have different educational standards than her home country, but surely, setting a wild creature loose to attack a class full of students wasn't part of that?

"You killed him!" Rather than being relieved, Jones's voice was horrified. His hands clutched at hair too short to grasp. "Rodney was our only specimen! You killed him!"

Penny's jaw dropped. "It just beat the shit out of—" she paused to do a quick headcount, *"five students!"*

Professor Jones swung his head around as if just noticing the havoc the gnome had wreaked inside the classroom. "Oh." His shoulders dropped, and he let out a breath through his nose. "I guess that might have been a bit ambitious for the first class."

Jones walked over to pick up the wooden box, heedless of the group of students still too stunned to do anything but watch.

"Ambitious? More like an indictable offense," Amelia muttered.

Penny was sure she'd spoken too quietly for the professor to hear, but he swung back around.

"You two." He pointed at Penny and Amelia. Penny's

heart dropped. Had she really just sworn at an instructor on her *first day*? "Good work."

If Penny's jaw had dropped any farther, it would have touched the stone floor. She caught Cisco smirking at her from across the room and quickly snapped her mouth shut.

Professor Jones gestured at Red. "You. Pick this mess up, and make sure you get every bit." He thrust the box into Red's hands, then, on his way out of the room, called, "Class dismissed," over his shoulder.

Penny glanced at Cisco, who had a hand pressed over his mouth. When a bubble of laughter swelled in her chest, she couldn't hold it back. Between giggles, she gasped, "What the hell just happened?"

There was a smattering of nervous laughter as Red started scooping bits of ceramic into the box. Penny knelt, picking up the tiny shards by her feet. Within a few minutes, the class had cleaned up the mess, and every bit of the psychotic garden gnome—or "Rodney," as Jones had called it—was carefully secured back in the box.

"Who the hell calls a murderous garden ornament 'Rodney?'" Clive asked. It set off another round of laughter.

"Forget the décor. I'm starving." Amelia yanked the door open and held it for Penny. "I was in the cafeteria yesterday. Cook said the full menu will be up today!"

Penny's stomach let out a noisy growl. "Take me there," she moaned. "My stomach just remembered I skipped breakfast. The last thing I ate was airport food."

Amelia shook her head. "I hope you're not expecting much better. Still, it's food! Let's go."

CHAPTER THREE

P enny followed Amelia upstairs and through the foyer of the old building now used as a college. The cafeteria was just off the main room, a dining room filled with two long tables. It had a wide serving window on one wall.

"Everything. Just give us everything," Amelia told the plump, elderly woman.

Cook wagged her finger at Amelia. "What did you forget?"

"Please," Amelia added, rolling her eyes good-naturedly.

"Um…" Penny looked at the deep trays of food, her mouth watering. "I'll have the same. Please!"

The cook dolloped meatballs, an assortment of steamed vegetables, some kind of baked pasta, bread, and gravy onto two plates, then slid them onto the counter at the end. "Here you go."

"Thanks!" Amelia snatched up both plates and nodded to a spot at the end of one of the tables. "Over there. We won't get anyone trying to shove past us at that end."

Penny followed dutifully, and the two girls were soon joined by Cisco as the rest of their class took seats scattered across the long tables.

"Good grub," Penny mumbled through a mouthful of eggplant.

"Mmmm, Cook has been here a month now, working on the menu." Cisco shoveled a pile of baked pasta into his mouth.

"Does 'Cook' have an actual name?" Penny asked.

"Yeah." Cisco swallowed a mouthful of food. "Cook." At Penny's glare, he explained. "Her first name is Millicent, which she hates. Her last name is Cook, which she is. And 'Mrs.' makes her feel old, apparently. She was pretty insistent that the students call her Cook, nothing else."

Penny stabbed the air with her fork, pointing it at him. "Spill."

Cisco froze. "What?"

"You knew about the training room." Penny held up a single finger. "Professor Jones knows you, and you know the *entire* history of Cook's name and how long she's been here." Two more fingers joined the first one, punctuating each point. "And when I ask you about it, you looked like I just caught you with your pants down."

"Hey, that's right!" Amelia threw down her cutlery and scowled at Cisco accusingly. "I've been here for a whole week and I've never seen Jones, and the very first thing I was told when I got here was that basement levels were out of bounds until classes started. And I only call Cook, *Cook* because you told me to."

"Look, I was here early, ok?" Cisco stared at his plate,

the heat rising over his face turning him a ruddy shade of red.

"Francisco! There you are!" Professor Madera headed toward them, her short legs and sharp heels clicking quickly across the floor.

"Oh, God save me." Cisco had gone from red to crimson. "Or kill me. Either. I don't care, just do it quickly."

"It's so good to see you making friends!" Madera smiled and bent down to kiss Cisco's dark hair. "Ever since he was little, he's had trouble fitting in."

"Aww, Francisco," Amelia crooned, voice shaking with suppressed laughter.

"Now, I have a faculty meeting this evening, so I won't see you at dinner. Make sure you call your father. He won't let me live it down if you forget." She patted his head and left, heedless of Cisco's tortured expression.

"Are you gonna tell us, or do we need to go grill Professor Madera about widdle Francisco's childhood?" Penny asked, unable to wipe the grin off her face.

"Fine!" Cisco balled up his napkin and tossed it on his plate. "She's my mother, ok? She *promised* she wouldn't tell anyone!"

"Well, technically, she didn't," Penny reminded him.

"I'm never gonna live this down, am I?" Cisco groaned.

The two girls exchanged a glance, then answered in unison, "Nope."

The early release from Defense class had given the

students a free afternoon. Curious about the building, Penny suggested they give her a tour. "I didn't see much when I got in last night. Besides, I'm sure Mister Teacher's Son will do a great job of showing us both around."

Cisco rolled his eyes, but Amelia enthusiastically agreed. "You have to see the library. It's amazing, and the grounds are huge! Come on, Cisco. Be nice to the new girl..." She gave him a cheeky smirk. "Or I'll tell your mom."

Cisco threw his hands up in defeat. "Fine! It's not like anyone else in the whole Academy is ever going to speak to me now that my secret is out."

Penny patted his shoulder consolingly. "It's not that big a deal, you know. It's only funny because you care so much."

The topic was forgotten once Cisco showed Penny the expansive library. Inhaling the scent of old books and running her fingers along the shelves of leather-bound tomes, Penny oohed and ahhed appropriately. "And we can borrow these any time?" she asked. She'd have to cram in as much reading as she could while she was here.

Cisco nodded. "They'll set up a real borrowing system once the next group of students comes in, but with only a few dozen enrolled, they didn't bother for this term."

"How'd you get recruited, anyway?" Penny asked. "Is it because your mom is teaching here?"

Cisco shrugged. "I fit the criteria. I don't think they would have let me in if I hadn't."

"*What* criteria?" Amelia asked. "My recruiter just shoved a letter in my hand and told me the first semester is free. I wasn't even sure what it was about until I got here."

"You enrolled in a school, knowing nothing about it?" Cisco asked. He ushered the girls out the door into the next room. Desks lined the walls, leaving room for the pool table in the middle. They passed through without stopping and emerged onto a long terrace framed by ornate balustrades.

"Well, they said it was free, then offered insurance for my whole family," Amelia explained. "My mom had cancer last year. It wiped out her savings, and she still needs another round of surgery."

"Fair enough." Cisco looked at Penny. "How much do you know?"

Penny thought back to that warm spring evening a few weeks earlier, feeling suddenly cold now that they were outside. The cab driver who'd dropped her off had laughed at her shivering in the back seat, insisting it was t-shirt and shorts weather. "The basics, I guess. I don't know why I was picked, though. I mean, I'm nothing special. Who would come all the way to Australia just for me?"

"Oh, I heard about that," Cisco said. "The agent who pulled you in got in trouble for it. He was down there for an international task force meeting and was supposed to pick up some bigwig scientist living in a small town. He spotted you on his way through and went back after the conference to pull you in, despite being told he was only there to scout for candidates."

"Why would he get in trouble for that?" Penny asked dubiously. "They're not going to kick me out, are they?"

"Nah. He asked for permission and got it; he just did it *after* he gave you the offer." Cisco chuckled. "Once they checked you out and realized you weren't a kook or a terrorist, they stopped caring."

"Why is the FBI linked to the Academy, anyway?" It was something that had been nagging Penny from the beginning, but Agent Crenel had dodged the question with expert ease. "Isn't that...kinda unusual?"

"Dean March is a former agent," Cisco explained. "I think she's still pretty close with the department."

"Oh. That makes sense, I guess." A gust of icy wind blew past, and Penny shivered again. "It's pretty out here, but I'm freezing."

"You wanna grab a coat?" Cisco asked.

Penny laughed. "You know where I'm from, right? Back home, we know it's winter if it takes more than a minute and a half to fry an egg on your bonnet."

"You...cook eggs in frilly hats?" Amelia gave a weak smile. "That's not weird. Not at all."

Penny thought for a minute. "Hood. The hood of your car."

"Oh!" Amelia looped an arm through Penny's. "Now, I get it. Well, winters in Portland aren't too bad, but nothing like what you'll be used to. And there's only one way to fix that." Her eyes sparkled. "Shopping trip!"

"The reviews online all say the best coffee is here," Amelia proclaimed. Her eyes searched the crowded coffee shop. "Look! There's a spot free!" She pointed to two stools under a large window.

"I haven't bought this many clothes in one trip in...well, ever," Penny admitted. She plopped the four bags of clothes on the floor beneath the table while Amelia quickly scooped up the two dirty cups and balanced them on her arm.

"That's why they gave you a stipend—to cover expenses like this," Amelia pointed out. She pulled her purse out with her free hand. "What are you having to drink?"

"Coffee. A latte. Do you want to share something to eat?" Penny scanned the display of sandwiches and pastries beneath a blue neon sign that said 'Coffee.

"I'll bring back cake!" Amelia had to raise her voice to be heard over the bustle as she headed to the counter.

Penny waited as Amelia chatted to the barista, first pointing at a tall, layered cake, then some oversized muffins. *It's not that much different from home,* she decided. Although her actual hometown, small as it was, had nothing like this hipster café, she'd visited enough of them during her year of traveling through Australia.

The hiss of frothing milk and the rumble of the machines hadn't changed, just the accents she occasionally picked out as bits of conversation passed her. She relaxed against the long table, closing her eyes for a moment to inhale the scent of freshly brewed coffee. Instead of the busy street outside, her mind conjured a picture of waves lapping white sand. Bondi. That was the last place she'd had a truly good coffee.

"Doesn't this look amazing!" Amelia's exclamation brought Penny back to the present.

In front of her sat a slice of cake. Or, maybe it would be

better described as a tower...seven layers of dark chocolate sponge separated by pale buttercream. The white icing on top was carefully dusted with fine chocolate shavings. Amelia brandished two forks, and Penny eagerly plucked one from her hand.

Penny carefully slid the little fork through the top layers of the cake. It got about halfway down before she pulled it away, the sliver teetering precariously. "This looks..." She put the fork in her mouth, and this time when she closed her eyes, it was in pure appreciation. "Incredible," she mumbled through the mouthful of crumbs.

"Immm mrphm, phrramt?" Amelia swallowed her own much larger bite, then tried again. "I know, right?"

"It's our most popular dessert," a woman said. She held up two mugs balanced on saucers. "Two lattes?"

Amelia nodded eagerly and thanked the woman as their coffees were delivered. Penny reached for hers, taking a moment to appreciate the swirling tulip in the foam.

"Perfect way to end the day," she mused. "Although I probably shouldn't be drinking coffee this late. I've been up for—" she checked her watch. "Oh, hell, way too long."

"Still jetlagged?" Amelia asked sympathetically.

"I guess. I only slept for a few hours last night after I got in. My body is screaming at me to sleep, but also telling me I should be getting ready for breakfast." Penny sipped the coffee anyway.

"At least you're not cold!" Amelia pointed out.

Penny wriggled inside her new leather jacket. The shopping trip had burned up a chunk of her money, but Amelia was right—she was now properly equipped for the weather on this side of the world. "You know, it's just occurred to me—where am I even going to put all this?"

"On your body, silly," Amelia giggled. She stabbed her fork in Penny's direction. "Look, it would be a sin to buy that jacket and not wear it every chance you get. It'll go on the door hook. The boots are for every day too, you can just—"

"I told you, I'm not giving up my old faithfuls," Penny insisted. "I spent *way* too much time wearing them in." They had indeed argued about it. Amelia had been forgiving of Penny's refusal to buy a pile of frilly, girly clothes, but the shoes had been a sticking point.

Of course, Amelia didn't know the clothes would only need to last the season. Penny bit her lip, thinking of the money wasted—but clothes were clothes, and a good quality jacket would keep her just as warm in the Australian bush on a cold night as it would in Portland.

Amelia scooped up the last bit of cake and pushed the plate away when she was done. "Fine. Your old ones are ok for class, I guess. The tall boots are for wearing *out*. Now we just need somewhere to go."

"Does the dining hall count?" Penny asked. She ducked the swatting hand that flew toward her head. "Hey! I'm serious. I don't know anyone in Portland. Hell, I don't know anyone in America! Where is a small-town Aussie girl going to find a social life in the big smoke?"

Amelia threw her hands up, exasperated, almost tipping over her mug in the process. "You ask your new best friend, of course! Look, I've already hit up a distant cousin. He's having a get-together Wednesday night to welcome me to town. Just something small and informal." She paused, taking a sip of coffee. "That red dress would be perfect."

"The red one. Sure." Penny grinned nervously. *That* dress had taken a lot of talking into.

Amelia didn't respond, just drained the last of her coffee, eyes twinkling.

Penny wondered what the hell she'd gotten herself into.

CHAPTER FOUR

When Penny woke at eleven the next morning, she silently thanked whoever had made the class schedules. She'd slept restlessly at first, only sinking into a deep slumber in the wee hours of the morning. The late start meant she had enough time to still get a solid eight hours of sleep.

She might not even have woken then except for the unrelenting tap, tap on her face. Penny shoved away Boot's insistent snout. "Fine! I'll get up. I know, you're bored, but you get to come out today, ok?"

She rolled out of bed and dressed lazily, taking her time to work the knots out of her long hair as Boots watched from the mess of blankets. Penny's curls hadn't adjusted well to the sudden weather change, puffing up around her face until she gave up trying to smooth them down and pulled them back in a ponytail instead.

Her favorite boots slipped on like gloves. So did her new jacket. Neither felt as good as the familiar weight of her serpent draped over her shoulders, though.

Boots had only been around for a few months, but she was Penny's constant, the thing that would never change.

By the time they made it to the dining hall for lunch, she almost felt human again.

"You girls, always skipping breakfast." The cook squeezed three burritos onto Penny's plate, despite her protests that two would be fine.

"Sorry, I slept through it," Penny explained. "The jetlag is still kicking my ass.."

Cook *tsked* at Penny's language, then leaned closer to look at Boots. "What does this one eat? We chased off the mice—bad for the kitchen. I'm sure I can find a supplier of snake food, though?"

"It's fine," Penny explained. "She sometimes tastes my food, but I've never really seen her eat. All she needs is water."

Cook motioned for Penny to wait, and a moment after she disappeared from the serving window, she reappeared with a large bowl of water.

"Off you go." Cook shooed Penny away. "Make sure you eat all that. You'll waste away if you're not careful!"

"No chance of that," Penny replied cheerfully. "Not with all this grub around."

Penny gave a timid wave to the small group of students at one end of the table, but they didn't notice her, too intent on their conversation. Without the distraction of companions, she ate quickly and, with nothing better to do, arrived at class early.

American Folklore was held in the room next to the previous day's history class. Penny took a seat near the front, ignored by the professor bumbling about his desk as she entered.

Clearly agitated, his silver-rimmed glasses had started to slide down his long nose, and sweat beaded on his forehead. His gray wool suit added to his scholarly appearance, despite the messy clutter strewn across the desk.

She watched as he rifled through pages, muttering to himself in increasingly frantic tones as he searched for something. "Bag. Bag, where's the bag. I know I put it here!" He ran one hand through thinning hair as he looked up, scanning the room.

"Uhh...sir?" Penny called. "Is it that one?" She pointed at a gray satchel perched on a chair in the front row.

The professor stared at her for a moment as if trying to process her words. Then, his head jerked in the direction she had gestured to. "My bag! Yes, that's it. Thank you, thank you. Err." He pushed his glasses back up with one finger and squinted at her, then Boots. "What is that thing? And who are you?"

"That's Boots. She's a rainbow serpent." Boots flicked her tongue in the direction of the professor, tasting the air.

"Ah. Lovely coloring, I'm sure. And you are?"

"Penny Hingston." When his confusion didn't break, Penny added, "A student?"

"Oh. Why are you—" He broke off and spun to check the tall grandfather clock in the corner of the room. "Class! Of course! It's almost time for class."

He shoved the paper into a pile, rummaged in a drawer until he found a box of chalk, and then hobbled over to Penny. She noticed the bulge of twisted toes that stretched out the top of one of his shoes.

"I am Professor Craster. Jim. Jim Craster." He stuck a hand out, and Penny reluctantly shook it. To her relief, it wasn't sweaty. "Ahh, good to see you're an eager student. What made you choose American Folklore, eh?" Craster didn't wait for her to answer, turning his back on her to return to his desk.

"It's a compulsory class, Professor," Penny explained. *Surely, he would know that?*

"Oh? Oh, good. They weren't going to include it, you know. Jessica said it should be relegated to the electives, but I told her!" Reaching his desk, he sat with a thump but raised one wrathful finger into the air. "I told her, we're in this country, and we're going to be confronted by its history! You can't ignore that, and to leave our students unprepared to face such things as the Sasquatch and the Chupacabra would be worse than foolhardy. It would be negligent!"

"Ah." Penny busied herself with setting up her notebook and pens, letting out a relieved breath when the other students began filing in, several giving her startled looks or coming over to exclaim over Boots.

Craster made it a point to approach each student, asking their names and introducing himself, and offering little snippets of information about the course to each student.

Penny quickly realized that although he was clearly disorganized, he was extremely passionate about the subject of American Folklore. Though his animated conversations caught her interest, Boots was less impressed. Within minutes, the serpent was curled up under Penny's desk, asleep.

When the clock chimed the hour, Craster knocked on the table to get the students' attention.

"Welcome to American Folklore!" he proclaimed, leaning back to hook his thumbs through his belt. "Now, I should start by mentioning there may be some crossover between this class and the Modern Myth unit. You'll get to that next semester, but for now, know why you are here."

He leaned forward to rest his hands on the desk, taking a moment to eye each student carefully. "This country has changed. It has been overrun! Creatures from myth and legend—and yes, some from nightmare—walk the streets."

A muffled laugh, quickly covered by a cough, pulled Penny's eyes to the back of the class. A boy near the back— Corey, she was pretty sure—rolled his eyes at the professor's exuberance.

"Unlike the myths of specific denominations, American conjurations will be impossible to avoid as the insurgency grows in strength." Craster either hadn't noticed the interruption or had chosen to ignore it. "You can avoid the leprechauns if you don't go to bars. Greek and Indian legends are less often seen on our soil, and witch-gods are strongest in Britain. But the ghosts, the horrors, Mothman, and the Horsemen...all those beings are here in our backyard, just waiting for a moment of distraction before they *pounce!*" Craster snatched at the air to punctuate his speech.

"The Wiccan movement is quite strong here, though, isn't it?" It was the first time the gum-chewing girl in black had spoken up.

Craster nodded. "It is. The belief system here seems less

tangible, though. Or perhaps, the believers relate their deities to the home country more strongly."

That made sense to Penny. Professor Madera had explained how the "conjurations," as Craster called them, were dependent on the level of belief or worship in the community. If enough people in an area believed a creature existed it would appear. There were exceptions, of course--creatures summoned through the Veil by other means--but the experts seemed to think this was how it started.

"So, if people here are trying to conjure a pagan god, will that affect things in Britain?" Penny asked.

Craster stared for a moment, then shrugged. "Am I psychic? I have no idea. We have no way to track that. Yes, Mara?"

"Professor, where do they come from?" Mara blushed as she spoke and slid down in her seat as soon as she was done.

Craster emerged from behind his desk to begin pacing lopsidedly back and forth. "Well, that is a question, isn't it? They claim they have always 'been,' that they have existed for as long as we have." He nodded as his voice turned introspective. "Yes, that's what they tell us. Is it true? Are they lying, or perhaps simply created with the collective memory of the human consciousness?"

His head snapped up, and he scowled at the class. "We do not know. We suspect that the entities have been living in a world next to ours." He held up both hands and pressed them together. "When the Event occurred, it pierced the Veil that separates our worlds. They are leaking through, one by one. And that's just the ones coming through by accident!"

"How do we know that?" Corey called. "What did you do, ask one of them?"

"Yes, of course, we did. How else would we know?" Craster irritably brushed off the question and hobbled back to his seat. "Enough about the state of the invasion. It's Professor Madera's job to teach you that. Now, who knows what a Sasquatch is?"

After the class finally ended, Penny had a fair idea of where many of the professor's quirks came from. After all, ten years living in the mountains alone, with no one to talk to while you hunted non-existent Bigfeet could make anyone a little screwy. *Although I guess it exists now,* Penny mused.

Craster had given them a little too much detail about the injuries inflicted on him when he'd accidentally stumbled on the beast two months ago. It certainly explained his limp.

Penny had just slipped the last of her study materials into her bag when Cisco leaned over her shoulder from behind. "Well that was a trip."

Penny shot a glance toward Professor Craster, but he was deep in conversation with Clive, who had shown great interest in the professor's exploits in the mountains. "It certainly was," she agreed. She stood and hoisted her backpack over her shoulder, nudging Boots awake with her toe. "Wake up, sleepyhead. We're going."

"And did you see that scar?" Cisco asked. He waited impatiently as Boots lifted her head and lazily made her way up Penny's leg. He sounded as thrilled as Clive had. "It went all the way up to his—"

"I know!" Penny cut him off. Boots settled around her

shoulders, and she headed for the door. "It was terrifying! I thought his junk was going to fall out. *That* would have scarred me for life." She shuddered as the unwanted image encroached on her mind.

"'Junk?'" Cisco asked bemusedly.

"Yeah. You know." Penny gestured to her nether regions. "Junk. Meat and potatoes. Knackers and tally-whacker?" She tried to stay deadpan, but couldn't keep her giggles from erupting as Cisco's eyes widened.

"I can't even tell you how much I love the Australian language," he said, awed. "Will you teach me?"

Penny looped her arm through his. "Stick with me, kid, and I'll turn you into a fair dinkum yobbo."

"That's a good thing, right?" Cisco asked. When Penny clamped her mouth shut, he tugged on her arm. "A yobbo? Yobboes are good? Like, they're really cool Australian dudes?"

"Sure." Penny rubbed her face to hide the grin. "Really cool."

Cisco pursed his lips, then shook his head. "I feel like you're setting me up. Hey, did Amelia tell you about dinner?"

"Dinner?" The sudden change of subject took Penny a moment to process. Still, when she double-checked her recollections, she had to shake her head. "I know she said a cousin of hers was going to arrange something, but I don't know any more than that."

"There's a really cool pub at the back of the Baghdad Theatre. He said to meet him there tonight." Cisco ducked his head, cheeks pink. "I think there are others going, but I don't know any of them. You in? We can share an Uber."

"Sure," Penny said. "I'll even teach you some Australianisms on the way so you can impress the girls."

Cisco punched the air with a hiss of satisfaction. "I'll be the best yobbo there!" He spoke with an exaggerated Australian drawl that sent Penny into uncontrollable laughter.

"You...you do...you do that, Cisco," she gasped. "Oh, my God, I...can't breathe."

Cisco chuckled, despite having to hold Penny up so she didn't collapse in the hallway. The pair caught a few strange looks from passing classmates, but all Penny could do was wipe the tears from her eyes.

The rest of Penny's afternoon was spent nestled in the Academy's library. Apart from the wide range of books, Craster had mentioned that the computer in the corner— one Penny hadn't noticed on her initial tour—had access to a government database setup to catalog the verified sightings since the Veil had been pierced.

Access I'll lose at the end of the semester. Despite her thorough enjoyment of the last two days, her resolve to take the money and run hadn't softened. *I'm here to learn how to protect Boots, not qualify for a cushy job working for the American government.*

She quickly figured out how to use it. The password was written on a Post-it note stuck on the screen, and the system itself was clunky and counter-intuitive but reminded Penny of the outdated software used in her old high school library.

With that in mind, she managed to navigate to the section she was looking for.

Southern Hemisphere > Oceana > Australia

She clicked through to the list of confirmed creature sightings and brought up the first listing for Rainbow Serpents. As it loaded, she absentmindedly fondled Boots' head with her hand. The serpent nuzzled it, still looking sleepy despite her long nap during the Folklore class.

Mythological source: Dreamtime legend

Sightings: four recorded, two confirmed

Locations: Alice Springs, Dalby, Larrabee, Uluru

Penny navigated to the Dalby listing. She had already figured out that the underlined locations were linked to verified reports.

Rainbow Serpent, Dalby. Superintendent Jamie Walker, AFP.

Reporting agent observed the subject near a local watering hole while on medical leave. The subject was initially still, but roused at the sound of a child in distress on the other side of the body of water. Agent claims the child, estimated age three, had slipped into fast-flowing water. Agent prepared to rescue the child, but the serpent appeared near the child "near-instantly" and proceeded to act as a flotation device, helping the child to safety. Subject then returned to its spot on the rock with similar speed.

Agent claims the distance traveled underwater was several hundred meters, and despite the subject clearly being an aquatic creature, it was not a distance possible to cross in such a short time. The agent also claims that

upon subject returning to the rock, no water residue was seen.

This, in combination with a previous unverified sighting, suggests the subject possesses the ability to translocate within water sources.

Penny sat back, thinking. She already knew Boots could use water as a kind of portal to other locations, and she had no doubt the serpent would run to the rescue if Penny needed it. It was something else that had caught her attention.

"Boots, are you cold?"

Boots lifted her head slowly, then tucked it into the coils of her body.

Penny bit her lip. Boots had been a little slower than usual since arriving in Portland, but her sleepiness today was unusual for her. Normally, Boots would happily laze on Penny's shoulders or curl up by a sunny window but would be awake and alert for most of the day.

"Let's get you warmed up, my love." Penny closed down the program she was using, making a mental note to go back to it later. She wanted to see what was written about her under the Larrabee section.

Hefting a reluctant Boots into her arms, Penny headed for the one person she could rely on being where she was supposed to.

"Cook?" Penny stuck her head into the dining room.

"You're a bit early for dinner, love, and too late for lunch." Rather than poke her head through the window, Cook pushed through the swinging door to the side, brandishing a flour-coated spoon. She spread her hands apologetically. "I could find you some biscuits if you're hungry?"

"No, I'm not," Penny reassured her. "It's Boots. I think the weather is a bit much for her. I wondered if you have anywhere warm she could stay for a little while? She won't be any trouble, I promise."

Cook eyed the serpent, who coiled up even tighter under the scrutiny. "Well, I suppose. I was about to put one of the ovens on for a big ham I'm doing for dinner. Won't hurt to pop it on a bit early." She waggled the spoon at Boots. "Come on. We'll have you warm and toasty in no time. Just don't you be climbing on the counters, or you'll get scorched. I don't think your young lady would like that, now, would she?"

"Go on, Boots," Penny insisted. To her relief, Boots uncurled and slithered to the ground.

"I have some old rice I can stitch into a bag," Cook said, holding the door open for her. "I can warm it up for her to sleep on tonight if you want?"

"That would be wonderful," Penny gushed. "Thank you, Cook!"

Shaking off her usual worry at being separated from her friend, Penny left the dining room. She hesitated. The computer file beckoned her, but now that Boots was taken care of, she realized the serpent wasn't the only one suffering from the cold weather.

"If you can't find a warm spot, make one," she decided. Penny jogged upstairs to the dorm rooms and soon came back downstairs, dressed for a run.

Cisco greeted her with a wave. "Going out?"

"Shaking out the collywobbles," Penny explained.

Cisco nodded slowly. "I'm going to pretend I know exactly what that means. Good luck!"

Bracing herself as she stepped outside, Penny wondered if it really had been a good idea. Chill winds tore at her lungs and her gait was wobbly, muscles trembling from the cold. It didn't take long for her to warm up, though, and by the time she came back an hour later, a thin sheen of sweat coated her body, and the sense of claustrophobia had vanished.

She stopped in the dining room to check on Boots.

"Oh, you're a good girl, you are. Such a clever thing!" Cook's crooning voice filtered from the kitchen.

"Cook?" Penny called.

"Come in, dear! Your wonderful Boots has been such a help."

Penny pushed the swinging door open and stepped into the heat of the kitchen. Cook stood at the counter, stirring a pot with one hand and scratching Boots' enthusiastic head with the other. "What kind of help?" Penny questioned.

"You wouldn't believe it if I told you!" Cook dropped the spoon and strode to a large cupboard, Boots slithering off the counter to follow at her heels. Cook yanked the door open, and Penny peered inside. The shelves were neatly stacked with bags of flour, spices, canned goods, and baskets of produce. All except the bottom shelf—it was stripped bare except for a messy pile of debris in one corner. "I had no idea we had an infestation."

"Infestation?" Penny asked, feeling a little green. She hated mice.

"Oh, they didn't touch anything we used for meals. It was all my spare flour bags. Those rotten little rodents were nesting down there, right at the back. Your Boots was only in here for about ten minutes when I opened it to get the marmalade. She darted in and made such a fuss! I was ready to chase her out when I saw her push a bag of rye over, and lo and behold, a furry little beast shot out."

"That's disgusting," Penny said, skin crawling. Then she winced. "No offense."

"Oh, they're foul little things, all right. But your Boots snapped them up in a couple of bites. If she hadn't found them, it could have been a much worse problem." Cook nodded happily. "I'll have the kitchen pulled apart and cleaned properly, don't you worry. But your sweet Boots is welcome anytime."

Penny thanked her, happy Boots was now alert and back to her normal self. "Are you coming with me?" she asked.

Boots let out a hiss as her body undulated. A moment later, she had wrapped herself into a messy coil, little face peeking out to stare at Penny between the ropes of her body.

"Fine. Traitor." Penny knelt and scratched the serpent's back as a sign of goodwill. "I'm off for a shower. Come up when you're done, you big sook."

As Penny headed to the dorms, her steps were light, and a smile pulled at her lips. Boots was happily settled, and her run had shaken off the dreariness of the weather. She almost—*almost*—wished she were staying.

CHAPTER FIVE

P enny tugged the hem of the slinky red dress down and pulled her jacket a little tighter.

"You look great," Cisco assured her for the third time.

Penny blushed. She'd spent the entire Uber ride complaining that the dress wasn't long enough and that she'd never worn anything so revealing before. "Thanks."

At least she didn't look out of place amongst the patrons swarming the Baghdad Theatre. They were varied enough that almost anyone could fit in—some in jeans and old t-shirts, others dressed as if for a 1920s flapper convention.

Cisco noticed the group of girls in retro dresses and eyed them appreciatively. "Wonder if they're with us?" he asked.

Penny snorted. "Keep dreaming." She looked around, overwhelmed by the bright lights and the cluster of people sitting outside nursing beers and cocktails. "Where to?"

"This way." Cisco took her elbow and guided her through the crowd. A few moments later, Penny's eyes stretched up to an incredibly high ceiling, trying to take in the rich balustrades and bright mural of the pub.

"Cisco! Penny, over here!" Amelia waved from a long table already crowded with guests. "Tammy, shove off. These seats are taken."

The blonde girl next to Amelia rolled her eyes but quickly vacated her seat. Penny gratefully slid in next to Amelia, Cisco beside her. "Thanks." She peered over Amelia's shoulder at the menu. "How's the grub here?"

"That means food," Cisco interjected. He looked around smugly. "I speak Australian now."

Amelia schooled her expression. "Wow, Cisco. That must have been very difficult to learn for someone of your intelligence."

Cisco thumped into his chair with a wounded expression. "I'm very smart, thank you."

"That's not what your mom says." Amelia waited for Cisco's cheeks to glow before erupting into laughter. "I'm sorry, I'm just joking. Your mom says you're really clever. Her clever little *Fran*cisco."

Worried that Cisco was about to burst a blood vessel, Penny coughed. "Where can I get a drink around here, anyway?"

Amelia motioned to a pitcher on the table. "The jug of margaritas is for us girls." She leaned around Penny. "Cisco, you want me to buy you a beer?"

Any ill will Cisco had held for Amelia's teasing disappeared immediately. "Sure. You know what I like."

"A Mexican for the Mexican?" Amelia asked with a grin.

"Damn straight," Cisco said, high-fiving her over Penny's head.

An hour later, the drinks had taken the edge off of Penny's nerves, and she was gladly recounting a story from her trip to Sydney.

"I swear to god, the roaches in that dive were as big as possums!" She held up her hands for those who hadn't seen an Australian possum, which, to be fair, was everyone at the table. "And this big biker guy saw it and started screaming. Nearly pissed his pants! But his mate was all 'I got this,' and he flicks out a knife and throws it, only it's all ass about face. The knife bounces off the wall behind the cocky and comes straight for the old codger in the corner."

"Wait up, I didn't understand half of that. Can you talk more slowly?" Tammy, the blonde Penny had unseated, filled her glass and peered into it as if hoping a magical translator would appear.

"An old fart." Penny grinned. She'd tried to pepper as much slang as she could into the conversation, much to the delight of her new friends. "Anyway, the knife grazes his ear, and he doesn't even flinch. He puts down his stubby, cool as ice, and stands up to—"

Penny's train of thought vanished as Amelia nudged her leg and nodded to the bar. Agent Crenel was chatting to the bartender. Both he and his companion were dressed in full FBI uniforms, and as Penny watched, Crenel spoke into his sleeve.

"What happened?" Tammy pressed.

"Uhh, there was a fight. Lots of blood, but the cocky got away." Penny's eyes followed Crenel back out to the foyer as she rambled.

"Wow, I really have to pee." Amelia shoved back from the table, her head darting in the direction Crenel and his friend had gone. "You coming, Penny?"

"Yup. Bursting."

The two women stood and hurried off, heedless of pleas for Penny to finish her story first.

"We *are* following the two special agents, aren't we?" Penny asked as soon as they were out of earshot.

"There he is." Amelia pointed to a door that was just swinging closed. "He went through there. Where'd the other one go?"

Penny was first through the door. She emerged into a kitchen to see Crenel speaking to one of the chefs.

"Ok, just make sure you let us know if you see anything." Crenel spotted Penny and Amelia over the chef's shoulder and quirked his mouth into a wry smile. "Thank you." He shook the man's hand and headed toward them.

"What's going on?" Amelia demanded.

"Why do you ask?" Crenel smoothly swept an arm out and guided the girls out of the kitchen ahead of a waitress carrying a loaded tray of food.

"Civic duty," Penny shot back.

"Well, it just so happens you two could come in handy," Crenel muttered. He led the girls to a secluded alcove, then gestured toward a narrow stairwell. "We got a call about a local coven. Well, we think it's more of a cult, really. They're holed up in the bathrooms, and they're trying to summon a local poltergeist."

Penny lifted an eyebrow. "They're in the ladies', aren't they?" Crenel's companion had been male.

Crenel touched the side of his nose. "Clever girl."

"So what, we get to bust in there and arrest them?" Amelia's eyes were round and sparkling. "Can we use force? *Lethal* force?" She looked around, then leaned in to whisper, "Do we get guns?"

Crenel snorted. "Against a couple of girls in bad makeup and oversized dresses?" He shook his head. "I don't think so. I just need you to take a look. If anything is going on, just pretend you're drunk and get the hell out of there. We can handle the rest."

Amelia giggled. "Well, *that* will be easy. I'm two-thirds there already."

"What are we looking for?" Penny asked.

"You'll know it if you see it." With that, Crenel shoved Penny gently forward. "I'll be waiting right here."

Penny stepped out and around the corner, only for someone to grab her arm. "Where'd you two buzz off to?" Cisco asked.

Amelia pranced by, tugging Penny's other arm. "We're going to the *ladies*, Cisco. Are you gonna follow us in to watch us pee?"

Cisco narrowed his eyes. "Something is going on." When faced with wide-eyed looks of innocence, he sighed. "Fine. I'm waiting here, though."

Penny descended first, squeezing to the side as a tall guy ran past them, wiping wet hands on his pants.

"Gross," Amelia murmured. "Seriously, hand towels exist for a reason, people!"

Despite her nonchalance, when they approached the women's bathroom, Amelia slipped her hand into Penny's. "Together," she whispered.

CHAPTER SIX

P enny pressed her hand to the door. Before pushing on it, she hissed to Amelia, "Follow my lead." She shoved the door open forcefully. "And did you seeeee his biceps?" Penny strode into the bathroom giggling loudly, doing her best to pay no attention to the black-clad cluster of girls in the corner.

"I know! Drool-worthy!" Amelia did her part, clasping her hands to her bosom as Penny approached the basins.

Penny turned on the tap and washed her hands. "Pity about the goatee. *So* nineties." She gave a dramatic shudder for effect, using the chipped mirror to watch the girls. They had quickly turned their attention from the intruders and huddled around each other, closing ranks—but not before Penny saw the huge, tattered book one of them clutched.

"Are you done?" Amelia whined. Her eyes darted to the corner, clearly uncomfortable. "That sexy bartender is *waiting* for us."

"I...really need to pee." They probably had enough to

take back to Crenel; the black robes and silver-lined hoods were enough for him to act on. She wanted a look at that book, though. "You go on. We don't want him to disappear on us."

"Uh-uh, girl. I'm not leaving here without you." Amelia held Penny's eyes for a moment.

Penny nodded. Her friend had her back, and she was glad. Crenel wouldn't abandon them if they didn't come back right away, and the more information they could get to him, the better.

Penny jerked open a stall door, then shrieked.

The white, semi-transparent body slumped against the stall wall lifted his head, blood still pouring from his throat as he gurgled incoherently.

"Penny!" Amelia's yell snapped Penny to attention, and she threw herself backward in time to see one of the cultists shove Amelia into the wall, sending her skidding off-balance.

"Hide the book!" A petite, dark-haired girl thrust the book at another girl as they pushed and shoved each other, trying to escape the ghost.

"Get her!" Penny pointed at the book's recipient, and Amelia, one hand clutching the arm she'd bashed against the porcelain bowl, lunged forward.

The mass of black hoods pressed together, and Penny lost sight of her target. Amelia turned to say something to Penny but dropped her jaw and froze. Penny looked back.

The mutilated ghost emerged, passing through the toilet door that had bounced shut. "Arrghgglllggghhh!" Sunken eyes rolled around to focus on Penny.

"Oh...*shit!*" Penny stumbled backward as it reached

toward her. "Run!"

She grabbed Amelia's arm on the way past, then dove to the side as the ghost picked up speed, floating past them.

"Follow it!" Penny yelled.

"That's a terrible idea!" Amelia hollered back, but she took off up the stairs behind it, toward the sudden outcry from above.

The growing screams spurred Penny on, and in moments, she'd burst through the upstairs door into the foyer.

Patrons of the Baghdad Theatre were yelling, screaming, and scrambling for exits. Two were jostling for a hiding spot behind a large planter, and one held up a chair in a defensive position.

"Cisco! You can't fight a ghost with a chair, you idiot!" Amelia cried.

Penny realized the chair-wielder was, in fact, Cisco.

"It's a ghost!" Cisco yelled, jabbing the chair toward the spirit. He swung it, but it passed through the apparition.

"Penny, you ok? This way." Crenel appeared in a doorway, gesturing hurriedly. "Someone has barred the kitchen, I can't get— What the fuck?" He'd finally noticed old cutthroat, whose attention seemed piqued by the newcomer. Crenel backed away slowly.

"Just the kitchen?" Penny asked, poised to run if the ghost turned her way.

Crenel nodded.

"Get to the bar," she said brusquely.

Cisco hesitated. "What, are we gonna fight this thing off with a bottle of tequila?"

Penny grinned. "Close."

Cisco's confused expression faded, and he barked a laugh. "Salt!"

Within half a minute, the three Academy students were armed with salt shakers, shoving their way past a fleeing crowd.

"This way!" Crenel's voice floated over the cries of alarm. "We've got a handful of suspects, and at least two apparitions. We need salt, string, and the GB equipment if it's nearby."

Penny arrived at his side just in time to hear the radio crackle. "We're en route. Over and out."

"Tell me what you saw," Crenel said quietly as he took the offered salt shaker.

"There were a bunch of them huddled together. They weren't doing anything when we got in. I think they'd already summoned it," Penny explained breathlessly. "They had a book. An old one."

Crenel paled. "What color?"

"Too old to tell. Black, maybe?" Penny glanced toward him. "Is that bad?"

Crenel shrugged. "It's the *Book of Thoth*, kid. We've heard rumors it was discovered but were hoping it wasn't true."

The ghost burst through a wall, moaning loudly. Despite his ability to pass through walls, the nearby concrete planter flew across the room when the ghost kicked it.

Penny dumped some salt into her hand and flung it at the spirit. It hissed and recoiled.

"Did you see who left with the book?" Crenel asked. He threw another handful of salt at the furious ghost. The tiny grains sizzled on its skin, leaving pockmarks, and melting a hole in its nose. The ghost retreated through the wall.

Penny hesitated. "Not really. They all looked the same. They know enough to keep it hidden, though."

A crash came from the kitchen, and the door burst open. People streamed out, screaming. Crenel nodded at the door, then ran toward it.

Penny took a breath to steel herself, then plunged in behind him. She jerked back as a whisk flew directly across the room toward her, missing her nose by inches.

The ghost stood on one of the stainless steel benches in the middle of the kitchen. Around him, pots, pans, and cooking utensils took to the air, hurtling toward the ghost but passing through him harmlessly.

"What in the hell?" Penny called to Crenel.

"I think they're on our side!" Crenel yelled back.

"Who? The utensils?"

"Smartass." Crenel ducked a badly aimed fork. "He's the one we need to deal with. I think the other stuff is down to some friendly neighborhood ghosts."

Penny's head swiveled around, looking for a weapon that would work. She spied a chopping board with a half-diced onion next to a steaming pot. Beside it, a bowl of sea salt glistened under the fluorescent lights.

"Distract him!" Penny called to Crenel.

"HEY!" Crenel yelled and waved. As the ghost turned to him, Crenel shot her a glance. "Be careful, kid."

Penny lunged across the counter and grabbed the salt. She scooped it into her hand and stepped forward, ready to throw it. Underfoot, a greasy, wet residue made her slip.

She tossed the salt as she fell, cracking the back of her

head on a bench hard enough that her ears buzzed. Cold liquid soaked the back of her dress, and the thought crossed her mind that the ghost could see straight up her skirt—not that he seemed to notice.

Thankfully,

"Penny!" Crenel's shout rang out over the noise.

"I'm fine!" she yelled, clutching a table for balance as she scrambled to her feet.

The ghost swooped to the floor and spun to face her, his face now melting and pulling away where, she assumed, the salt had hit its target.

Behind him, a soft wind whirled in a circle, disturbing the fallen seasoning. Penny eyed it warily. *It's salt,* she reasoned. *It's not gonna hurt me.*

"Feel tough, asshole?" she goaded, trying to keep the ghost's attention focused on her, even as she tugged her dress back down over her ass. If nothing else, distracting their target would buy Crenel time to act. "Picking on a poor, innocent girl. Shame on you!"

His rotting lips pulled back in a snarl, the effect made even more threatening by the loose flap of skin hanging off his chin.

Penny growled back.

From the corner of her eye, she saw the salt gusting around in a tiny tornado. It lifted, then swirled toward the ghost.

"You know what?" Penny said calmly. "I'm not gonna miss you at all." She stepped back as the saltnado slammed into the ghost. Tiny holes tore through him, and his body twisted and shrank. With one last violent scream, he vanished.

The salt fell and scattered across the floor. "How the fuck did you do that?" Penny asked.

Agent Crenel, face as white as the streaks in his hair, shook his head shakily. "That wasn't me."

Penny gasped as something moved behind her. She lurched forward and turned, to find a kitchen cloth slowly dragging itself onto the floor, settling on the puddle of spilled soup she had slipped in earlier. Slowly, the kitchen came to life, utensils floating to benches, fallen chairs righting themselves, and empty pots returning to cupboards.

"Looks like those girls raised more than one spirit," Crenel said. "We were just lucky the rest weren't malignant." He took Penny's arm to steady her, helping her untangle her feet from the cloth wrapped around her new boots.

"Uh, thanks for the cleanup?" Penny said to the empty air. The cloth dipped once, then scooted away.

Crenel frowned. "You've ruined your dress."

Penny shrugged. "I knew I should have stuck to jeans."

The agent shook his head, unable to let the matter go. "You're a civilian acting for the department. That's how I'll spin it for them, anyway. We can reimburse that." He pointed out the far door. "The exit is that way. You should go check on your friends. All we have to do now is clean up, and that's a job best left to the professionals."

"What about the bitches who summoned this thing?" Penny asked. "And the ghost. Ghosts. Is he just...gone?"

Agent Crenel sighed. "The girls will be long gone by now if they've got half a brain between them. The book, too."

69

"Damn." Penny wasn't well versed on the FBI, but she could guess someone's ass would be hung out to dry for that. "And old Cutthroat the Psychopath?"

"Gone, most likely. He could pop up again, but based on what we know of the location, he'll just loiter around the bathrooms giving people the willies."

Penny tugged on his arm as he made to leave. "What do you mean, the location?"

Crenel chuckled. "We've got the history of every ghost sighting in Portland. This place? It's notorious for spirits. My guess is our friend with the slit throat was probably a suicide. An old stagehand from back in the day who haunts the bathrooms, spying on girls. It's not the first time he's been seen here."

"That's disgusting," Penny said, horrified. Bad enough an actual creeper perving on girls in the loo, but an invisible one?

"The rest of them took care of it." Crenel waved his hand around the room to indicate the invisible helpers. "Old kitchen staff. Everyone who works here confirmed that there's a benevolent presence hovering around the kitchen and making sure everything runs smoothly."

Penny still had questions. "So, the girls with the book. Were they trying to bring something over, or just incite what's already here?"

Crenel shrugged. "Who knows."

"Right." Penny hobbled to the door, back stiff from her fall. It swung open to reveal two agents.

"Goddammit, Stu, what's going on here?" The taller agent, a woman with tight curls and bright red lipstick, clicked her tongue. "Can't keep you outta trouble for a hot minute, can they?"

"No, ma'am, they cannot." Crenel flicked his thumb toward Penny. "Karen, this is Penny Hingston."

"Oh!" Karen ran appraising eyes over Penny. "Was she worth the demotion?"

"Demotion?" Penny asked.

"For taking on unofficial business while on a job." The agent lifted a sculpted eyebrow. "You don't think he flew all the way across the world on the government's dime just to recruit a kid for college, did you?"

"I was there, and I did my job." Crenel laughed. "I just happened to take an afternoon of personal time in the middle. Anyway, if the pay doesn't drop, it's not a demotion. They just lumped me with an idiot partner for a few months."

"Tell me about it after you've partnered with Curry for a week." Karen smirked. "I'd swap with you any day." She stuck a hand out to Penny, who shook it timidly. "Special Agent Karen Delouise. How is school going?"

"All right, I guess." Penny shrugged awkwardly. "We only started this week."

"Ah." Agent Delouise gave Penny a dismissive nod. "Well, good luck with it. Crenel, you gonna tell me what in sweet Jesus is going on here? We have equipment assembling outside. Is that still needed?"

Crenel tipped an imaginary hat at Penny, then turned his attention to Delouise, giving her a terse but accurate description of the evening's events.

Penny slipped out of the kitchen into the foyer. It was mostly empty now. A few chairs still sprawled on the plush carpet and a palm tree had been knocked over, leaving a crescent-shaped trail of dirt as the pot rolled away. Its mate had been luckier; although the second pot had been disturbed, as evidenced by the freshly piled dirt at the base of the ribbed trunk of the palm tree, it was still upright.

Nearby, a mound of black cloth sat discarded in the corner. Penny picked it up and held it by the corners. It was a hooded cloak. "Looks like someone was eager to blend in with the crowd," she mused.

Penny wandered back toward the theatre entrance, cloak bundled under her arm. She would pass it on to Agent Crenel, but she didn't want to interrupt him just yet. Instead, she settled down on a cushioned bench facing the door to the kitchen.

A couple walked past her, excitedly talking about the disturbance although their heads were each buried in a phone.

"It's uploaded!" The guy, sandy-haired and grinning, high-fived the girl.

"Babe, if that takes off, we'll be rich with all the views!" They paused for a passionate kiss.

Penny grimaced but suppressed the urge to tell them to get a room. As they left, Penny caught the traces of an argument from outside.

"Ma'am, it's for your own safety. You can't go back in!"

Penny leaned over for a better view. Police milled outside, stringing up a flimsy taped barrier to prevent anyone from entering the theatre. Although most of the crowd beyond them seemed content to watch, flashes dotting amongst them as they snapped pictures from their phones, one girl angrily faced down her opponent.

She wore tight jeans and a dark tank top, and Penny shivered in sympathy. The girl must have left her coat inside, although it was a purse she was fighting over with the cop.

"Hey!" Penny called out, getting the officer's attention. "You're not kicking me out, right?"

With a pained expression, the officer shook his head. "We've been ordered to prevent anyone from entering, but the people inside are in charge of evicting anyone still there." He quickly sidestepped to prevent the girl from darting past him.

"I'll get your purse and throw it to you," Penny called.

The officer sighed in relief, but the girl snarled. "No, I need to go in myself. Let me through!"

She shoved the police officer. Another quickly grabbed her from behind, and between them, they restrained the angry girl.

"I don't have time for this shit," one officer growled. "You're under arrest." He spun her around and flicked a pair of cuffs from his belt.

"I need that book!" The girl screeched before lunging forward, freeing one arm that was quickly grabbed by the second officer. He held it tightly over her head. The girl clenched her dirty fist in frustration.

Dirty...hands. Book? Penny stared for a moment, then gasped. "The palm tree!" She spun back toward the theatre and started running just as the girl wriggled past the cop. The girl's hand, streaked like she'd spent the day in the garden, had sent her head spinning. "I'm such a wombat. How did I walk past that?"

A hand yanked her wrist, jerking her back on unsteady feet. "Get away from it, bitch!"

Penny dropped her stance and flung her body back, easily breaking the smaller girl's grasp. She ducked a wild punch, then grabbed the outstretched arm, twisting her body around and flipping the girl onto the floor.

Outside, the sound of fighting grew. Penny threw a quick glance toward the officers, who were now struggling to hold back a wave of angry people. "Crenel!" Penny screamed.

The kitchen doors burst open, and Agent Crenel appeared, Special Agent Delouise behind him. It took him barely a second to parse the scene. "Backup in the foyer, STAT. More beat cops, and I need three officers here now!"

The momentary distraction was Penny's undoing. When the cultist's forehead connected with her nose, the pain sent her vision spinning as heat blossomed across her face.

"You sneaky bitch!" Penny croaked as the girl tried to scramble away from under her. Penny let her twist around, trying to get to all fours. Then, she looped an arm around the girl's throat and pulled. The forward movement stopped as limp hands scratched at her arm.

"Get off her, kid." Penny looked up to see Delouise standing over them, a pair of handcuffs dangling from one hand and a stun gun in the other. "Trust me, you don't wanna be touching her when this goes off."

Penny sprang away, and the girl lurched forward. She had taken about three steps when the stunner clicked. The tiny prongs flew forward, connecting with her arm, and she dropped to the ground, convulsing.

Outside, the fighting grew louder. Satisfied Delouise had the girl under control, Penny dashed back to the small atrium with the two potted plants. She gave the fallen one a cursory glance—no, too messy. Nothing hidden in there. She dug her hands through the loose dirt of the other. Nothing!

Dammit. She'd been so sure.

"What is it?" Crenel's voice behind her made Penny jump.

"That girl—she's one of them." Penny suddenly remembered the cloak. She picked it up where it had dropped in her scuffle. "I think this is hers. It would explain why she's out in this godawful weather without a coat, anyway."

"And?" Agent Crenel pressed. His eyes continued to search the room, occasionally flicking back to the disturbance outside. More police officers had lined the barricade, and Penny spied three protesters lying face down on the concrete, hands cuffed behind them as they flailed on the ground.

"Her hands were dirty." Penny gestured to the pot. "And the soil in the pot was disturbed. I thought—"

Crenel didn't wait for her to finish. He shoved the tree, sending it rolling on the carpet, a pile of loose dirt flying to join the half-circle made by the other pot. He leaned down and yanked the plant out.

"Lesson number one, kid: always trust your gut. If it fails, it just means you haven't dug deep enough." Crenel thrust a hand into the bottom of the pot and drew out a cloth-covered square. He shook the dirt off, and the fabric dropped away to reveal a tattered book.

"Oh, shit!" Penny's jaw hung open for a moment before

a grin spread over her face. "I was right!"

A guttural scream interrupted anything else she might say. The girl, now standing and cuffed, struggled in vain as Delouise held her tight.

"Hey, Walker! This one's ours. Take care of her, will you?" Agent Delouise shoved the girl into the waiting arms of a uniformed officer. Free of her prisoner, Delouise strode over to where Penny stood with Crenel. This time, her glance was accompanied by a small smile. "You did good, kid."

Crenel handed her the book, and Delouise hefted it appreciatively. "I told you she was worth it."

"Crenel, how exactly are you wrapped up in the Academy?" Penny asked bluntly. She'd had enough of the pussy-footing around, and figured her efforts this evening had given her the leverage she needed to insist on an answer.

Delouise snorted, and Crenel looked at his feet. Neither answered.

"Really?" Penny sighed in defeat. *Guess I was wrong.*

"Penny!" Amelia's head popped through a doorway. "I've been looking everywhere for you!"

Penny waved at Crenel and Delouise. "That's my cue. I'll see you guys around?"

"Only if you're in trouble," Delouise said crisply. "So let's hope not."

"I'll be knocking around the Academy at some stage," Crenel said. At Delouise's lifted eyebrow, he smirked. "They gave me the liaison job. No, I don't know why, either."

"God help you all," Delouise muttered. She glanced at Penny. "Make sure you give him hell."

CHAPTER SEVEN

Penny stumbled into class the next morning, still wearing the smeared remnants of last night's mascara. She had a purple bruise blossoming from her lower back to her mid-thigh, although that, at least, was easily covered by her usual uniform of worn jeans.

To her surprise, the professor was nowhere to be seen. Penny carefully eased herself into an empty seat near the front, next to Red. She leaned past him so she could see Cisco and hissed to catch his attention.

"Cisco! Where's Amelia?"

Cisco thumbed the empty doorway. "First aid room. I don't know what you two were doing last night, but that bruise down her arm was pretty vicious."

His remark reminded Penny of her own throbbing ache. *I swear it didn't feel that bad last night.* "And the professor?"

Cisco lifted his hands. "No idea. No one has seen her this morning."

"Am I in your way?" Red leaned forward to insert his

grinning face between Penny and Cisco. "Because I feel like I'm interrupting something really important."

"Not at all, Red," Penny said. "Just glad I didn't miss the start of class."

"The start?" Red snorted. "This class ain't happening. It's been fifteen minutes! Either someone messed up the schedule, or they're havin' a laugh. I'm outta here, friends." He stood, stacked his things, and marched out of the room with a backward salute.

Two more students followed, leaving the rest to shuffle in their seats uncomfortably while they waited. After another ten minutes, Penny started shoving pens back into her pencil case. "Red was right," she told Cisco. "I'm going back to bed."

Footsteps in the corridor made her pause, and a moment later, Special Agent Crenel strode in, a folder in one hand and his phone in the other. He slipped the phone into his pocket and slapped the folder on the desk.

"Good morning, class. You've probably figured out I'm not the lovely professor Katie Marcus."

"You'd look great in a dress, though," Kathleen called from the back.

Crenel just gave her a smooth smile. "Thanks for the vote of confidence. However, your dean asked me to slip by on my way out to— Well, I'm here to let you know classes today are canceled. They'll resume as normal Monday. Have a great weekend, kids, and don't get into too much trouble."

Crenel stepped back to avoid being crushed by a half-dozen students who, spurred by the lure of a long weekend after twenty-five minutes of boredom, rushed for the door.

Penny waited for the rest to wander out before approaching the agent. Cisco hovered behind her, listening.

"Where's the professor?" she asked.

"She's the only expert in mythological items we have on hand," Crenel said. He didn't explain further, leaving Penny to fill in the gaps.

"You need her to look at the book I found?" she asked.

"What book?" Cisco finally spoke up. "What the hell *else* did I miss last night? Apart from the ghosts. Exactly *how* did you and Amelia get involved in that again?"

Penny coughed. "I wouldn't say we were *involved*." She realized she hadn't seen Cisco after he'd fought the ghost off. "Where'd *you* go last night, anyway?"

Cisco blushed.

"No shame in running from something like that, son," Crenel assured him. "I damn near crapped my pants as well, and I've faced that kind of thing before."

"Don't sweat it." Penny refrained from teasing Cisco. She had, after all, screamed like a girl when she'd first come face to face with the ghost.

"Listen, Penny, I wanted to thank you for your help," Crenel cleared his throat before speaking. "That book is a huge win for us."

Cisco's head bounced from Crenel to Penny, then back again. "*What* book?"

"Take care, kid." Ignoring Cisco's questions—in fact, ignoring him altogether—Crenel picked up his papers and walked out.

"Penny? Come on!" Cisco's desperation would have been funny if he weren't so earnest. "You have to tell me!"

"Ok, fine." Penny sank back down into her chair and gestured for him to do the same. "It went down like this…"

It was another week before Penny got to meet the elusive Professor Katie Marcus. Penny had to admit, she was quite impressed. The professor's mousy appearance and quiet demeanor belied her passion for mythological artifacts, quickly made apparent as Marcus introduced her students to a very recent find.

"I almost had to mortgage my soul for permission to show this to you," the professor explained, holding up the very book Penny had fought so hard for the previous week. "This, students, is none other than the *Book of Thoth*."

"Is it like a book of shadows?" Kathleen asked, flicking back her new dreadlocks. She'd had them done the previous weekend and took every chance she could to show them off. "Every witch has one. It's, like, a list of spells they've made up."

Professor Marcus just smiled. "It does have similarities. The *Book of Thoth* is an Egyptian artifact, but it *is* full of spells."

"How was it used to summon the ghosts?" Penny blurted.

Rather than admonish Penny for speaking out about classified events, Professor Marcus clapped her hands. "That's exactly what I was hoping you would ask. I take it everyone knows of the events that led to the discovery of the book?"

The professor's eagerness wasn't diminished by the

blank faces that met her question. "Well, I suppose most of the details are irrelevant. What you need to know is simply this—the group that procured this artifact used it to summon upwards of four ghosts. They didn't mean to, and in fact, the ghosts already existed to some degree."

She leaned forward conspiratorially. "What we theorize happened is this. One of the spells in the book—marked with fluorescent pink pen, so probably a recent notation—was one that calls to the undead. It seemingly can't be used to raise them, although there are other spells that will do that. This spell was used to summon forth the ghost that had been haunting the bathrooms, but its power extended further than the participants in the ritual expected it to."

Corey made a woofing sound. "That's 'cos dudes are strong, yo. Overpowered!"

Penny rolled her eyes. The bro club he and Jason had formed reeked of arrogance, the two eager to attack anyone they deemed as inferior to them—which seemed to be everyone.

"The young women who created the spell may have been overpowered," Marcus admitted with a tight grin at Corey's scowl. "They are a very industrious young group."

"That spell seems awfully unspecific." With the attention of the class turned his way, Red blushed. "I mean, if the people using the book knew there was a chance it'd summon a bunch of ghosts they didn't want, why would they use it in the first place?"

Professor Marcus pressed her lips tightly shut. Then, she put the book down carefully. "The motivations of the people who found this book are not the subject of this class. Suffice it to say, they have been dealt with. Now, any questions about the book itself?"

"It's just a book," Kathleen said dubiously. "Does this mean all magic is real now?"

"Not quite. The archetype of the 'magical book that provides a power source' is a common one." Marcus walked over to the board and started scribbling on it with a piece of chalk, listing titles as she wrote them.

"*The Coven. Blair Witch*—the second one, not the first. *Nowhere Boys*—Penny, you might know that one?"

Penny recalled a vague memory of an Australian tv show some of her self-defense students had talked about after class. She hadn't seen it, though.

Professor Marcus continued. "*Charmed*—that one is quite well known. *Supernatural*, very well known... " She placed the chalk down carefully. "And of course, that doesn't even begin to touch upon the crossovers with the *Necronomicon*."

"So, the only people who can use this fancy book are tv geeks or emo girls who listen to heavy metal and chant spells to make guys' dicks fall off?" Jason asked.

Heddy stood, stacked her books, and stormed out of the room while Kathleen squealed in outrage. She spun around in her seat, scowling. "I'll have you know I'm a dedicated Wiccan, and I only listen to country music." She turned back to her seat, throwing herself back in the chair with a flounce.

"Your theory has merit but was proven incorrect, Jason, although I am glad we have a Wiccan in the class," Professor Marcus said. "One of the things you will need to learn as part of your studies is the concept of conditional belief—although you should note, this is only a working concept at this point. If enough people believe, it will appear behind the Veil and has the potential to slip through. Once it has, anyone can use it—*if* they can see it for what it really is. That is a whole other kettle of fish!"

"I don't believe in leprechauns," Clive protested. "I still saw one at a party a few months ago."

Marcus looked at Clive over her glasses. "The events that we are witnessing could have an unprecedented effect on the belief systems of the general population."

Professor Marcus clasped her hands behind her back, pacing back and forth across the room as she spoke. "A year ago, I would wager none of you believed in the Easter Bunny. However, most of you probably believed that an Easter Bunny mascot could attend a corporate event, yes?" Most of the heads in the room nodded.

The professor continued. "There is a specific type of plasticity in the brain unique to those in your approximate age group. From around the age you begin to assert your independence, up until the age most people discard their faith for such fairytale concepts as justice or the overall fairness of life.

She lifted her head and ran her eyes over the room. "Sometimes, it lasts into adulthood—sometimes not. However, your ability to rationalize unusual events combined with your ability to accept even the strangest things, when presented with enough proof, make those of you in this classroom particularly suited to the specific coursework we are covering. In short, you have the capacity to *believe*."

The room was silent, the students listening, enraptured,

and the professor knew it was because they'd witnessed the impossible already. "Everyone here has seen enough over the past months to understand that *something* is happening. Myth and legend are becoming fact. Creatures that never before existed now walk amongst us. You have seen the proof, and you have accepted it. Part of my job, and the job of every professor in this building, is to teach you how to interact with those from beyond the Veil."

"So, we can cast a spell from the book?" Kathleen asked.

Professor Marcus nodded. "We believe so. We haven't had the chance to test it yet. A quick glance shows most of the spells require reagents that don't exist or at least haven't appeared on this side of the Veil yet."

"Can a curse hurt someone who doesn't believe?" Trevor pressed. "My dad doesn't believe in any of this. He was at that bar with the leprechaun, you can see him in the YouTube clip. He swears it's fake, that he was just talking to a regular, short man. He was green, though! My dad doesn't remember that bit at all."

Professor Marcus nodded. "Unfortunately, rigidity of the mind is no protection. You may not be able to see the short-statured man in your local bar as a leprechaun, but he can still tip a beer over your head. At that point, a flex-ible mind may reveal the truth—we've learned that those under threat can often see the reality of what they face, instead of the mundane veneer their mind normally cloaks it with. But disbelief is not protection, I'm afraid."

An awkward silence fell. After a moment, Professor Marcus reached beneath the heavy desk and withdrew a solid wooden box. "Let's move on, shall we?"

Penny immediately winced. The box closely resembled

one she had seen in another class. That class had ended in her being attacked by a psychotic gnome. Looking around, Penny realized she wasn't the only one who'd come to that conclusion. A couple of the other students were nervously pushing themselves away from their desks, as if ready to run.

Noticing the reaction of her students, Professor Marcus tittered a laugh. "Oh, it's not going to hurt you, I promise." The lock on the box clicked open, and Professor Marcus lifted the lid. A moment later, she drew out a blackened, withered hand, placed the book inside, and locked it again. "Does anyone know what this is?"

Blank stares were her only answer. Penny squinted, wondering if the disembodied appendage was about to start skittering toward her. Nothing happened.

"This is a Hand of Glory," Professor Marcus explained. Holding the gruesome item aloft, she walked over to the windows and drew the heavy blinds. Once closed, Penny had to stifle a hint of concern. Not even a sliver of light peeked through the edges.

Once the room was devoid of natural light and only the humming fluorescent bulb overhead was left, the professor walked over to the door. She closed it with a click, then reached for the light switch. "If anybody is afraid of the dark, I suggest you speak up now."

The switch clicked, and the room was plunged into darkness. "You'll find most of the classrooms in the Academy are sound- and light-proof," the professor explained. "This comes in handy in several ways, but today it's to show you a demonstration of how the hand works."

Penny heard footsteps as the professor walked around

the room, seemingly unbothered by the darkness, "One of the benefits of the hand is that it allows the bearer to see in complete darkness. To demonstrate this, we are going to pass it around the class. If you are touching the hand, you will be able to see without a problem. If you are not, please stay seated. We don't want any accidents to occur, do we?"

"Woah!" Penny recognized Clive's voice. "It's like daylight! Or maybe infrared? I can't see colors, so I guess it's not infrared."

"So far, we haven't been able to quantify what exactly allows you to see with the device," the professor answered.

Penny sat patiently, listening to the gasps of awe and exclamations of disgust as the item was passed around the classroom.

When it was her turn, Cisco quietly explained what he was doing. "I'm going to take your hand first," he told her. "Then I'm going to put the glory thing in it. As soon as you're touching it, you'll be able to see. Don't take it off me completely until I'm back in my seat, though." He laughed nervously.

Penny felt warm, living fingers touch her hand, cupping it carefully. Then, something dry and hard grazed the skin of her fingertips. The sudden blossoming of her vision took her by surprise.

Even though Penny had been expecting it, the clarity of her sight was beyond what she had imagined. Although the room was as bright as it had been earlier, her eyes needed no time to adjust to the sudden disappearance of the void that had swallowed her sight when the room went dark. As Clive had mentioned, the colors in the room were washed out—muted shades of gray and brown, with anything brighter indistinguishable.

Penny held one end of the hand while Cisco grasped the other, carefully moving back to his chair and gripping the desk.

He nodded to her, then let the hand go.

Penny watched until he had awkwardly slid into his seat again before she took a moment to look around the room. She had never used infrared goggles, so she didn't know what that would be like. This seemed like it would be pretty close, though, based on what she'd seen on tv. It certainly wasn't heat-sensitive—her fellow students were no brighter or clearer than the coldest, darkest corners of the room. "What was it used for?" Penny asked as she made her way over to the next student's desk.

"Thieving," Professor Marcus said simply. "It's the holy grail of a medieval thief. It lets you see in the dark, sneak around the house without having to light candles or lanterns—or switch on a light. We're not sure where the myth originated from, likely the Middle East. The item itself is the desiccated hand of a former thief."

Just as the professor finished her explanation, Penny touched Mara's arm, intending to give her the item.

Mara shrieked, flailing her arms in the air. "Get it off, get it *off*! I'm not touching no dead guy."

Penny snatched back her hand. "That was *my* hand, Mara."

"I don't care!" Mara had shrunk back in her seat, eyes wildly darting around the dark room. "That thing you're holding is a piece of *dead human*!"

"It's not really —"

Mara cut off Professor Marcus's explanation. "It's close enough," she snapped. "And I'm not touching it. You can't pay me enough. I don't care if you fail me out of this class, if *anybody* brings that dead piece of flesh anywhere near me, I'll...I'll punch you in the face!"

Penny hid her grin, even though no one could see it. Mara was standing a few inches away from her desk now, whirling around in a blind frenzy and shaking her finger at a classroom full of students who couldn't see it. Penny waited for Mara to calm down a little. The girl took a step forward, reaching for her desk. She was facing the wrong way. Mara leaned further forward, groping.

Then, she lost her balance. Mara's arms windmilled as she tried to regain her balance. A fist caught Trevor's chin and he yelped, frightening Mara even more.

Penny reached out and yanked on Mara's elbow, pulling her upright. "Woah, girl. You're gonna take out the whole class if you're not careful." Mara flinched, but Penny was able to set her back on her feet.

"If you touch me with that thing, I swear..." Mara scowled blindly.

"It's okay. I won't let it anywhere near you." Penny guided Mara back to her seat.

"Me next!" Kathleen called from next to Mara. Excitement shone from her eyes, and Penny eagerly handed the impossible object to her classmate, who made sure she helped Penny get back to her seat as she had done with Cisco.

It wasn't long before the hand of Glory had made its way around the classroom and back to Professor Marcus. She opened the blinds, letting light flood the room again. As she unveiled each of the windows, the professor made a point to unlatch each one, although she left them closed. Finally, she flicked the old yellow ceiling light on as well. Penny blinked the spots away from her eyes as they adjusted. She saw the professor jiggle the handle of the door, apparently making sure it was unlocked, then set the hand down on her desk.

Professor Katie Marcus grinned at her class. "As miraculous as the hand of Glory is, it possesses another use as well. Can anyone hazard a guess as to what it does?"

There was a pause before Clive called, "Does it cast a spell of silence?"

Marcus smiled. "That would certainly be handy while you're robbing a house, but no."

"Can it pick locks?" Red asked.

Again, Professor Marcus shook her head. She looked down at her desk and pulled open a drawer. After a moment of rummaging, she withdrew a small box of matches. It took two strikes to light one, but when she leaned forward and touched it to the blackened hands to light the single outstretched finger, it caught quickly. Penny watched the tiny flame gutter and dance. A trail of breezy smoke wafted into the air above it, twisting like a dancing snake. Despite her interest, Penny had to smother a sudden yawn.

"This particular spell only works under certain conditions," the professor explained. Her voice sounded dull, and when a second yawn cracked Penny's jaw, there was no hiding it. Beside her, Cisco rubbed his eyes.

"Any surrounding locks must be disengaged," the professor was saying. She gazed around the class, a smile twitching at her lips. "As you can see, the effect is not instantaneous. However, it is quite fast. In fact, I suspect most of you are only seconds away from—"

Penny's eyes fluttered open as she slowly became aware of the hard surface pressed against her cheek. She slowly moved her lips and blinked hard. When she lifted her head, it was to see her classmates sharing the same sleepy, befuddled glances. Penny glanced at Cisco and giggled at the wet smear across his cheek. "You drooled," she told him.

Cisco blushed and scrubbed at his face, then wiped a sleeve over his desk. "What the fuck just happened? I thought it was just me, but I somehow doubt an entire class just happened to choose to take a nap at the exact same time." He lifted his arms and stretched back, screwing up his face.

Penny glanced toward the front of the class. The hand of Glory was no longer burning. "Did you just...roofie the class?" Penny asked.

Professor Marcus giggled. "I prefer practical demonstrations, yes. I guarantee no harm came to any of you while you were sleeping, though." She paced to the front of her desk, waiting for the last remnants of sleep to fade from her students. "Quite a handy skill to have if you are about to break into a place, no?"

The professor waited until the rest of the class was conscious and alert. She picked up a slim stack of papers from the desk and began handing them out to each student. "Class isn't supposed to end for another ten minutes, but you could all do with a break. Go and have some lunch. Next class will meet on the patio for an outdoor lesson."

Penny took the piece of paper Professor Marcus handed her. It was titled *The Hand of Glory*, and a brief look confirmed that it was a study guide for the artifact.

As students began to make their way toward the classroom door, Professor Marcus called over the noise. "This is information you will be tested on, so make sure you keep your handouts and study them. A little more research into each topic wouldn't hurt either!"

CHAPTER EIGHT

"I can't believe Mara wouldn't even touch it. She's such a baby!" Amelia sank her teeth into the fat chicken burger that had been served for lunch. Despite getting let out from class early, Cook had been well prepared to accept the sudden influx of students into the dining room.

"Maybe it's a phobia?" Cisco spoke through a mouthful of food.

Penny motioned to his mouth, where a smear of mayonnaise decorated his lip. Cisco used his t-shirt to wipe it away. "I bet your mom would kill you if she saw that," Penny commented.

The mention of his mother sent Cisco bolt upright, swiveling his head around to make sure Professor Madera was not actually present. Seeing the room empty apart from the class, he relaxed again. "Don't scare me like that," he said, "or I'll push you off the rug."

"Rug?" Penny questioned.

Cisco smirked. "You'll see."

The doors to the dining hall burst open and another

group of students filed through, the sounds of the conversations filling the dining room.

"I don't care if it *is* a phobia," Amelia said. "We're here to learn. Eventually, we can be kicked out of this place and will have to face these things on our own. We are gonna need all the help we can get."

Penny nodded in agreement. The altercation they'd had at dinner the previous week still weighed on her. Apart from Boots, it was the first real contact she had with any of the mythical beings. She had to admit, it hadn't left a great impression on her. "What else do you think they've got?" she asked. She directed her question at Cisco, knowing he would be most equipped to answer it.

He caught her glance and gave her a wide grin. "If I told you, I'd have to kill you."

Amelia punched him in the arm, hard enough to make him yelp and wince. "If you don't tell us, I'll tell your mom you're being a dick."

Cisco cursed in mock outrage and threw his hands in the air. "Fine. I don't know all of it, but I've heard they've got an Asclepius Staff down there."

Penny scooted forward to the edge of her seat. "Really? How does it work?"

Amelia, mouth full of burger, tugged Penny's arm and gestured furiously. Unable to make herself understood, she gave a hard and painful swallow before speaking. "Don't leave me out. I want to know what it is!"

"It's a healing staff," Cisco said. "Greek, I think. You know the symbol on everything medical? The snaky thing around a staff? One touch, and it can heal anything."

"That's a caduceus." Amelia scowled. "And anyway, if

they've got that, why the fuck did I get a tube of shitty bruise cream last week?"

"Caduceus—*Caduceiae?*—have wings. And anyway, maybe they thought you needed to learn a lesson?" Cisco shot back.

"I imagine they want to keep it a secret," Penny said. "I mean, that kind of thing could go missing real fast."

"What, you don't know?" Cisco asked. "It's one of, oh, maybe a dozen in Portland? That's where all these miracle cures are coming from in the hospitals."

Penny frowned, thinking. "That kinda makes sense. I mean, the staff is on a ton of ambulances, right? And on letterheads and buildings? If these things are dropping out of the sky where they're most integrated into society, I can understand them appearing in hospitals."

"Well, if that's how it works, how in God's name did Professor Marcus get her hands on that creepy-ass thief of glory thing?" Mara noisily slid her tray onto their table, pulling back a chair with a screech before setting herself down. "I mean, it's not like we've got a thieves' guild right around the corner."

"Hey, Mara," Amelia said. Penny guessed she was feeling bad about her earlier comments, calling Mara a baby. "You've got a good point. That thing is just weird."

"It's disgusting!" Mara agreed. Her face twisted. "There's no way I'm touching something that came off a dead man."

"You know that's not technically correct, right?" Cisco interjected. He took another bite of his lunch, crumbs flying everywhere as he continued to speak. "It's only a myth. It's not like someone actually walked up to a dead guy and lopped off his hand."

"I don't care, it's still disgusting." Mara shrugged, face surly. "My brother hid a dead squirrel in my bed once. I cuddled it and everything, thinking it was our cat. When I woke up…" She shuddered. "Ugh. Never again."

"Oh. Mara, I'm so sorry. "That must have been traumatic!" Amelia touched Mara's arm. "I can see why the hand would upset you."

"But it's not real!" Cisco insisted. "It's like a movie prop or that synthetic meat stuff. It's close, but it's not *real*."

Penny watched the exchange with amusement. Cisco's argument made sense to her, as everything they've been told about the objects suggested they had simply popped into being in another plane of existence once popular belief took hold. "It's such an obscure piece of mythology, though," Penny mused, thinking of their earlier conversation. "I wonder why that appeared, and not something a little more well-known."

"Like what?" Cisco asked. He licked the grease from his fingers with a loud smacking noise.

"Like lucky horseshoes or rabbits' feet." Penny shrugged a shoulder. "You know, the kind of stuff people still believe in."

"Maybe it's just random." Mara was watching Cisco's attempts to clean himself up, distaste curling her lips. "Cisco, have you *ever* heard of soap and water?"

Cisco froze halfway through the act of lifting his shirt to wipe his face again. He flashed a chagrined smile and dropped it. "What can I say, I was never fully domesticated." He pressed his hands on the table and stood to head for the bathroom, leaving two shiny handprints behind where he had touched the table.

Penny sighed. "Men!"

The other two girls at the table nodded.

"Oh, crap, it's time for class." Mara picked up her half-eaten burger. "Although I'm making it clear—if it's more corpse stuff, I'm gone."

"Any guesses about what Cisco was hinting at?" Amelia asked Penny as they left the table. Mara remained behind, quickly stuffing her lunch into her mouth with dainty fingers as she tried not to make a mess.

Penny shrugged and pushed the doors of the dining room open, heading toward the covered balcony where Professor Marcus had instructed them to meet for the next lesson. An answer popped into Penny's head, but she quickly shook it away.

"There's no way they've got a..." Penny's voice trailed off.

Outside, hovering about a foot off the plush green grass of the grounds of the Academy, stood Professor Marcus. She balanced unsteadily as the carpet holding her up undulated and began to drift closer to them. "It is. It's a magic-fucking-carpet." Penny had to resist the urge to spin her head around to look for an adorable street urchin and his Middle Eastern princess.

"Good afternoon, students. I hope you all enjoyed your lunch?"

Penny was the third student to step on the flying carpet. It hovered just in front of the top step leading down from the balcony. She gingerly walked onto it, then sat, tangling her fingers in the tasseled edge and gripping it tightly.

"One lap of the Academy grounds, please," Professor Marcus said, her tone crisp and clear.

The carpet shot into the air until it was level with the Academy roof. When it steadied for a moment, Penny let go with one hand to quickly wave at her friends standing below. At that moment, the carpet took off, moving fast enough for the wind to whip Penny's hair across her face as it rounded a corner.

Below, the Academy grounds spread out farther than Penny had guessed from the limited balcony view. A wooded area hid a dilapidated tennis court, and what looked like a neglected herb garden sprawled beyond a small duck pond. The carpet turned again, and this time, Penny leaned into it, feeling more secure.

They came to a halt in the position they had started. "Your turn to take the proverbial wheel, dear," Professor Marcus said. "Pick anywhere that isn't underwater, on fire, or underground, please. This is a demonstration only, not a safety test."

"And it can go anywhere?" Penny asked. "Instantly?"

The professor murmured an affirmative response, and Penny bit her lip. Did she dare? *Hell, yes I do,* she thought. "Uluru."

The carpet took off at incredible speed, leaving Penny's eyes blurred and watering. She blinked hard, unwilling to loosen her grip on the carpet's edge to wipe them. Instead, she rubbed her shoulder across her face. The frigid air that tore at her skin changed, although it didn't warm. Instead, it dampened as the light surrounding her dimmed.

Penny squeezed her eyes shut and tried to shake away the blindness. When she opened them again, she saw that stars dotted the sky and soft clouds partially obscured a swollen moon.

"Pity about the time zone difference," Professor Marcus commented behind her. "I imagine this is quite the sight in the middle of the day."

The carpet zipped through the cool night air. It was barely warmer than Portland despite the seasonal difference, but the air was heavy with moisture. "Looks like rain," Penny said. "It won't ruin the carpet, will it?"

Marcus laughed. "It's been through worse. Besides, it's only light."

Penny swallowed back the lump in her throat. She was still half a country away from her hometown, but it *smelled* like home. "Can we go down for a closer look?" she asked.

Before the words had even left her lips, the carpet angled downwards. The soft glow of the shadowed moon cast eerie shadows over the landscape, highlighting the dips and mounds of the landscape and picking out the scattered, twiggy bushes that dotted the otherwise barren ground. Though not what she had expected, Penny was struck by the cool beauty of the Australian outback at night.

"Look!"

Penny looked at where the professor pointed to see two kangaroos bounding across the dirt away from them.

"We must've startled them," the professor said.

"This is incredible." Now that the speed had dropped a little, Penny felt confident releasing the edge of the carpet. She spread her arms wide, letting the dusty air kiss her skin.

"Certainly better than the top of Everest," Professor Marcus said dryly. "The view there is nice, but I do like having oxygen to breathe."

Penny snorted a laugh. "Let me guess. That was Corey's choice?"

Professor Marcus didn't confirm, but her soft laugh let Penny know she was right on the money. "I'm afraid we must return now, dear. Back to the Academy, please, carpet."

Penny grabbed the edge of the carpet just in time to prevent being swept off as it lurched into the night.

"Strike. Strike. Strike." The staccato beat of Professor Jones's instructions rang through the training hole. "Strike. Oh, for God's sake, not like that." Jones snatched the blunt stick from Red's hand.

"Sorry, Professor," Red mumbled.

Four weeks into the term, Penny had realized that even the *thought* of combat made Red squeamish.

He had already professed his desire to join the more scientific branch of the mythological agency being set up by the government.

Despite this, Professor Jones had insisted every one of his students would need to pass defense in order to move on to future classes. "You never know what's going to jump out of the shadows. No point being a scientist if you're going to end up a dead one."

After the things she had seen over the previous month, Penny was prone to agree.

Despite a teacher with the attitude of an angry dishcloth, Defense was one of Penny's favorite classes. She relished the opportunity to move, and to pit herself against the other students—especially Corey and Jason. The two boys had experienced the blunt end of Penny's training weapons more than once and hadn't enjoyed it one bit.

Professor Jones held a staff over one shoulder like a javelin. He took three quick steps, jabbed the staff into the face of the training dummy, then pulled it back and swung it around sharply to connect with the dummy's torso.

The realistic figure shuddered with the impact, and a rush of fake blood poured onto the floor where the cracked ribs punctured the transparent gel, quickly slowing to a slow trickle.

"*That's* how you kill a Naga." Professor Jones handed the stick back to Red, who held it up. Even from across the room, Penny could see from its crooked angle that it had fractured.

"Apart from the peace-lover and the bookworm over here, you're all progressing well," Professor Jones stated, gesturing at Trevor and Red. He clasped his hands behind his back and paced as he spoke. "I think it's time to test you out in the field."

"Ah, professor?" Cisco asked, sounding nervous. "Is that in the curriculum?"

Professor Jones met his eyes with a manic grin. "What's that saying, that it's better to ask forgiveness than permission?" He eyed the students as if daring them to protest. "Let me rephrase. We're going to take a camping trip. It's entirely voluntary—no one will be forced to come."

He ignored Red's relieved sigh. "But if you don't come, you *will* fail the damn class. Got it?"

Cisco groaned in frustration but nodded along with the rest of the students.

"And if *any* of you go running to your mamma," the professor's gaze was definitely directed at Cisco this time, "you'll also fail."

"What are we hunting, Professor?" Penny asked.

The professor's eyes gleamed. "Sasquatch."

CHAPTER NINE

In the end, it wasn't Cisco who ratted out the professor. Clive had made the mistake of begging Cook for some extra food to take on their adventure. Unable to resist bragging about the upcoming trip, Clive had told her everything.

Cisco told Penny that from there, Cook had complained to the dean. Not about the mission – no, Cook had absolutely no interest in what the students were learning – but that she hadn't been warned she would have to cater for twelve students camping in the woods for two nights.

In the end, the excursion went ahead, but with the caveat that it truly was voluntary and that no one would be downgraded for not attending. Penny arrived at the meeting place with Cisco and Amelia. Corey, Heddy, and Red were already waiting.

"Only six of you?" The outrage in Professor Jones's voice was palpable.

"Jason decided he had better things to do," Corey spat. "Fucking coward."

The professor looked downcast. "And the others?" he inquired hopefully.

"Clive was coming, but he got cursed in Acquisitions class earlier today. Trevor stayed back to try and help them reverse it." Penny handed Jones the note Professor Marcus had written out for the two students, explaining that Clive was in no condition to travel, and Trevor's uncanny affinity for investigative magic would be useful.

The professor scowled. "And are you just here to wave your friends off?" he asked Red, who'd angled himself to stand behind Cisco so he wouldn't be noticed.

Red blushed. "No, Professor. I want to go."

Jones narrowed his eyes. "I'm *apparently* obligated to tell you that you won't lose marks if you stay home."

"Yes, sir, I know. But...you're right. After what happened to Clive, I can see why I need to know how to protect myself, even if I'm only working in a lab." The gentle giant shrugged. "Besides, I suck at fighting. I figure I need all the extra credit I can get."

"You're not wrong there," Professor Jones muttered. He plastered a fake, cheery grin on his face and motioned toward the front door of the Academy. "Our chariot awaits."

The "chariot" was a stretched VW Kombi van. Penny eyed it with trepidation. A trip in that would possibly be more harrowing than facing down an actual Sasquatch if indeed they found one.

"Professor? That wouldn't seat twelve students." Heddy

stuck her head in the back to confirm. "Did you cancel the bus?"

"Cancel it?" Jones started throwing the students' bags under seats. "This *is* the bus. You would have squeezed in."

"You're kidding, right?" Amelia scorned. She met the professor's glare without backing down. "That thing looks like a deathtrap."

Jones finished loading the equipment and strode around to the front. "Old Sally has been hauling my ass around this country for the last thirty years, and she's never missed a beat. You give her the respect she deserves." Professor Jones' lips moved as he patted the nose of the vehicle.

Penny couldn't quite make out what he said, but she'd lay money down that he was apologizing to the car for the affront.

The six students piled into the Kombi, picking their way over bags of camping equipment packed into random corners and strapped on the seats. Penny had clutched her own duffel bag protectively—Boots was inside, nestled amongst layers of flannel and wool. A large cooler was wedged into the very back seat and Penny wondered if Cook had won her battle to cater for the expedition.

"Off we go!" Professor Jones threw himself into the front seat, twisted the key, cursed as the engine stalled, then tried to start the van again. This time it started and the professor laughed joyously.

"What is he *on* this morning?" Amelia muttered into Penny's ear. "Whatever it is, I want some."

Penny leaned forward to tap Cisco's shoulder. "Cisco,

are you sure they vetted all the teachers' backgrounds before employing them?"

"I'm starting to think not very well," Cisco answered. He cringed as the radio blared to life. "If he's gonna keep up with this music for the whole trip, I'll report him for grievous bodily harm to a student."

Penny didn't recognize the song, but the high-pitched country drawl was loud enough to make her eardrums ache. "This is gonna be one hell of a trip," she said, grinning.

Despite the unconventional approach of the professor, riding into no man's land in a rickety old van was something Penny had done many times before. During her high school days, she often escaped with a bunch of friends to a nearby watering hole, setting up tents for a couple of days and exploring the nearby caverns for fun.

This time? This time she was with new friends, a new place, and there was every chance she was going to see something incredible.

By the time Penny was tucked into her sleeping bag that night, her excitement had well and truly worn off.

She twisted uncomfortably, clutching the synthetic covering closer to try and ward off the biting cold. It didn't work. The soaking ground felt like ice, and the damp ate into her bones and chilled her to her core.

Penny rolled over again in frustration and was rewarded with a sharp hiss. "Sorry, Boots."

"This is pretty shitty, isn't it?" Amelia remarked.

"Cold, wet shitty," Heddy whispered.

Despite the low turnout leaving them with spare tents, the girls had elected to share anyway They were banking on the theory that many bodies would make extra heat, keeping them warm. The cheap, flimsy tents did little to hold that heat in, though.

"You're damn right it is." Penny gave up trying to get comfortable and sat up instead. "It's colder than a witch's tit, and I can't for the life of me get comfortable. I swear to God, Jones picked the lumpiest spot in the damn forest to set these tents up."

"We still have another night to go." Amelia heaved a dramatic sigh, then Penny heard the rustle of her sleeping bag and the sound of the zipper being undone. "Be right back."

Penny quickly struggled out of her sleeping bag. "You're not going anywhere without me. Coming, Heddy?"

Penny quickly re-evaluated her estimation of how much warmth the tent held. As cold as it was inside, nothing prepared her for the icy rush that hit her when she stepped outside. "Yikes!" She wrapped her arms around her chest. "This takes glass-cutting to a whole new level!"

"Is that Australian for 'oh gosh, it's terribly cold out here?'" Amelia asked. "If it is, I agree wholeheartedly." She began picking her way through the underbrush toward the middle of the small clearing they had set up camp in.

"Where the hell are we going?" Heddy asked. "You know people die of hypothermia, right?"

"Don't be so dramatic," Amelia scoffed. "Anyway, I'm off to find something to warm our bellies. Or at least, something strong enough that we don't care about the cold anymore."

She didn't elaborate further than that, but Penny was starting to develop a theory about where they were headed. During the bus ride, Cisco and Red had very circumspectly slid a bag under their seat, resting their feet on it when the bouncing of the van made the bag clink.

Her suspicion was reinforced when Amelia approached the boys' tent.

Amelia flicked the side of the tent. The low mumble of voices from inside was quickly followed by clinking glass. A moment later, the front of the boys' tent rustled as the zip was pulled down. "Who's there?" Cisco called in a hushed voice.

"It's us, you idiots. You didn't put the booze away, did you?" Amelia shone her flashlight in Cisco's face, and he held up a hand to protect his eyes from the blinding light. "We didn't come for the good company, you know."

"We didn't know it was you!" He moved aside to let the girls squeeze into the tent.

"Who the hell else would it be?" Penny asked. She maneuvered into a cross-legged position and took the plastic cup Cisco offered. She sniffed the amber liquid and guessed it was whiskey.

"Professor Jones?" Cisco said acerbically. He held up a bottle of Coke to Penny, and she nodded. "Nice flannels, Heddy."

Heddy grinned. "Goth doesn't stop when you sleep."

Amelia had already gushed over her black pajamas with a cute, skeletal cat pattern.

Penny rolled her eyes. "You really think Jones will care

if we have a few drinks? It's not like we're underage." She grinned, then took a sip, closing her eyes for a blissful moment. Although the Coke was flat and the drink a little stronger, somehow the torchlight and nylon walls made it taste far better than it would at home.

"Speak for yourself," Red mumbled, his face turning the same color as his name.

"What? How old are you?" Penny asked.

"I'm twenty-one in three weeks' time!" Scowling, Red threw back the last of his shot and filled it up again.

"Aww! He's just a little whippersnapper," cooed Amelia.

Red grumbled something in reply, but Penny didn't quite catch it. From his tone, she guessed it was something rude.

"I just turned nineteen," Heddy said quietly. "I don't wanna get you guys in trouble. Can I have a Coke?"

Penny passed Heddy a bottle while Cisco rummaged for a cup. "I keep forgetting you guys have to wait so much longer than we do to drink," she lamented. "I've been getting shitfaced for the last three and a half years."

"That's *so unfair!*" Amelia groaned. "Three years? I only had my first legal drink last month!"

"What?" Red snapped. He tossed a rolled-up sock at Amelia's head. "You just called me young!"

Amelia tossed the sock back at Red, missing his head and hitting his cup instead.

Red cursed, looking down at his lap where the sticky liquid had soaked his jeans.

"Oh, dammit. I'm sorry, Red." Amelia's apology sounded sincere, but her eyes glinted, and a sly grin touched her mouth. "You want me to help clean that up? I've got a towel back in my tent."

Penny's jaw dropped, and Red blushed even harder than he had before.

Amelia just laughed. "God, you're such prudes." She winked at Red. "Come on. It'll only take a minute."

"Oh, my God, did you just insult me *again?*" Red screeched. He grabbed an unopened bottle and stood, or tried to. Hunched over in the tent, he stepped on Penny's hand while trying to make for the exit. "Shit, did I get your fingers? Sorry Penny." He glanced back at Cisco. "I'll be back. But I'll be gone *at least* three minutes."

"Oh, a challenge." Amelia passed Penny her already-empty cup and clambered out over her friend.

Penny grabbed her arm and pulled her close. "If you get *anything* on my blankets, I'll leave you out here for Bigfoot to eat," she told them in a low voice.

"We'll find a quiet spot in the woods. Have fun, you three," Amelia said with a wink. She saluted and backed out carefully.

"Did he step on you?" Heddy asked.

Penny held up her hand. "Yeah. Not hard, though."

Cisco snorted into his cup. "That's *not* what she said."

Penny giggled, heat from the whiskey already flooding her cheeks. "I bet." She glanced at the open tent flap, seeing nothing but darkness. "Do you think they'll be safe out there?"

"Red is chicken. They won't go far." Cisco eyed Penny's cup. "Need a top-up?"

"Are you trying to get me drunk?" Penny asked, grinning.

Cisco quickly waved his hands. "No! Not me. Boy scout's honor."

Heddy twisted her mouth. "Were you even a scout?"

Laughing, Cisco shook his head. "No way. They were too uptight for a kid like me. One *hundred* percent rebel, I was."

"And now?" Penny's voice dropped, her question a serious one. She gestured a hand toward the bottle stashed by his side.

Cisco passed her the whiskey. "Mom had cancer last year. She was lucky—a few weeks of chemo and she was cleared. But I had to take her to the appointments. Penny, I met a lady who lost *everything*. Her life savings, her house. Until then, I hadn't taken it all seriously, you know? I just kind of thought Mom would always be there, that someone would always be looking after me."

Penny nodded. She had been drifting through life, too. Hell, this whole trip was on a whim and she still had no idea if she would stay. "I guess that kind of thing really makes you think."

Cisco nodded. "Life sucks when you're an adult. In some ways, anyway. I realized I'd better start thinking about my future. Good job, financial security, insurance."

"My dad died of cancer," Heddy told them in a small voice. Before the others could say anything, she waved her hand. "We weren't close. He wasn't an asshole, but we only spent a few weeks a year together after my parents split. But the cancer? It was expensive. My mom ended up paying his rent for the last six months, just so he wasn't homeless."

"I guess I've never really thought about it," Penny said.

"But my parents will get old one day. They're happy now, but traveling. I've honestly never considered what comes next for them."

They all fell silent for a while, sipping their drinks and contemplating uncertain futures.

"What are you two gonna do when you graduate?" Cisco finally asked. He twisted around and rummaged in a bag while he waited for the girls to answer.

"Government work," Heddy said. She shrugged. "I know I act like a rebel, but that doesn't mean I want to throw my life away."

"Penny?" Cisco nudged her with his knee.

The question took Penny by surprise. "I don't know. I mean, I don't even know if I will."

Turning back, Cisco tilted his head questioningly. Penny explained Crenel's offer. "I told him I'd give it a shot. One semester. After that, I have to choose whether I'll stay —but I don't think I will."

"You can't leave. What would you do back home, anyway?" Cisco finally found what he was looking for and pulled out a bag of Doritos. He popped it open and tipped it toward Penny.

She sniffed the bag cautiously. After being stuck in the airport for four hours on arrival waiting for her ride to the Academy, she'd found Doritos in America were *not* the same as Doritos in Australia. She plucked a chip out and popped it in her mouth.

"I don't know," she admitted. Then, she gasped as the spices from the corn chip started to bite at her mouth. "Oh, shit." She downed her drink and held the empty cup out for Cisco to refill. "Spicy!" she explained in a choked voice.

Heddy snorted her drink into her cup, and Cisco chuckled as he poured Penny another drink. Penny emptied it, then sucked air into her still-burning mouth. The burn receded and she waved her face, panting. "What the hell is with American food? At this rate, I'll be dead before the semester is over."

"Spicy?" Cisco shook his head in wonder. "You haven't *tried* spicy."

"Yeah?" Penny grimaced. "Let's keep it that way."

"I'll tell you what," Cisco leaned back into a more comfortable position. "I'll take you to a nice place I know. It's a little cantina, hidden in a back street. The food there is amazing. Once you taste it, you'll never want to go home."

Penny gave him a skeptical look. "Mexican food is spicy," she reminded him. "My tongue is about as tough as a newborn kitten."

"They have some stuff even *you* can handle," Cisco promised. "And if that fails, I'll have my mom cook for you."

The idea of having Professor Madera cook for her made Penny giggle. "Right. I take it you can't?"

With a wounded expression, Cisco threw his hands up. "I can cook! Pretty damn well, too. But no one beats Mom's paella. *No one.*"

"Ok, fine. Somewhere in the US, there's good food. But after this semester, I don't get a cost of living grant, and tuition isn't covered." Penny spread her hands. "I'd have to get a job. Who would look after Boots?" She shook her head. "It just wouldn't work, Cisco."

"I'd babysit for you." Cisco's face squinched as he reconsidered his words. "Snake-sit?"

"Serpent-sit," Penny amended. "Thanks for the offer, though. I just...don't know if I can stay away from home for two whole years," she admitted.

She was surprised to find herself giving it serious thought, though. *What if I did stay?*

"Homesick?" When she nodded, Cisco patted her knee. "We'll just have to make sure you have so much fun you don't have time to think about going back. And maybe you can visit on breaks."

Penny snorted. "Yeah, if I find a sugar daddy to pay for the flights."

Cisco tapped the side of his nose. "Or, make friends with a guy whose mom knows the owner of a magic carpet."

Despite feeling stupid for not even considering that, Penny's spirits lifted. "It beats an eighteen-hour flight, that's for sure." She jabbed a finger at Cisco. "You could come too! Mrs. Chu would love to meet you." Then she frowned, reconsidering. "Then again, she'd be planning our wedding within five minutes of seeing us together. That woman is obsessed *with* marrying me off."

"Who's Mrs. Chu?" Cisco poured two last drinks, draining the whiskey bottle empty. He held a Coke out to Heddy, then chuckled when he saw she'd fallen asleep, slumped over a duffel bag, and snoring lightly.

"I guess it's safe to reveal my secret Australian identity, then," Penny joked. Sighing happily, she told him about the eccentric owner of the Chinese Kitchen, the resident drunk, the kind publican, and the rest of the larger-than-life characters of Larrabee.

Cisco listened loosely, eyes widening when she told him she taught self-defense and laughing at her portrayal of Jerry and his altercation with Boots.

"I can see why you love it," Cisco conceded when she stopped, lost in her memories of her hometown. "But there are good things—and good people here, too."

Penny smiled. Despite a pang of homesickness and the knowledge her time here was limited, she had to admit that right now, she was glad to be where she was. "I know. I've already met some."

CHAPTER TEN

Penny woke the next morning with a pounding headache. She sat, wincing as it thumped harder. A quick glance at Amelia showed her roomie was no better off.

She wondered how Heddy was doing—since she had refused to leave the warmth of Cisco and Red's tent, curling into Red's empty sleeping bag for the night instead.

"How are you holding up?" Penny asked gently.

Amelia sat up, then clutched her stomach. "Ohhhh, God. I'm gonna be sick." She pressed her eyes shut as Penny scrambled for a bag. "It's ok. I can hold it in...I think."

"Did you two finish that whole bottle between you?" Penny asked.

Amelia nodded. "Looks like we're hitting the hay early tonight."

"Don't bet on it," Penny argued. "The boys brought enough grog to last a week. If you don't mind liver failure, anyway."

Laying back down on her sleeping bag, Amelia groaned. "No way. Never again."

"Wait until tonight," Penny assured her. "You'll change your mind."

Amelia yanked her pillow over her head. "Probably. But until then, I'd like to die alone, please."

Penny reached for the tent zipper but jumped back when a loud, metallic clang pierced the air. It sounded a half-dozen times in rapid succession, loud enough to penetrate Penny's hands clasped over her ears. Beside her, Amelia whimpered.

"Get up! We don't have all day!" Professor Jones's voice rang out when the cacophony had stopped. "I heard the shenanigans last night. That's no excuse—if you want to act like adults at night, you work like adults the next morning."

"All right!" Red yelled nearby. "Enough with the banging, though!"

A hand groped Penny's leg, and she looked down to see Amelia blindly searching for something, pillow still clutched tightly over her head.

"Pink bag," Amelia moaned. "Tylenol."

Penny spotted the lifesaving purse tucked in a corner of the tent and fished out the small bottle of painkillers. "Here."

Amelia swallowed two of them dry. "Gods, I'll kill that bastard myself if the Sasquatch doesn't."

Hiding a smile, Penny emerged into the morning sunlight. She winced, realizing she should have asked Amelia if she had enough Tylenol to share.

Cisco waved at her from across the clearing, stirring a

bowl over a steel camp table. Nearby, the blue cooler sat with the lid open. "Do you know how to build a fire?"

Penny nodded, wandering over to see a small stack of firewood was already set up in a neat pile, the previous night's ash and charcoal swept into a pile beside it.

"Catch!"

Penny spun just in time to see Jones toss a box of matches her way. She reached out, the tiny box bouncing off her fingers and falling to the ground when she fumbled it. "A little warning next time, hey?"

"A wildebeest won't give notice before it charges." Jones's face held just a little too much glee.

Before long, they had a cast iron skillet perched over a crackling fire. The aroma of herbs and mushrooms filled the air.

Cisco stirred the eggs. "It's almost ready." He nodded to the table. "Penny, can you grab the plates?"

Penny helped Cisco dish out the scrambled eggs as Jones dangled bread slices over the fire in a claw-like contraption to toast them.

Corey and Heddy finally appeared, one looking bright and bushy-tailed, the other paler than the ivory makeup she usually wore.

They sat together on a fallen log, but when Corey leaned over and said something to Heddy, she shook her head in disgust and went to find another place to sit.

She eventually parked herself on the bare ground beside Boots, who'd curled up in the warmth of the fire and took the plate Penny handed her gratefully.

"You ok?" Penny asked. "Or do we need to feed someone to a hungry Myther?"

"It's fine." Heddy sighed. "I'm pretty used to it now."

"Is that breakfast?" Amelia shuffled over, face pasty-white and eyes red.

At least she's not green anymore, Penny mused.

"Save some for me!" Red appeared from the trees, zipping up his jeans as he ambled over.

He glanced at Amelia, and their eyes met for a brief second. Red immediately looked away, blushing. Amelia just rolled her eyes. Despite any awkwardness, the two somehow managed to end up sitting next to each other, perched on a fat log with plastic plates balanced on their knees.

Cisco sauntered over to Penny once the skillet had been lifted off the fire. "How's it taste?"

"Oh, my God," Penny gushed. The smell had been tantalizing, but the actual taste sent a shiver of deliciousness down her spine. "It's amazing! If you learned to cook like this from your mum, I'm *definitely* coming over for dinner."

"I can't take all the credit," Cisco admitted. "If Cook hadn't packed every spice known to man, it'd be plain-ass eggs for breakfast."

"You did good." Penny stopped talking to cram the last bit of egg-laden toast into her mouth, then brushed the crumbs from her fingers to reach over and high-five Cisco. "Bloody good work, mate."

Jones congratulated Cisco as well but hustled the students to finish. "We have work to do," he reminded them.

Once breakfast was cleaned up and packed away, Jones ensured everyone's backpack was packed with water, lunch, a map and compass, and a small first aid kit.

Next, he lined them up. "What we hope to face today is a monster long rumored to be present in these hills. Sightings have been plentiful, but always brief, with little real information to divulge its nature."

He paced back and forth, shaking his finger as he spoke. "We know that it's wily. *Intelligent!* It is strong and fast. Are six children and an aging soldier up to the task of capturing it?"

He ignored the scowls and Red's muttered protest about being a "fully-grown adult, thank you very much."

"We must outsmart the beast," Jones continued. "And succeed where that fool Craster failed. We must be swift and work as a team. Most importantly, we must be armed." He marched over to the van, shoving a side door open and dragging out a flat, padlocked box.

"You brought *guns?*" Amelia demanded. "That was *not* on the travel brochure!"

"Forget the guns," Penny murmured. "Did he just call Craster an idiot?" She had already come to like the eccentric old professor.

"This'll be awesome!" Corey's excitement was not entirely unexpected, but Penny couldn't suppress her eyeroll.

"Don't worry," Jones called. "No bullets, just tranquilizer darts. If you get hit by one, you'll probably survive the event."

"Probably?" Penny asked dubiously.

Jones stood, brandishing a long, skinny rifle. "Well, I can't guarantee it. These babies were designed to take down a five-hundred-pound beast, not a school kid."

"Do I look like I'm fucking twelve?" Red snapped, his patience worn thin.

"Hey, just because you lost your boyhood last night, doesn't make you a man." Jones sighed, cutting off Red's stammered protest. "Boy, when you're fucking in the woods, it's best to do so quietly. You never know what kind of beast will take interest. If I hadn't been out there guarding the campsite with one of these, you might have both been killed!"

"Oh, God." Amelia sank her face into her hands. "I wish Bigfoot would just eat me already and put me out of my misery." Her face was, to Penny's amusement, as bright as her new lover's.

"Hey, at least you had fun." Penny nudged Amelia in the ribs. "A *lot* of fun by the sound of it."

Amelia lifted her head enough to smirk. "You have *no idea* how much fun."

Finally, armed with dart guns and minds reeling with Jones's convoluted instructions on how to use them, the team of hunters advanced toward the trees. They walked single file, following the path Jones cut for them through the thick growth. His machete set off a run of jokes on what a 'knife' was as Cisco and Red tried to outdo Penny's Australian accent.

"Ssh!" Jones's urgent whisper and raised hand cut the chatter in an instant. "This is the spot."

Cisco moved to one side to give Penny a clear view into the small clearing. She lifted her rifle, mindful not to point it at any of her friends as she swept it side to side, taking in the piles of chewed-on bones and piles of detritus that scattered the ground.

Corey was a little less careful. Finger on the trigger, he held the scope to his eye, waving the muzzle wildly.

"God damn it, kid!" Jones growled. He stomped over and fixed Corey's stance and grip. The boy took the correction surprisingly well.

"It just looks like a dirty campsite." Red's voice rang out too loud in the quiet, wavering with uncertainty.

"Look." Cisco pointed at a set of claw marks running in jagged lines down a tree trunk.

"What did that?" Amelia asked in a whisper. Her rifle was butted against her shoulder, her finger resting safely on the outside of the trigger guard.

Penny realized she'd allowed the barrel of her rifle to drop and quickly corrected. She wasn't a total stranger to guns, but that one time she went out shooting wild pigs in the outback didn't exactly compare to hunting a Sasquatch.

Jones thrust his dangling rifle behind his back, creeping forward with his knife held out in front of him. He carefully made his way over to a pile of bones, then circled it, facing the forest. Once satisfied that they were alone, he bent down and snatched up one of the bones.

"These aren't human teeth patterns," he hissed at Red.

Red took the bone between two fingers, holding it aloft with his disgust clearly written across his face. Even in the dappled light filtered by thick foliage, Penny could see the deep scores where teeth had gnawed the bone. Jones was right. There was nothing human about those marks.

"*WHERE ARE YA?*" Jones's sudden bellow sent rifles waving in frantic fear. "*COME OUT, YA YELLOW BASTARD!*"

The panicked beating of Penny's heart hadn't slowed

when the forest sent its own answer. The trees trembled as an angry screech hammered her eardrums. Moments later, the trembling turned to violent shaking as something very large rushed the clearing.

"Bigfoot!" Cisco jerked his weapon toward the commotion. "Fire!"

Penny registered the *thunk* of a dart hitting wood before realizing he'd discharged the rifle already. She looked around, fear anchoring her feet to the ground even as she stood exposed in the clearing.

Red was nowhere to be seen. Amelia's sharp intakes of breath gave away her hiding spot behind a fallen tree.

Jones...well.

The professor had climbed a half-rotted stump and stood hollering at the forest, beating his chest.

Something large and brown slammed into him, landing on top of the screaming professor and finally silencing the yells.

The Sasquatch was tall, covered in heavy fur that accentuated its bulging muscles.

Penny gulped when it turned its head toward her, its black lips pulled back in a snarl that exposed its sharp white teeth.

"Shoot it!" Cisco fired again, then yanked another dart from his belt. His rifle shook in his hands, rattling as he tried to load it.

The Sasquatch turned toward Cisco and growled.

Cisco's eyes followed the threat. Then he fumbled, cursing when the dart rolled to the ground.

"Oh...shit." Penny yanked her gun up and fired twice,

one round after the other. Both shots missed, one *thwapping* into a tree, the other sailing into the forest uselessly.

Two thumping steps brought the monster face to face with Cisco. Penny snatched at her belt. "Stay still," she hissed. "Just stay still, Cisco."

Cisco seemed unable to do otherwise. He stood trembling as the furred face drifted toward him. The beast sniffed at Cisco with a flattened ape-like nose, seeming to relish the scent.

Penny freed the dart and carefully tipped her weapon up so she could reach the chamber. Eyes on Cisco, willing the beast to wait, she heard a *snick* as the dart slipped into place.

The sound caught the beast's attention. It turned its head, green eyes and cat-slit pupils running over Penny's body with ruthless intelligence.

"Hey! Over here, Hasselhoff!" Penny's eyes jerked to Amelia, who stood on the fallen log waving her arms.

The Sasquatch roared and swung an arm, knocking Cisco to the ground as it turned and bore down on Amelia.

Amelia squealed and dove back behind the log. "Hurry up!" she squeaked. "I don't want to die!"

Penny lifted the rifle, looking down the scope at the lumbering beast. She followed its momentum and let out a slow breath. She squeezed the trigger.

The dart hit the Sasquatch in the flank, pink flights jutting out. It didn't slow.

Penny's heart skipped a beat. *Should have loaded two.* She grabbed for another dart.

"Hey, sexy!" Cisco yelled. He scrambled to one knee then lifted his gun. "Don't turn your back on me!"

Whirling, the Sasquatch bellowed. Its eyes darted from Cisco to Penny, then spun back to a cowering Amelia.

Penny fumbled her next dart and cursed when it rolled away across the ground. "Shit! I dropped it!" Penny yelled.

The Sasquatch turned to her as if understanding her predicament. It snarled, then dropped to a crouch.

"Run!"

Cisco's shout loosened Penny's feet at last. She turned and ran, flying into the forest, jumping over roots and rocks, ducking under large branches and letting small ones slap her harmlessly in the chest.

Behind her, the clumping footfalls and heavy breathing of the Sasquatch pursued.

Penny ducked behind a tree, veering off to the left. The crashing stopped, giving her a brief moment of hope before the thundering chase resumed.

"Penny! Back this way!" Cisco's voice filtered through the pounding of her heart. Penny followed it, all sense of direction skewed but trusting her ears to guide her.

A bellow rang out behind her. Penny burst into the clearing and leaped over the fallen tree. Ahead, Amelia, and Cisco stood, rifles aimed toward her.

"*DUCK!*" Amelia screamed.

Penny dropped to the ground, her momentum propelling her into a slide. Behind her, the Sasquatch roared. Time slowed once more.

Guns fire.

Thock! Thock!

Penny twisted her head, following the arc of two bright darts as they silently sailed the short distance between her friends and their foe.

Both hit, embedding in their target's flank.

The Sasquatch lumbered forward, eyes wild.

Penny rolled to a squat. The beast took another step and reached for Penny with a monstrous fist. She threw herself backward, any attempt at gaining her footing gone.

Time stopped as she sprawled on her back.

Or perhaps, Penny realized after a moment, *it wasn't time that froze.*

The Sasquatch stood, teetering on unsteady feet. It looked down and blinked.

Then it fell.

When Penny came to, it was to the stench of dank, wet fur, dog breath, and a dry, flickering tongue tickling her cheek.

"Urgh." She turned her head to escape the smell, but it followed her, permeating her nostrils with eye-watering potency. *I guess it isn't snake-breath, then.* In a display of uncanny intuition, Boots gave an irritated hiss and head-butted Penny's cheek before slithering away.

"Penny?" Amelia's face appeared over her. "Are you ok, hon?"

Penny reassembled the scrambled pieces of her mind to check. *Legs? Still attached. Arms? Moving. Boots? Annoying the shit out of me, so clearly fine. Breathing ok, except for...* "What crawled into my nose and died?"

"It's Sassy. He's a bit fresh." Amelia pulled back so Penny could sit up.

"Sassy?" Penny rubbed her head. It throbbed harder than it had when she'd woken up that morning. She sat where she had fallen, body-slammed by the monster when it slipped unconscious from the tranquilizer darts. Her ass and back were wet from the damp leaf litter, and dead leaves hung from her matted hair.

"I named him. Sassy the Sasquatch." Amelia grinned and gestured to the still-sleeping pile of fur splayed on the forest floor, where Boots had gone to investigate. "Cisco thinks it's a territorial thing. Like, he's stinking out the other Sasquatch in the area."

"Other Sasquatch?" Penny jolted to her feet, unsteady but alert for danger. Boots jerked her head up and wriggled back to Penny, head raised in concern.

"Steady, girl." Amelia pulled Penny's wrist. "Figure of speech. We haven't seen any others lurking about."

"Oh." Still dazed, Penny blinked to focus her eyes properly. Boots nudged her knee. "What about you, love? You didn't bite him, did you?" She had no idea what effect the tranquilizer might have on Boots if she did. In fact, she wasn't even sure how the serpent had found her. Penny had left her basking by the fire.

"It's ok. I kept an eye on her while you were out." Amelia crouched down to coo at the serpent, who replied with an elegant dance. "I don't know when she turned up. I saw her checking out Sassy, but she seems fine."

"Hey! Sleeping Beauty is up!" Red emerged from the trees, Cisco trailing behind.

"Which one?" Cisco asked before peeking over Red's shoulder to check.

Red snorted. "The less stinky of the two." He walked over to kick the comatose beast. "Did he move while we were gone?"

Amelia shook her head and patted a rifle on the ground next to her. "Not yet. It's only been a few hours, though. How long are these things supposed to last?"

Red and Cisco both shrugged.

"Uh, guys?" Penny glanced around, seeing no one else in the clearing. "Where are the others?"

"Corey got hurt," Amelia said gently. Penny tried to get up, but Amelia gently pressed her back down. "He'll be fine. Heddy is looking after him."

Penny squashed down a trickle of unease that Heddy was 'looking after' someone who so clearly disliked her. "And Jones?"

Cisco pulled a disgusted face. "Jones bailed. He came back after we took down the giant gerbil. He had some excuse about a faulty gun, but it was bullshit. When things got tough, he ran."

"No!" Penny choked back a laugh. "Mr. Tough Guy? Seriously? I thought he said he was a professional hunter!"

"He was, he just never found anything," Cisco clarified. "And when he did, he realized he's as yellow as an egg yolk."

"Yeah. And when he finally found his balls and came back, he left again to call for backup." Amelia seemed as unimpressed as Cisco. "Apparently, the genius didn't think we'd actually find the Sasquatch we came looking for. Now we've got one, and no way to get it home."

Penny's eyes widened. "We're taking it *home*?"

Red walked over and stuck his hand out to Penny. She grabbed it and let him pull her to her feet. "I know you guys think he's trash, but give him a break, ok? He was scared."

"*You* weren't." Amelia stepped closer to Red and looped an arm around him. "Red hid in the trees and shot from behind," she explained to Penny. "That's the only reason he fell when he did. By the time Cisco and I got our rounds off, Mr. Bigfoot here had enough rounds decorating his ass to double as a *Mardi Gras* costume."

"Wow." Penny grinned at Red, admiration blooming. "Good work, mate!"

Red looked away, abashed. "It was nothing. Couldn't let the hairy fecker get you, after all."

"I'm glad you were here." Penny smiled, then rubbed her face. "Man. I must have really conked my head. My ears are ringing!"

Amelia looked up, frowning. "I don't think it's you."

The low, rhythmic whine solidified into the thud of a helicopter overhead. Penny looked up, wondering if it would pass over the tiny patch of clear sky over the clearing. It didn't, but the staccato beat grew until the leaves nearby stirred gently.

"It's landing nearby," Cisco called over the noise. "I'm guessing he's why."

He pointed over Penny's shoulder, and she turned to see Jones standing by a tree, yelling into a handheld radio. Without missing a beat, he tossed a pile of ropes at her, then jutted his chin at the fallen Sasquatch before stomping back into the forest.

The roar of the blades slowed to a rhythmic thud, and finally, the chopper stopped. Moments later, shouted words filled the void.

Penny tossed the rope to Cisco. "Give me a hand?"

Cisco nodded and planted one foot on the sasquatch. "Red, lift his head."

By the time the troop of heavily armed intelligence agents thundered into view, the sasquatch was trussed up like a Sunday roast.

Penny looked down approvingly. "Better than a date with Tom Cruise," she mused.

"You've been on a date with Cruise?" Amelia cocked an eyebrow. "Honey, the guy is nearly old enough to be your *grandad*."

Penny took a moment to process what Amelia had said. "Roast lamb? Sunday dinner?" At Amelia's blank—and increasingly worried—expression, Penny gave in. "It's an old tv ad from back home. A girl wins a date with Tom and passes it up for a roast lamb dinner."

Amelia just shook her head. "Girl, I never thought I'd say this, but you come from a place that's even crazier than America."

"Take him, boys." Jones stood back, thumbs hooked through his belt loops.

"Excuse me, Professor, but I'm leading this operation." Dressed in tactical gear yet somehow looking as classy as she had in a skirt and heels, Agent Delouise shot Jones a withering look before addressing her team. "Travis, check the subject's vitals. Tuck, make sure that rope is secure. Max, question the civilians. Find out what *really* went down here."

Jones mumbled an apology and shuffled back toward the trees.

Penny turned her back on him, covering a smirk. She'd

bet her Boots that he'd told them he was responsible for the capture.

The agent ducked his head politely and pulled out a notebook and pencil. "Ma'am, my name is Max Townsend. I'd like to ask you a few questions about what happened here today."

Penny's smile widened. "Sure, Max. I'll tell you everything I remember."

CHAPTER ELEVEN

Three weeks flew by in a blink. Penny slipped into the rhythm of academy life, her time between classes usually spent with Boots, Cisco, and Amelia.

The coffee shop Amelia had taken her to on their first outing had become a regular hangout, ever since a young barista had whispered to Penny that she could provide a little cup of milk for her "friend."

Although dubious at first, Boots had quickly decided she was a fan of hot, frothy milk, to the point of trying to lick it off Penny's coffee. "What have I done?" Penny pulled Boots away, but the serpent persisted. "You've had yours! No coffee. It's not good for snakes."

Amelia lifted an eyebrow. "How do you know?"

Pursuing her lips, Penny considered the question seriously. "Because if she keeps stealing mine, I'll turn her into a handbag."

Boots hissed and disappeared under the table. A moment later, the tip of a rainbow tail crept up the side, groping its way toward the little pot of plain milk. Penny nudged it over, and the serpent expertly pulled it down without spilling a drop.

"Wow." Amelia eyed the macaroon on her plate, knowing Boots had enthusiastically tasted the crumbs last time she'd ordered one. "You're lucky she's not a klepto, Penn. That's talent!"

"Don't give her ideas," Penny chided. "Did you know she's been sucking up to Cook for fresh cookie dough?"

Amelia giggled, then sobered as something occurred to her. "Penny, she hasn't been pooping in our room, has she?"

"Yeah, of course she has. It's ok, I made sure she doesn't use your good shoes. Just those blue flats. You don't wear them often."

Amelia's outrage was quickly smothered by Penny's hysterical laughter. When Boots popped her head up, curious what the commotion was, Amelia started giggling too.

"As if I'd let her use your shoe as a dunny," Penny wheezed.

Amelia laughed harder. "I don't even know what you just said, but I love it, you crazy chick."

When they finally recovered their composure, Penny wiped the tears from her eyes. "Amelia, I can't thank you enough," she said seriously. "I mean it."

Amelia pulled a face. "What for? You paid for the coffee."

"For...being you." Penny twisted her coffee cup in circles on the table. "We came here with no idea what to expect. I didn't know anyone. After that *first* night, you'd be well within your rights to hold a grudge."

"Well, you did make me late to my very first class,"

Amelia pointed out. "But I suppose I can forgive that. I mean, you have excellent taste in coffee and men."

"Men?" Penny frowned. At Amelia's expression, she sighed. "Mate, if you roll your eyes any harder, they'll fall out of your head."

"Cisco? Mr. Tall, Dark, and Ripped like a Greek god?" Amelia threw up her hands, exasperated. "I'm not *blind*, Penny!"

Boots, sensing her friend's discomfort, climbed up into Penny's lap and butted her chin.

"See? Even Boots thinks it's obvious," Amelia proclaimed.

"Dude, we're just friends. Mates. Like you and me. There's *nothing* sexual going on." Penny bit the inside of her cheek, trying to will away the heat rising to her cheeks. Then, she leaned closer. "What do you mean, 'ripped like a god'?"

Amelia almost knocked over her coffee in her excitement. "Oh, I totally forgot—you didn't see!"

Penny waited, but Amelia was already lost in thought. "Amelia! See what?"

With a sly smile, Amelia explained that after they'd pulled Penny out from beneath the sasquatch, Cisco had stripped his shirt off to clean the mud and hair off her face. Amelia clasped her hands to her bosom, swooning. "Not an ounce of fat on that boy. And his tan is just…" Tipping her head back with a hand on her forehead, Amelia collapsed back in her chair.

Penny watched the theatrics, blushing again when she realized half the busy cafe had their eyes on Amelia too. "What about Red?" she asked.

Amelia smirked. "That beautiful boy is all mine—Cisco's not my type. Why? Are you jealous that I looked?"

Penny coughed to hide a laugh. "You can look all you want, Amelia. Cisco and I are just mates."

Amelia gave a very unimpressed nod. "Sure, hon. You keep telling yourself that. Just don't come crying to me when Kathleen swoops in and takes him off you."

"What?" Penny snapped. Then, trying to regain her nonchalance, she added, "I didn't know Kathleen was interested."

"Does it matter?" Amelia asked coyly.

Penny resolutely shook her head, ignoring a small prickle of jealousy. *We're just friends,* she reminded herself. *I'm not going to be here much longer, anyway.*

For once, that reminder didn't come with a rush of relief. Instead, a pang of sadness swept over her. She had enjoyed Amelia's company, teasing notwithstanding. She would miss her new friend if she left.

When I leave, Penny amended. *When. Not if.*

Amelia screamed. "Penny!"

Penny blinked and looked up from the library desk. "Mmmm?"

"We're going to see The Dead Adonis!" Amelia waved her phone at Penny, too quickly to be read.

"What? Is that for an assignment?" Penny racked her brain. None of their classes had touched on Greek mythology. That wasn't due until next year.

"No, you doofus. The band?" Amelia sighed and jerked

her phone back. A minute later, a song blared out from the tinny speakers.

Penny snapped her laptop shut and closed her eyes, listening to the tune. Then, she shook her head. "Never heard of them."

"They're a local band, but they just signed a contract with one of the big labels. Penny, don't you pay any attention to the real world?" Amelia perched on a stool. "Ugh, whatever. I'll just have to make you listen to all their songs before Friday."

"What's Friday?" Penny was beginning to think she had missed the first half of the conversation.

"The *party*." Amelia held out her phone again, this time passing it to Penny to hold.

A series of text messages ran down the screen. Penny quickly scanned it.

Tammy: Hey babe! Ger snagged TDA for his bash this wknd!

WHAAAT?!?!?! WHEN?

Tammy: Fri @ 9. U coming? Bring that friend of urs, the one who knows Thor.

Who?

Oh, Penny? The Aussie chick? She's fab, but I don't think she knows him.

Tammy: Damn! Oh well, she cool anyway. C U then!

Penny raised an eyebrow. "I know *a* Hemsworth, but not any of the famous ones," she clarified.

Amelia brushed off the statement with a flick of her hand. "Doesn't matter. I'm more of a Momoa girl anyway."

"Ah. So, we're going to a party?" Penny rolled her shoulders back and stretched. "I suppose... Midterms will be over by then—by the way, how'd you do on the defense test?"

Amelia groaned, sitting down with a thump. "Terrible. But if I tell you what's coming, it's an auto-fail. Just...be careful, ok?"

"Wow." Penny was confident she had aced the Mythological Items class written exam and felt as prepared as she could be for the Acquisitions practical. So far, though, no one had been able to talk about the secretive Defense test, held in the training room one student at a time.

Amelia leaned over. "Whatcha working on?"

"Database additions." Penny had exhausted the entire swathe of information the institute had on Rainbow Serpents in about forty-five minutes of reading. "Madera offered me extra credit if I add everything we know about Boots."

Frowning, Penny tapped out the last paragraph of her addition and clicked Update.

Submission *pending*.

Madera and the dean would both have to sign off on the added information before it appeared in the listing, part of the vetting process for all new information.

"Ugh, I could do with some of that." Amelia thumped down next to Penny. "My brain is *terrible* with dates and figures. It'll be a miracle if I do anything but scrape by in History."

Done with the database, Penny clicked around the screen, absentmindedly hitting the 'latest updates' tab. She leaned in. "Wow. There's a ton of vampire info being added this week."

Amelia leaned over her shoulder. "Boston?" That's

where all the updates were originating. "Weird. Maybe they're having an outbreak?"

Penny snorted. "They're Mythers, not chickenpox."

Amelia punched Penny's shoulder. "You know what I mean. Your sense of humor has dried up from all that computer work—you wanna come hit some targets?"

The archery range had only been set up the previous week and had proven popular amongst the students. "Sure. There should be some targets free this late in the afternoon."

CHAPTER TWELVE

Penny knocked on the door of the training room, trying not to fidget as she waited for Professor Jones to open it. The Defense Class professor had barely spoken to her since the camping trip. Penny guessed it was because she had ratted him out.

She had heard—from Cisco, who had heard from his mom, who got it straight from the Dean herself—that Jones was on his last warning.

When Penny expressed surprise that Jones had kept his job at all, Cisco admitted it was only due to a dearth of qualified professors able to teach the subject. Word on the campus grapevine was that if a better candidate came along, Jones's job might not be all that secure after all.

When the door finally creaked open, she stepped inside, butterflies exploding to life in the pit of her stomach. "Good afternoon, Professor Jones." Penny looked around the room, hoping for a hint of what was to come.

A heavy, locked chest sat alone in the center of the

room. The nearby walls held the usual array of practice weapons.

Perhaps the biggest surprise was Professor Jones himself. He was dressed in full combat gear—Kevlar vest, a full-face helmet, and heavy padding on his arms and legs.

"Choose your weapons." The professor tossed Penny a duffel bag. "You can take anything that will fit in this bag. Once the test begins, these will be the only weapons you may touch. If you use anything outside of your initial selection, you fail the class."

"But what am I fighting?" Penny eyed the wide selection of weapons, knowing that any creature she might face would probably have its own specific method of destruction.

No point picking up a gun if your enemy was a vampire. At the same time, a wooden stake would do nothing against an angry zombie.

"If you're out in the field and run into something unexpectedly, do you think it's going to wait for you to run back home and assemble your kit?" the professor asked acerbically. "Choose. Your. Weapons."

Penny took a hesitant step toward the nearest wall, one adorned with a selection of weapons used for vampire slaying.

"You have two minutes."

The sudden sense of urgency was all Penny needed. She ran for the wall, grabbing one of each type of weapon.

Two wooden stakes, an ancient blessed sword, one silver dagger, two water pistols filled with holy water, a bag of salt, knuckle dusters, a hand axe, and a pair of scissors—excellent for cutting off malevolent shadows.

"Set the bag down over there. Arm yourself. You have thirty seconds." Professor Jones pointed to an area about twenty meters away from the chest. Penny dragged the bag over as fast as she could, hesitating before drawing out the blessed sword, strapping the holy water and salt to her belt, and fitting the knuckle-dusters on her left hand.

"Five, four, three..." As he counted down, Professor Jones strode over to the box and slid a key into the large padlock. "Two, *one*." The padlock slid up and the professor jumped back, stumbling on his heavy attire. The lid to the chest sprang open.

Penny dropped into a defensive stance, gripping the sword with two hands. She waited, nerves twisting tightly in her gut.

A music box chimed the hollow tunes of an ancient lullaby as a thin, childlike voice called, "Play with me!"

Penny's stomach fell to her boots. "No fucking *way*."

A small creature shot out of the box, flipping in the air and landing in front of it. Patchy ginger hair fell over large, painted eyes and onto white wooden cheeks. The tiny doll wore a red pinafore over striped stockings and held a sharp knife in one hand.

"Is that a *haunted doll?*" Penny squeaked. She swallowed hard, trying to muster back the confidence she'd walked in with. It didn't work.

Unable to help himself, Professor Jones confirmed it. "You have *no idea* how hard she was to find. Do you know what kind of a catch an actual urban mythological creature is? I had to —"

Penny lost whatever else the professor said, his words

AMY HOPKINS & MICHAEL ANDERLE

drowned out as her sword clanged with the psychotic doll's dagger.

"Hi, I'm Annie." The doll's head tilted jerkily to one side. Her frozen, painted eyes bored into Penny's soul. "Be my best friend?"

"She's *terrifying*!" Penny spun, trying to keep the fast-moving creature in her sights. Annie, laughing in a high pitch that sent shivers down Penny's spine, sprinted forward again.

Penny flung her sword up to block her, knocking the little knife out of her hands. Unfortunately, the doll had already attached to her leg. Blunt teeth sank into her calf. Penny shrieked.

"Your mouth is painted on, bitch!" Penny yelled. "How do you have teeth?"

Desperate to dislodge the tiny nightmare, she reached down and grabbed the doll's hair. She flicked it and tossed it across the room, where it slammed against the wall and crumbled to the floor in a heap, hinged joints askew.

Panting heavily, Penny let the tip of her sword drift toward the floor.

"That wasn't very nice!" Penny's stomach lurched as Annie contorted and jerked, pulling herself back up to her feet and shuffling toward her on a splintered leg. Tiny points of red glowed in her eyes and her vacant smile had contorted into a frown, made all the more surreal for the blood that dripped down the tiny chin.

"I'm gonna get killed by a motherfucking doll," Penny groaned. Although she hoped the idea of legal liability meant the professor would stop the exam before that happened, she had no guarantee that he would. Something about Professor Jones made it seem somewhat unlikely that he cared that much about procedure.

"How do I kill it?" Penny called to her teacher.

"What? Don't kill her! I still haven't fixed my gnome."

"Asshole," Penny muttered. Her back pressed against a row of rope weapons hanging on the wall behind her. "So, how am I meant to stop it?" she yelled, hoping against all odds that her teacher would divulge some actually useful information.

"However you want." The padded monstrosity that was the professor shrugged. "Just don't damage her, please."

Annie lurched closer, dragging the broken leg behind her. "What, don't you want to play with me?"

"I was more a Pokémon kind of kid," Penny explained.

The red embers glowing in Annie's eyes flared. "You're saying you don't like dolls?" Her voice dripped with fury.

With a movement too fast to see, Annie lifted her arm and flicked the knife forward. Reacting purely on instinct, Penny dove to one side. A sting in her ear told her how close she had been to losing an eye. "I wouldn't like to be paying the insurance for this place," she mumbled.

Now weaponless, Annie began using her hands to drag herself along the floor faster.

At least she can't reach the knife, Penny consoled herself as she continued edging away.

The doll stopped. She lifted her head, violent red eyes meeting Penny's. "I don't like people who don't like dolls."

She pounced, wooden body shooting through the air like a bullet. Penny ducked, but not fast enough. The doll connected with the top of her head, a chunk of hair ripping from her scalp as Annie grabbed it to halt her momentum.

Penny screamed; the thought of the creepy little doll touching her was almost scarier than the prospect of death. All such notions were quickly abandoned, however, when a sharp pain bit into her shoulder. Penny shrieked.

She scrambled with her hands, trying to pull the vicious little monster off her neck. Annie had a good grip on Penny's flesh with her teeth and a handful of hair. Unable to maneuver the sword in a way that didn't risk her own neck, Penny punched the doll with her fist. The knuckle-dusters crunched against Annie's skull. Over and over again, screaming in pain, Penny hammered the doll to a crumpled mess.

Finally, she let go. The doll slipped to the floor.

Penny stomped on it with her heel. "Take that, you creepy little shit." Tears dripped down her face, and blood tickled as it ran down her arm and back.

Finally, Penny's adrenaline began to ebb. She stepped back, examining the crushed pile of debris that had been the horror movie doll. Her eyes lifted to the professor.

Professor Jones leaned against the doorway, arms crossed and posture relaxed. *I just beat the shit out of his doll,* Penny thought. A sick pit of worry grew in her gut. *He should be furious, not relaxed.*

Confirming her fears, the pile of splintered wood and torn fabric quivered.

"Oh, for fuck's sake."

Now seriously injured, Penny wondered if she had any chance of winning this fight. Her eyes fell on the duffel bag. Without knowing Annie's specific weakness, Penny had no doubt that any injury she inflicted upon her wouldn't have a permanent effect.

"Come plaaay." The creepy whine sent a shudder up Penny's spine as the doll reassembled itself, this time without the broken leg.

"Wow. Guess I really fucked that up!" Penny darted away as the doll came for her, then blocked an attack with her boot, thrusting Annie away with a solidly planted kick.

The doll stumbled, rolled, then came to a kneeling position beside the open chest. Though small, the glowing red eyes that peeked out from beneath patchy, synthetic hair were utterly terrifying.

"Talk about a Pandora's Box," Penny noted. "Wait… *Oh!*"

Without giving her brain time to dismiss the incredibly stupid idea it had plucked from the sky, Penny wiggled her fingers. "Sure, devil spawn. I'll play with you."

Annie grinned, although it looked more like a snarl to Penny. The doll scrambled forward on hands and feet, and Penny waited until she was little more than arm's reach before ducking sideways.

"Can't catch me!" she cried. Fear tightened her voice, spoiling the sing-song effect she'd been going for, but it didn't matter.

Annie rounded on her with a growl as Penny backed up slowly, unwilling to take her eyes off the tiny monster for a moment. Her calf throbbed and each small movement pulled at her shoulder where the blood had begun to thicken, sticking her shirt to her skin.

"I love playing catch. Catch n' kill!" Annie jumped and landed a few feet in front of her.

"You know who else loves to play?" she asked. "That guy." She pointed at the professor. "You probably don't want to play with him, though. He thinks you're kinda ugly, and no fun at all."

Annie's head turned slowly, eyes rigid, until she faced backward. Penny swallowed hard. *That's some exorcist-level shit right there.*

Professor Jones held up both hands. "Woah, now. I never said that. I love you, Annie! You're the best in my collection!"

It was the wrong thing to say. "Collection?" The doll asked, the words low and menacing.

Jones didn't back down, pleading his case as he backed toward the locked door. "Yeah. Sure. I've got heaps of little trinkets like you. Nothing this scary, though."

"Collection?" Annie repeated.

She moved so fast Penny couldn't follow the blurred streak that shot across the room. Jones screamed and staggered back as the small beast pounded into the padded armor. Annie howled with maniacal laughter, then plunged the knife into Jones's chest, ripping through nylon and scattering white fluff on the floor.

Shit, how'd she get the knife back? Penny didn't have time to figure it out. On light feet, she bolted across the room, reaching the two just as Annie turned to see Penny's outstretched fingers reach for her throat.

Penny grabbed the doll by the scruff. The knife plunged into her hand, and she cursed but didn't let go. "Get. In. That. *Box*!"

Blood trailed on the floor as she dragged the doll to the center of the room, fighting Annie's frantic attempts to shake her off. Though she was small enough to hold aloft, she pushed against Penny as though her feet were secure on the floor. Twice, Penny had to use her second hand to stop the doll escaping, quickly snatching it back before she lost a finger to Annie's furiously gnashing—although painted—teeth.

Penny shoved the doll toward the box. Annie threw her arms out, grabbing the corner to stop Penny jamming her all the way in.

"Die, bitch!" Annie hissed.

"Annie, that's no way to speak to a lady," Penny grunted. She pried the wooden fingers away, then realized the knife jutting from her hand had pinned her to the doll. "Balls! You're a persistent little psychopath, aren't you?"

She flicked the doll off and slammed the lid shut, then jerked the knife out of her hand with a yell of pain.

Panting, she sat on the box, feeling it tremble beneath her as Annie tried to beat her way out. "Professor? You might wanna lock it."

Jones looked up, pulling a pale hand away from his chest. Some of the filler in the padded chest was tinged with red.

Yikes. I didn't mean for him to get hurt. Penny glanced down at the smeared blood on the floor where she'd struggled to dislodge the doll and rolled a stinging shoulder. *Then again...*

Jones shuffled over and clipped a padlock onto the box with one hand, the other still clutched to his wound. The kerfuffle inside stilled immediately, and Penny wondered what magic the lock held.

She was too tired to ask, though.

"That's...that's over now, at least." Jones didn't look her

in the eye. He hobbled over to a cabinet in the corner and pulled out a black staff wound around with silver rope.

He propped it on the wall, then struggled to take his shirt off, discarding the armor to reveal a shallow scratch down his sternum.

Penny resisted the urge to ask how it had even bled enough to stain the flocking on the padded vest. Jones touched the staff to the wound. When he turned back, his skin was unmarked.

He threw the staff to Penny, who caught it with a pained gasp.

"You'll lose points for endangering a teacher," Jones snapped.

"How could I possibly endanger the defense instructor?" Penny asked coldly. "Especially with a tiny doll. I mean, if the doll was dangerous, then setting it on a first-year student might be considered reckless, no?"

She bit her lip, hard, to suppress the rest of what she wanted to say. *Especially for a professor whose job is already under threat for endangering students.*

Jones muttered something under his breath. Then, louder, he told her to use the staff and head to the dining room when she was done.

He left, slamming the door behind him and leaving the box of psychotic doll with Penny.

She eyed the chest. "Go fuck a dingo, Jones." She eyed the staff, realizing the "rope" wound around the main body of the staff was actually a snake. Its head rested on the top, eyes glinting with silver wisdom. "The Asclepius staff!" She remembered her discussion with Cisco and touched the snakehead to her hand.

Muscle writhed and skin pulled, knitting back together to repair the damage Annie had inflicted. Goosebumps ran up Penny's arm as the wound healed, leaving no trace of injury beneath the already-drying river of blood that ran to her elbow.

"Pity it doesn't fix clothes, too," Penny muttered as she inspected the damage to her leg. Frayed threads of denim had matted with the sticky blood that still oozed as she prodded it. "Ugh. Wouldn't want to get that stuck in there."

Unwilling to bank on the staff removing the foreign material from her wound as it healed, Penny looked around for a sharp blade, chuckling as she realized she was surrounded by them. She selected a short, utilitarian dagger with a paper-thin edge, using it to slice off the leg of her pants at the knee.

Once the wound was exposed, Penny picked out the threads she could see. Then, she healed it. Like her hand, the process made her skin contort and ripple, though it was less startling the second time.

Penny touched the staff to several smaller wounds on her legs and torso, healing bruises and scrapes she had endured during the fight. She left her shoulder until last, unsure how well she could heal a wound she couldn't see.

Just as Penny was wiping away the dry blood to inspect the now-healed flesh, the training room door flew open.

"Penny! I'm going to *kill* Jones. Sadistic bastard." Amelia looked half ready to run to Penny, and half eager to go and punch the defense professor in the teeth.

Penny snorted. "Yeah, he's a real knob. Before you go kick him in the 'nads, though, can you help me take my shirt off?"

Amelia hurried over and helped Penny peel off her ruined shirt and tend to her shoulder wound. The staff did its trick, and once the last painful wound was healed, Penny sagged with relief.

"That feels amazing." Tired, drained, and filthy, Penny still felt like a million dollars. "I'd forgotten what it feels like to not be in pain."

"He deserves to lose his job," Amelia snapped. "Crazy son of a bitch."

"Has Cisco had his yet?" Penny asked. "And how'd you get through it, anyway? I thought I was going to die! Or at least fail the class after I smashed that little fucker to pieces."

Amelia winced. "Cisco was the first up. He checked on me after I did mine. I guess you didn't pick the flamethrower?"

Penny shook her head. "Nope. But I can see why that makes sense." Her brain tripped over the long list of beings sensitive to fire. "Damn, I'm such an idiot!"

"Nah, if you beat that creepy little monster without it, you're a damn genius." Amelia helped Penny to her feet. "Lunch?"

Penny's stomach answered before she did, growling loudly. "Wow, I'm starving!"

"It's the staff," Amelia explained. "One of the side effects from healing."

The door handle rattled and twisted. Penny gritted her teeth, expecting Jones, but it was Cisco who stuck his head in. "Penny! Did you— Uhh. I'll just...wait outside."

He vanished, leaving Penny bewildered. "What's his problem?"

"I dunno." Amelia cupped her hands around her mouth. "*CISCO!* What's your problem?"

He crept back in, one hand firmly over his eyes. "Just...you know. Penny's not wearing a shirt."

Penny gasped and looked down at her bare, blood-smeared midriff. "Oh." She folded her arms over her chest, grateful she'd worn a sports bra under her shirt but painfully regretting her choice to wear a white one that particular day. "Well, shit."

Cisco turned his back and wriggled out of his black t-shirt. He passed it over his shoulder. "Here. That'll get you back to your room, at least."

Blushing madly, Penny pulled Cisco's shirt over her head, trying not to inhale the scent of his deodorant too deeply, just as she tried to ignore the rippling muscles down his back.

That is to say, she tried.

Unsuccessfully.

The sudden rush of blood to her cheeks almost made her swoon. Hunger had set in deeply now, along with loss of blood and the draining of adrenaline. Her head swam, her stomach cramped, and her body felt light as a feather.

"You good there, Penn?" Amelia asked quietly.

"Hungry," Penny groaned. "Falling-down hungry."

"Of course, you are," Cisco said. "How many times did Jones have to use the staff on you?"

"Jones?" Amelia snapped. "Jones ran off like a pussy. When I got here, Penny was healing her own damn wounds."

Cisco sucked in a breath. "Did he explain the risks?"

Penny shook her head vacantly. "I just used it...a couple

of times. Like, two or three. Or maybe four? Yeah. Four chickens sound good. Roast ones, with lots of gravy."

"You get the food, I'll get her to lie down," Amelia said in a clipped voice. "Make it a big meal. *Then* we go to the dean."

Once her stomach was swollen with food and she'd washed off the blood, Penny began to feel human again. She sat on her bed, blanket pulled to her chin, Boots snuggled in her lap. The serpent had fussed and flitted until Amelia had told her off, instructing Boots to "sit down and stop making a fuss."

Chagrined, Boots had obeyed. She seemed much happier now that Penny was coherent again.

"Do you feel up to seeing the dean now, hon?" Amelia asked, putting a hand on Penny's knee.

Penny bit her lip. She wasn't one to complain, and she didn't really know if Jones had broken any rules—after all, the Academy existed to teach the students to deal with supernatural threats. Some degree of danger had to be expected, right? But Amelia's explanation that incorrect use of the Asclepius staff could lead to death had set her temper afire.

"No need." Cisco licked his fingers, salty from the packet of potato chips he'd polished off once Penny finally proclaimed she was full. "I ran into Mom in the dining hall. She guessed something was up, so I told her everything. Don't be surprised if the dean's already—"

There was a knock at the dorm door.

"Come in," Penny called warily.

The door opened and the dean stepped in, her heeled boots clicking on the floorboards. She wore a vibrant red suit that matched her glasses, a look that made her seem young despite the platinum hair knotted in a neat bun and deep wrinkles lining her face.

"Penny, dear. I hear you had a little trouble in the Defense exam?" Dean March's eyes swept the room, landing on Cisco, who was sitting cross-legged on the floor. She stared at him for a minute, then turned away, ignoring his presence. Boys were not allowed in the girls' dorm, after all.

"I...got a little hurt. And the staff... Well, I didn't know it—"

Dean March raised a hand. "Perhaps this will be best done alone. Thank you, Amelia and Cisco."

At the clear dismissal, both students scurried out of the room and shut the door behind them.

Suddenly alone, Penny bristled. Was the dean here to help her or chastise her?

"Tell me everything."

Boots raised her head to examine the dean, undulating her body in a mesmerizing pattern. To Penny's surprise, the serpent leaned forward and butted her head against the woman's cheek, a sign of affection usually reserved for Penny and her closest friends.

The gesture gave Penny the confidence she'd lacked moments earlier, and she listed the events of the testing from start to finish.

The dean listened, nodding occasionally, only a soft intake of breath denoting her surprise when Penny detailed her wounds. Her mouth hardened when she learned Professor Jones had abandoned a wounded Penny when the ordeal was over.

She didn't pass judgment, only nodded when Penny was done. "We will have to speak to Professor Jones." Penny bit her lip, wondering if, when it came down to it, her word would be trusted over Jones's—or if his track record would be enough to indict him.

"And we will check the security cameras, of course." A hint of a smile touched Dean March's lips. "They're in every classroom. Dreadfully expensive to retrofit a building this old, but perhaps worth it in the end."

She picked up Boots, who had slithered halfway into her lap, and set her on the bed. "Look after Penny, will you?" The dean looked Boots in the eye as she spoke, sounding as if she thoroughly expected the snake to understand every word.

Of course, as far as Penny knew, she did. "Thank you, Dean March."

"Take care, dear. And good luck on the rest of the exams." Dean March closed the door gently behind her as she left, leaving Penny to contemplate the exchange.

The dean was often seen, but only glimpses. Walking by a classroom or appearing in the dining hall to address Cook, or occasionally seen from a distance, walking the grounds. She rarely engaged with the students directly, but somehow...

Somehow, Penny had the impression she cared about every single one of them.

CHAPTER THIRTEEN

Penny looked up at the tall, pillared mansion with more than a little trepidation. Deep shadows, high-lighted by a series of lampposts that followed them up the driveway, gave the building a startling clarity. "Are you sure this is it?" she asked.

She adjusted Boots over her shoulder, worry knotting her gut. She didn't normally bring Boots out like this, but Amelia had insisted. Boots fed on Penny's nerves, flicking a nervous tongue out to taste the air.

"Of course, it is." Amelia picked her handbag up off the car floor and turned to the driver. "Thanks for the ride!"

"Please remember to leave a review," the Uber driver announced in a bored voice.

Amelia gestured impatiently. "Sure. Cisco, hurry up!"

Cisco huffed and hauled the bulging duffel bag out of the car and strapped it over his shoulder. "You know this bag is heavy, right?" He eyed the building suspiciously. "Anyone this rich should be able to afford to cater their own damn party. Why'd we have to bring our own drinks?"

Amelia brushed off the question. "Gerry said to bring *one* drink. You're the one who chose to bring a whole carton!"

"Well, he didn't come to that conclusion on his own, love." Red slammed the last car door shut, then patted Cisco's shoulder appreciatively as it rolled away. "You've got two strapping lads out for a night of fun. Do you really think one wee bottle of whiskey would get us by?"

"Amelia, this whole thing is weird," Penny said in a low voice. "He wants our grog for an 'offering to the gods'? Which god? With everything going on right now—"

"Oh, don't be a prude." Amelia looped an arm over Penny's shoulder as they arrived at the door. "Gerry is *totally* trustworthy. I'm sure it's just a figure of speech. Unless...oh, hell, I hope it wasn't a costume party!" She looked down at her black cocktail dress in dismay. "What if it is?"

Penny rolled her eyes and headed for the door. The heavy brass knocker probably cost more than her outfit, she realized.

The door swung open, and a wave of sound tumbled out. Loud music mingled with voices, and somewhere, a dog yapped. The girl in the doorway squinted under the bright lights. "You here for the party?"

Reading her lips as much as listening, Penny nodded. She glanced at Amelia, who was already pushing past, wonder etched on her face.

"This...is...amazing!" Amelia quickly stepped back to tug Penny's arm, leading her inside.

The marbled foyer looked like something out of a history museum. Greek statues lined the wall nooks, lit by tiny LEDs underneath. The floor itself was polished to a shine, the heavy marble dense under her heels. Whoever owned this place clearly had a passion for history and the money to flaunt it.

The group of friends followed the girl through a side door and down a hallway. Ahead, Penny caught sight of the party. She followed Amelia, glancing back to check Cisco was right behind her.

He was, although he didn't look as impressed as Amelia.

He saw Penny watching him and hurried to catch up, leaving Red trailing behind. "Take it easy in there, ok?" he cautioned. "Just until we see what's what."

The hallway opened out into a large entertaining area, one side open to a patio and pool, beyond which a band was setting up their instruments. The centerpiece was a huge stone statue of a Greek god, his hand holding a goblet aloft, and a tiny satyr cavorting at his feet.

"Gerry!" Amelia called. She waved her friend over. "Over here!"

Gerry sauntered over, his vibrant plum-colored suit reflecting the nearby lights off the shiny fabric. "Amelia!" He clapped his hands exuberantly, then pulled Amelia into a hug. "I'm so glad you made it. We're going to have so much fun!"

"Gerry, these are my friends. Penny, Cisco, and Red. That's Boots."

"Stunning!" Gerry clapped his hands again, squealing in delight at the Rainbow Serpent. He reached a hand toward Boots, who opened her jaws and gave a warning hiss.

"It's a little busy for her," Penny explained. "She's not really one for parties."

Gerry pouted. "Poor little thing. Well, just let me know if there's anything you need. Food, drinks," he winked at Cisco, "or a dance partner. You brought the offerings?"

Cisco pursed his lips but patted the duffel bag. "You got a fridge?"

"Oh, the fridge is stocked. That is for something *else*." Gerry spotted someone in the crowd he wanted to see and quickly waved goodbye, swaggering away with flair.

The music blasting from the stereo speakers was interrupted by the screech of a guitar.

"Eek! They're starting to play." Amelia spun, grabbing Penny's arms. "These guys are amazing, and so hot!" She put a hand to her chest, eyes glittering with excitement.

"Hey, what am I? A pork chop?" Red asked.

Amelia giggled. "A girl can look, silly. You're the only one I'll be dancing with, though." She linked her arm through Red's and dragged him outside.

"I wish I'd known it was going to be a pool party," Cisco said, watching a few partygoers strip off to dive in.

Penny shivered. "Are you insane? It's like *four degrees* out here."

"It's more like forty." Then, Cisco frowned. "Oh, right. Your people don't speak Fahrenheit."

"My people?" Penny raised an eyebrow, one hand on her hip.

Cisco chuckled. "You know what I mean."

It became difficult to hold a conversation as the band started playing. Penny had to admit, they were pretty good. On the other side of the pool, she could see Amelia dancing with Red.

Penny's feet were itching to dance, but the idea of walking out there alone? *Nuh-uh.*

Of course, she had a potential dance partner standing right next to her, if only she was brave enough to ask.

"Cisco, do you wanna... I mean..." Penny's eyes darted around. "Where do you reckon that fridge is? I'm dying for a drink."

Cisco glanced around. "I'll see if I can find it for you. Don't go anywhere—this place is huge, I'll never find you again if you run off."

Penny spotted a nearby couch and perched on the arm of it. She let the music wash over her as she watched the partygoers. "It's a far cry from the old backyard barbie," she mused.

As hard as it had been adjusting to life in America, she'd never felt quite as out of place as she did now. Surrounded by rich kids, party kids who clearly felt at home in this ridiculous mansion where the booze flowed freely and—she realized with horror—you could go skinny dipping, and no one would even bat an eyelid. The naked girl she had spotted squealed as her equally naked male friend pulled her back into the water.

"There's nothing wrong with a barbie," a voice said behind her. "A few slabs of beer, wine for the ladies. Good food, hot sun, and good mates, right?"

Penny shot to her feet, awkwardly turning to face the man who'd come to stand beside her.

The way he had described the image that had been in her head was eerily perfect, though any of her Aussie mates would have conjured the same. This guy, however... She couldn't quite place his accent, but she knew he wasn't

Australian, despite the perfect patois. His bronze skin contrasted with the white toga he wore, setting off the Greek-like godliness of his face.

It's like someone Photoshopped his face in real life, Penny thought, startled. She stammered, trying to form a response.

The newcomer laughed. "Be at ease. This is a party! Your friend is returning, so I'll leave you be."

Penny glanced over to see Cisco returning with two large plastic cups. When she looked back, the strange man had vanished.

"I didn't know what you wanted," Cisco explained, "so I brought a cup of beer and a cup of cider." He frowned worriedly. "If you want the hard stuff, I can go back and get you something else."

Penny shook her head, thanking him as she reached for the cider. It was sweet and crisp, and made her cheeks flush after just a few sips. "This tastes amazing," she said.

Cisco chugged his own drink, letting out a breath of satisfaction when the cup was empty. "I don't know *what* that was, but it's not bad." He eyed his empty cup.

"You might want to take it easy, big guy." Penny gave him a gentle shove. "Do that too many times, and I'll be holding your hair back while you puke out the window of a taxi."

"Who, me? Never!" Cisco shined a sunny grin her way. "I'll take your advice on board, though. Come on, let's go get something to eat. You won't believe the food they've got out."

Penny sipped her drink, trying not to spill it as they walked back to the kitchen together.

A sandy-haired jock pushed past Penny as they maneuvered past other partygoers, nudging her arm and almost spilling her drink.

Cisco reached out to steady her, clasping her elbow. He didn't let go as they continued on.

Penny didn't complain, but the cider was certainly going to her head—her cheeks felt like they were on fire.

The huge kitchen island was covered in cheese boards, meat trays, and an assortment of savory pastries. Between the platters, large trays of chips and dip protruded in a way that seemed almost artful.

"See? I told you it looks amazing." Cisco plunged a corn chip into a bowl of bright red paste. He closed his eyes and groaned as the food met his tongue. "This is fantastic," he muttered.

Penny eyed the table. She selected a couple of small pastries, each one twisted into a different shape. She put one into her mouth, and her taste buds crackled with delight as it exploded with warm, gooey cheese.

"Is this what it's like to be rich?" Penny murmured to Cisco. "A party at my place is a six-pack and some burnt snags. If you're lucky, you might get some soggy trifle for dessert."

"You'd like the parties at my place," Cisco teased. "The 'snags' there might be a little spicy for you, though."

The conversation turned to school and their recent exams. Cisco was feeling confident that he'd passed all of his subjects, excelling in history and acquisitions.

Penny also felt confident she had done well, but she was worried about her final grade for defense. Professor Jones hadn't been seen on the Academy grounds since her conversation with the dean.

"What if I have to take it again?" she fretted. "It was terrifying! I don't think I could go through it a second time."

Cisco smiled at Penny. "I'm sure you passed, and your grade will stand. There's no way they'll let Jones stay after that, but they're not gonna make you go up against that crazy doll again. That was just insane." He sighed in regret. "I should have mentioned it to Mom when I took my exam."

"Why didn't you?" Penny asked. She harbored no ill will toward him for it. She was simply curious.

Cisco shrugged. "She's been grading exams, and I've been studying for them. Our paths don't cross much these days."

"This week has been rough, that's for sure." Penny stretched, realizing the cider had relaxed her tight muscles for the first time in days. "I'm glad we came tonight. This is fun." She held Cisco's gaze while she spoke, and despite the heat rising in her own face, she was gratified to see him blush.

"It's time! Come on, people. It's time for the main event!" Gerry's high-pitched call caught Penny's attention. He fussed and waved his hands, leading a group of muscle-bound guys inside. Gerry pointed at the statue, then pointed to a spot out on the patio. "Don't break it!"

A minute later, the huge stone statue was safely relocated to its new home. Guests clustered around to watch, many of them clearly excited about what was coming.

Penny wished she knew what it was. "What do you

think he's doing?" She accepted the cold cup of cider Cisco passed her.

Cisco was as curious as Penny. "I don't know. Party game?"

Penny had lost sight of Gerry, but he appeared a minute later, wheeling a large trolley laden with bottles of alcohol.

Gerry pushed it to the statue, then grabbed a stool from a nearby table. He climbed onto the stool to call out over the crowd. "Mighty Bacchus, we offer these gifts, that you might grace us with your super fun and amazing presence! Let's get this party *started!*"

"He's not..." Penny began. Someone in the crowd started chanting Bacchus' name.

"He is," Cisco confirmed. Gerry opened the first bottle of wine and poured it over the statue. The red liquid splattered as he missed the cup, and yet somehow, the stone goblet never overflowed.

The music rose, but when Penny glanced at the band, their instruments were dangling untouched as they watched the spectacle on the patio. "Cisco? Where is that music coming from?" It didn't have the same digital quality as the speakers that had blasted earlier. This was live.

"Watch," Cisco whispered. "Watch when he pours."

Penny turned her attention back on the statue. Bottles of rum, whiskey, vodka, and wine scattered the ground, some smashed into jagged shards, and yet, the statue was pristine. All traces of spilled wine had vanished, and the cup still would not overflow.

As another slug of amber liquid dribbled over the statue's face while Gerry cheered the crowd, the stone absorbed the alcohol, sucking the fluid up and leaving no trace behind.

"It's almost full!" The girl who had squealed leaned a hip onto Gerry's stool as she rose on her tiptoes to peer into the goblet.

He just poured about twenty bottles of grog into an oversized cup, Penny thought. *How is it* not *full?*

Defying physics, the cup did indeed overflow, dribbling deep red liquid over the dais. It trickled onto the floor even as Gerry stopped pouring. The girl shoved past Gerry and pressed her empty cup against the flow. She took a sip and rolled her eyes. "Best. Wine. Ever."

"Beer!" Gerry yelled. The flow didn't stop, but dark amber liquid gushed over the red, frothing down in clumps. Gerry filled his cup, raised it, and called a toast. "To our esteemed host...BACCHUS!"

The beat of the music stopped and a beat of silence reigned. A girl's voice gave a rough, echoey laugh.

I know that voice, Penny realized. The quick techno beat that followed it brought a smile to her lips as the intro to Pink's *Get the Party Started* blared.

The crowd parted, and through the void, a man ran to the statue, high-fiving people as he passed them and jumping into a slick slide as he neared the end.

Penny immediately recognized him from their earlier conversation. *Not hard when he's dressed in a glorified bed sheet.*

He bowed and clapped, mimicking his own applause. "You know the rules, party-goers. *There are no rules!* No bad vibes, no inhibitions, just party 'til dawn!"

The crowd screamed and pushed each other, trying to get closer to the urn to fill their cups.

Bacchus encouraged the stampede, filling cups that appeared out of nowhere and tossing them out, drenching anyone who happened to be standing underneath.

"That's...something," Penny said, trying to keep track of their host and his god through the swarm of people. "What do we do?"

"Well, we can't go without Amelia." Cisco looked at Boots. "Do you think Boots could find her? It's chaos out there."

Boots immediately slithered off Penny's shoulder. "Be careful!" Penny called after her. There were a lot of stamping feet in the direction she was headed.

"Boots doesn't seem to have a problem with crowds," Cisco said.

Penny gave him a quick smile. "I took her to a music festival once. Everyone thought she was one of the acts, the way she danced. I think she liked the attention."

Cisco pulled back, confused. "You said earlier that she doesn't like parties."

Penny winced. "That was a polite way of saying 'I don't think she likes Gerry.' It's not his fault. He wouldn't know that she hates being grabbed like that."

They sat and waited, watching the crowd writhe and sway to the music, which had changed to a hypnotic trance beat. Those who had reached the statue had taken on a dazed, glassy look, many of them stripping off their clothes and getting intimate with whoever happened to be nearby.

"Wow. This isn't awkward at all," Cisco said, coughing.

He gestured to a couple who were going at it on a nearby couch, the guy's bare ass in the air.

Penny snorted a laugh, trying not to spit cider out of her nose. "At least Amelia's nights out are never boring!"

"Speak of the devil." Cisco pointed into the seething crowd of horny young adults.

Amelia headed their way, Boots wrapped around one arm and draped over her shoulder, the other arm looped around Bacchus.

Penny groaned. "Just what we needed."

The old god had lost his manic energy and transformed back into the studious man Penny had chatted with earlier. "Penny! Cisco!"

Penny gave him a tight smile, then grabbed Amelia's arm. "We were just going."

Amelia pouted. "Going? Penny, no way! This is the best party I've ever been to!"

"It's dangerous," Penny hissed.

Amelia shook her head resolutely. "It's not. Gerry has these parties all the time. No one gets hurt, I swear. It's just lots of booze, no hangovers, no drugs."

"You knew he'd be here?" Penny asked, too horrified to care if Bacchus heard.

Rolling her eyes, Amelia heaved a dramatic sigh. "I knew you wouldn't come if I told you. Penny, it's fine, I swear. Bacchus looks after everyone. He's a *party* god, not the god of death."

"Well, technically…" Bacchus shrugged. "But that was a long time ago. I promise I'm here to protect. I provide the wine, the music, and the guarantee that nothing will go wrong."

Penny raised a skeptical eyebrow. "A bunch of horny, drunk, uninhibited twenty-somethings, and *nothing* will go wrong?"

Bacchus took her hand. "I was born in a time when wine was the liquid of the gods. When loss of inhibition was the birth of creativity, philosophy, and the betterment of intellect." He shrugged again, the movement making his toga slip a little and reveal a few more ripped muscles. "Sadly, much of that history has been forgotten. I serve here as my lesser self, but I have not forgotten my origins —unlike many others who have crossed into this world."

Penny blushed and looked away. "What made *you* special enough to come over?" she asked.

"Penny! You can't be rude to a god!" Amelia admonished.

Penny turned back to him, her mind whirling. "No, I'm curious. Really. What made you come back? Were you forced over, or did you just...appear? Do you still have worshippers?" Despite the study they had done, so many aspects of the mythological invasion were unsure.

It was made worse by the variables—some Mythers appeared seemingly by chance. Others were summoned or, according to Crenel, forced through by other means.

"I have worshippers now, yes." Bacchus didn't seem to mind the question. In fact, his eyes lit up with a different kind of excitement than he'd shown as the statue. "Gerry here is one, and there are some weird, boring kids in black who have summoned me a few times. They were less fun. I haven't *quite* disappeared from memory. Your movies, television shows..."

Bacchus' face rippled into that of a slender man in a

white coat wearing an outlandish green-feathered hat, then morphed back.

"I know that face," Cisco whispered in Penny's ear. "From a tv show. I don't remember what it's called—emo guy gets into magic school and doesn't bang the gorgeous chick he should have."

"Right," Penny said unenthusiastically. She didn't admit the particular show he was referencing was one of her all-time favorites. "How did it happen?" she asked Bacchus.

"How did what happen?" Bacchus asked smoothly.

"How did you cross the Veil?" Penny ignored Cisco's tug on her elbow. "You know, how did you become *real?*"

"I was always real." Bacchus smiled and held up a wine-glass. He'd been empty-handed a minute before. "The questions you ask are not fit for a sober mind to understand. Drink with me. Drink, and I'll tell you everything."

"Not a chance," Cisco snapped. "Penny, this isn't safe!"

Boots rippled her scales, smoothly moving from Amelia's shoulder to slither around Bacchus.

"Yes, it is," Amelia giggled. "See? Even Boots trusts him. It's fine. He won't hurt her." She leaned closer to Cisco. "Aren't you curious?"

Cisco struggled with the question for a minute. "Fine. Yes, I am. But not if it's going to cost a quart of my blood, or a YouTube video of me," he glanced around and spied a girl dancing drunkenly with the refrigerator, "doing that."

"You question the sanctity of my entertainment?" Bacchus asked. His face softened, and he lifted a shoulder. "You are wiser than most. *I* wouldn't trust me, even though I'm entirely trustworthy." Perfect teeth sparkled in a bright grin.

Penny grabbed the wine from his hand. *Here goes nothing.* She downed it in the space of a breath, barely giving herself time to savor the incredibly smooth sweetness of the godly drink.

She closed her eyes a minute as the magically-imbued alcohol flowed through her veins. Her muscles softened, her anxiety eased, and her head felt a little floaty. "I feel good," she admitted. She opened her eyes, then narrowed them suspiciously. "And not at all like taking my clothes off."

Bacchus smiled. "There was a time when imbibing the drink of the gods was more congruent to the meeting of higher minds, of elevating understanding. It was only later that..." He glanced at the girl Cisco had pointed to. She leaned in to kiss the refrigerator. "Well, that it became *that.*" He shrugged. "Both are fun, at the appropriate time, but I do miss the older times."

He plucked the wineglass from Penny's limp hand and passed it to Cisco. She knew it would be full before her friend took it from the mysterious god, but somehow missed how it happened. It was empty, then it was full. There was no in-between, no moment of transition.

The small group retired to a quiet room, Bacchus stopping to deeply kiss a trio of drunken dancers on the way. Two of the humans started making out while the other watched, entranced.

The god caught Penny's glance. "The third didn't wish to participate. I don't coerce the unwilling, just encourage those who desire it."

That eased a little of Penny's worry, although if she were honest, there was very little left to begin with. Her head buzzed pleasantly, and in the quiet, dark room she heard her own thoughts as they mulled the possibilities that had brought the god to her world.

Bacchus flopped down on an overstuffed yoga cushion and drew a large, shallow bowl from behind him. "For you." He sat it on the ground, and Boots slithered in. "Spiced wine, my Dreamtime friend?"

The serpent rolled and twisted happily as he poured a steaming mix into the bowl, the wine dribbling from his hand despite the absence of a vessel. Boots cavorted as Penny watched. She'd never seen the snake so happy, and wondered how much of it was the wine, and how much was simply the presence of someone like him.

A warm glass was pressed into Penny's hand, and she looked down in surprise. "Try it," Bacchus insisted. "You'll like it, I promise."

Penny sipped, letting the nutmeg and clove roll over her tongue. Something in the brew had a little kick, not spicy enough to burn her mouth, but with the heat to make her throat tingle.

Warmth lapped at her skin, washing over her in waves.

"I will tell you a story," Bacchus said. "But it is a long one. It begins a very long time ago…"

———

Penny awoke in a cloud of pillows. Lifting her head, she saw she'd fallen asleep on the couch, but someone had tucked her in with cushions and a soft blanket. When she stretched, her toes bumped flesh. She lifted her head to see Amelia stir restlessly.

Relaxing back into her cocoon, Penny stretched her mind back to the night before. Even the memory of Bacchus's wine made her feel warm, and she closed her eyes, drifting comfortably. As he'd promised, she felt no hint of a hangover. That deal was totally worth it.

Her eyes flew open. "Our deal," she murmured. Wide awake now, she searched her memories of the evening.

The wine on her tongue, Boots' glee, Bacchus's soft hands rubbing her feet as he talked. It all held perfect clarity.

"Amelia?" Penny snapped. "Cisco!"

Cisco grunted and rolled over in his nest of blankets on the floor. "Huh?"

"Cisco, what did Bacchus tell us last night?" Penny nudged Amelia again with her toe. "Amelia, do you remember?"

"What? No, I'm too tired. I don't remember." Amelia yawned but sat up, rubbing her eyes.

"Cisco?" Penny pressed. "Do you remember?"

"Yeah, sure. He said that when the old Greeks...um. When they…" His face creased in concern.

"Oh, that sly fucker," Penny cursed. "He *cheated!*"

She felt the echo of laughter run along her senses. She looked around but saw nothing. A moment later, any hint of another presence had vanished.

Penny groaned and leaned back, snuggling into her pillow. "That was the perfect opportunity, and we blew it."

Amelia squeezed Penny's foot. "No, I don't think so. He obviously doesn't want us to know, so he wouldn't have told us anyway."

"Seems a bit unfair," Cisco said. "I feel pretty good, though, considering."

"Me too," Penny admitted. "Do you remember how much we drank?" She didn't have a perfect idea—every time she'd sipped from her glass, it had been full—but she knew it was a lot. "I should be puking in the gutter about now."

"Me too," Amelia admitted. "I can't even feel that bottle of tequila I had before the party got hectic."

Penny's jaw dropped. "You drank a whole bottle?"

Amelia giggled. "Yeah. Gerry promised I wouldn't feel it this morning. He was right!"

Penny snuggled deeper into the warmth of the blankets. She could hear people stirring outside over the whir of a coffee grinder. "Mmmm. Coffee."

"Time to get up?" Cisco asked. He looked like he had no intention of moving.

Penny rolled off the couch, blankets tangled around her legs. "As appealing as it would be to sleep all day, that coffee smells amazing." She reached for the door, cut short by a soft thump on the back of her head.

Amelia smiled sweetly, a second pillow held up ready to throw. "You *were* offering to bring one back for me, right?"

"Sure." Penny sighed. "Cisco?"

The blanket over his head nodded.

In the kitchen, Gerry was playing the part of the gracious host. He darted back and forth behind the expensive coffee machine, frothing milk and pouring shots. Penny held up three fingers and when he nodded, slid onto a barstool and waited.

"You're new in town, right?" Gerry asked as he poured

the first coffee. He'd dropped the dramatic persona from the previous night, making his pink hair seem incongruous with his flannel pajamas.

Penny nodded. "I've been here a while now."

"How do you like the good old Land of the Free?" He flicked the milk jug to make a delicate fern pattern, then slid it over to her.

Penny wrapped her hands around it, savoring the warmth and aroma. "It's good. I miss home, though."

"What's it like in the land of drop bears and crocodile men?" Gerry poured ground coffee into the machine, then realized he didn't have enough.

Penny waited for the whine of the grinder to stop before answering. "Hot. Like, so hot, you can feel your skin fry when you step outside. The smell is different. It smells clean and sharp, even though you're covered in red dust all the time."

"Sounds...hot and dirty," Gerry said. He grinned to take any sting out of his words. "I hear the beaches are good."

"We have some nice ones," Penny admitted. "But the best ones are the beaches no one else knows about. You need a four-wheel-drive to get to those, and you can stay for days and not see a soul."

"Coming to a place like Portland must be a huge change," he said, passing her a second coffee.

"It's...different." Penny blew across the top of her cup and took a sip. "I mean, Sydney has more people, so it's not so much that... It's just weird to be in a place where everyone has an accent."

"Hey, *you're* the one with the accent." Gerry winked. "This one's nearly done."

"I guess that's true," Penny thought about it. "You know what, maybe that's part of it. Back home, I'm just Penny. Here, I'm the weird girl with the accent."

"And the magic snake," Gerry pointed out.

"And the snake," Penny agreed. "Most of the people back home are too old and stubborn to see her. I think she likes it here, she gets more attention."

"Does she, um, need breakfast?" Worry crossed Gerry's face, quickly clearing when Penny shook her head.

"She only eats for fun." She took the third coffee from him, carefully balancing two in one hand while she sipped from her own. "Thanks, mate. For the invite last night, and for the coffee."

"Any time." Gerry's grin was genuine.

CHAPTER FOURTEEN

Penny stretched in bed, yawning before tapping her alarm. It kept screaming, so she hit it again, clumsily shoving it off the desk and yanking the power cord from the wall. *At least that shut it up,* she thought.

After a quick mid-semester break, classes had returned with a new schedule, one that was more intense than the previous timetable.

With a start, she remembered why the alarm was blaring. "Shit. Classes are on today." She tossed a pillow at Amelia's bed.

"I'm awake, dammit." The blanket muffling Amelia's voice suggested that hadn't been the case for long. "How much trouble do you think we'll get into if we skip first class?"

"With Madera? *Too* much." Penny rolled to her feet and started tying her hair up without bothering to brush it. She rifled through the pile of clothes on the floor for a clean top, finally finding one under Amelia's bed. "Wow. How did our room get so messy?"

"Vacation. You don't clean on vacation." Amelia dropped an arm out from under her blanket to pick up the pair of jeans she'd discarded the night before. "We'll fix it on the weekend." The blanket wriggled as she pulled them on beneath it.

"It was only a week! Besides, you didn't *go* on vacation," Penny pointed out. Amelia hadn't admitted it, but Penny suspected she had changed her plans and stayed at school after finding out Penny would be knocking around the Academy by herself.

Fortunately, it hadn't just been the two of them. Cisco hadn't left either, the Academy being home to his mother. Red had also hung around for all but a weekend, flirting with Amelia and occasionally disappearing with her until the early hours of the morning.

"Exactly." Amelia stood and shook out her hair, then grabbed a makeup case and sat cross-legged on her bed. "If I wasn't here, I wouldn't have made a mess."

"Fair point."

Boots slithered out from under Penny's pajamas, flicking them onto the floor with an irritated hiss.

"Oh. Sorry, Boots." Penny reached down and offered her hand for the snake to nuzzle.

"Two sessions with Madera in a row." Amelia groaned. "Don't get me wrong. I love Mama Cisco, but she makes us *work*."

"Did you notice the defense lesson is in the morning?" Penny asked. "I bet that's so Professor Craster can make sure Jones hasn't killed anyone during class."

"Not that it will do any good." Amelia paused to apply lipstick. "I bet Jones hates us for ratting him out."

"He passed me," Penny pointed out.

"You passed. The dean probably gave you the grade herself while she hung old Jones up by his toenails for what he did to you." Amelia kissed the air, then smiled widely into her mirror.

"Is that a new color?" Penny asked.

Amelia turned her grin on her friend. "Why, yes, it is. Not that Red noticed yesterday when I left it all over his...um. Well, he didn't notice anyway." She threw the tube to Penny, who caught it with one hand. "It's the new one from Ferocious Beauty."

"Candy Bomb," Penny read off the bottom before tossing it back. "It suits you." She shoved her books into her bag.

Though she'd enjoyed the break, she honestly couldn't complain about going back to class—not even to a double period of Introductory Myth and Legend.

The short reprieve had driven home how much fun she was having in class. Even that bastard Jones couldn't curb her enthusiasm.

"Come on." She clung her backpack on her shoulder. "You coming, Boots?"

Boots emerged from Penny's makeup kit, her tiny serpentine face somehow looking guilty.

"Nah, Princess Boots wants a makeover!" Amelia leaned down to touch her nose to the snake's. "You're perfect just the way you are, sweetheart. No makeup can match those gorgeous colors of yours!"

Boots rubbed her head on Amelia's chin, coming away with a tan smudge between her wide-set eyes. Amelia giggled and wiped it off.

"My snake is better at being a girl than I am." Penny sighed. She glanced down at her old jeans and basic t-shirt.

"You're perfect, too." Amelia laughed. "*Really!* Cisco wouldn't have the patience for someone as precious as me. I'm way too high maintenance. You do you, babe."

Penny couldn't hide her grin. Most of her girlfriends back home had pushed Penny to be more feminine, something she'd resisted as much as possible. "You know you're the best friend I've ever had?"

Sure, Amelia had taken her shopping and encouraged her to dress up for special occasions, but she'd quickly realized Penny was comfortable as she was. Rather than give up the fight, their trips to the mall now involved Amelia hunting out practical outfits and utilitarian shoes for her friend.

Amelia just rolled her eyes. "You won't think that when you realize I've made you late for class."

Penny flicked a glance at her watch, yelped, and raced out of the room, Amelia's laughter ringing behind her.

Professor Madera opened the lesson by handing out the end-of-semester assignment. "This semester we have two six-thousand-word dissertations. One on the theory of the appearance of the Mythers, and another on the potential worldwide ramifications if it continues unchecked."

Penny scanned the front page as Madera explained the requirements.

"Each piece will account for twenty-two percent of

your final grade. The remainder will be made up during the written exam, same as last time."

A smattering of groans ran through the students as she passed, dropping the papers on each desk.

Madera paused and swept her gaze over them. "Some of you may believe this to be an uninteresting class. There is no playing with magical trinkets, beating each other with swords, or hunting monsters. However, the knowledge you gain will give you the edge you need to turn this invasion into a new age, one where humans and our guests from beyond the veil can live in safety and harmony."

"Or at least not get us killed," Clive muttered, his voice just reaching Penny's ears.

Madera gave him a knowing smile. "I'm glad you agree, Clive."

Assignments set, Professor Madera spent the rest of the class guiding the students through developing their premises, as well as introducing them to the content that would be covered in the exams.

"If any student has difficulties, I expect you to see me for help," Madera called as the students swarmed out of the room at the end of class. "You know where to find me!"

When they arrived at Items Acquisitions class, Professor Marcus apologized for not having their assignment briefings ready. "I still have a few more things to work out," she explained. "But the class will be working in groups, so now would be a good time to start thinking about your options."

Once they were settled, Professor Marcus pulled a white screen down and flicked on a projector. A newspaper headline was illuminated, though most of the article was cut off.

Excalibur Found Again. New King Crowned In Britain.

"The spate of Excaliburs that began with the first parting of the Veil has increased three-fold this year," Marcus began. "The British government is fielding claim after claim to the throne."

"Who was crowned?" Mara asked. "Why would they crown someone? That's just stupid!"

"They were crowned 'King of Chess,'" Marcus explained with a patient sigh. "The media *does* like to bait with their headlines." She began pacing, a habit she'd established the first day of class. "So far, all those who have found Excalibur have been coincidentally bestowed the title 'king of' something within the next few days. One found a plastic crown in a box of cereal, another won an online multiplayer game, another won a scratch ticket jackpot called 'the crown jewel.'"

"So pulling the famous sword from the stone gives you...nothing?" Clive looked disappointed.

"For now." Professor Marcus stopped behind her desk, tapping it with a fingernail. "There is a real concern that one of these so-called kings will suddenly find a birth certificate tying them to the royal line, or—worse—they will get the idea that waging war on the monarchy is a good idea."

"What about the swords here?" Penny asked. She knew at least two had been drawn in America, along with three in African countries, one in India and one in her own home country.

"Again, the biggest concern is that it will exacerbate the

current political upheaval." Professor Marcus sighed. "Students, we have entered a new age, and the world is struggling to catch up. It was bad enough that laws hadn't progressed to adequately deal with the sudden surge of internet capabilities." She paused. "This will be worse."

The words created a pit of unease in Penny's gut. They'd already discussed some of the ramifications with Professor Madera. Things like the legal protection of innocent creatures like Boots, balanced with protection for those who hunted the more malevolent creatures passing through the Veil.

"What do we do?" Penny asked. The question surprised even her. *We? Who is "we?" I'm leaving in a few weeks!*

The assertion rang less true every day, but she shrugged it off. Admitting she wanted to stay brought a host of logistical issues that she simply didn't have time to deal with right now.

"We work," Marcus declared passionately. "We study hard, we learn as much as we can, and we advocate for change." A smile touched her lips. "When change comes, it comes quickly. We will be ready, and we will take advantage of that the best we can." Her eyes met Penny's. "After all, it's why we are here."

CHAPTER FIFTEEN

Penny had looked forward to the next class with Professor Marcus the next morning, only to find out when she arrived, that the class had been canceled due to the professor's absence.

"Meeting," Cisco explained. His brows were a knotted mess of worry. "Something's going on with the faculty, but Mom won't tell me what it is."

"Let's sneak out, then," Amelia proposed. "If I go back to bed, I won't wake up for Folklore this afternoon. Coffee?" She looked at Cisco and Penny expectantly.

Cisco shook his head. "I'm gonna hang back and see if I can get any info out of Mom. Have fun, though." He turned on his heel and walked away.

Penny couldn't resist Amelia's puppy-dog eyes. "Ok, coffee it is. Just let me get my coat."

"I can't believe you're still cold!" Amelia tailed Penny up to their room. When Penny emerged carrying only her purse and jacket, she raised an eyebrow. "Boots not coming?"

Penny shook her head. "I saw a cat on the grounds last night. She got a bit excited, I think she's hoping it comes back."

Amelia's hand flew to her mouth. "So she can *eat* it?"

"No!" Penny's laughter trailed off. "At least, I don't think so."

The girls trotted quickly downstairs and emerged into the crisp Portland morning.

"What's all that?" Amelia asked, nudging Penny with her elbow.

Penny turned away from the door and followed Amelia's stare. Three women and a man stood on the street corner, arguing with two police officers. The group scowled, and one of the women pointed toward the Academy.

"Weird," Penny said. Something about the group—their high necked blouses and long skirts in shades of pastel and beige, and the man's crisp white button-up shirt—made her skin crawl.

"Ignore them." Amelia scoffed, although her usual confidence was absent. "They're probably just tourists."

The line of black-clad women standing outside the coffee shop would have given Penny pause on *any* given day, but after the mysterious absence of Professor Marcus and the group of watchers outside the Academy, it set her heart racing.

"Amelia, what's going on?" She pulled on her friend's arm, but Amelia was having none of it.

"Let's go check it out." Shrugging off Penny's horrified look, Amelia plunged forward. "We might learn something, Pen. I bet your handsome agent would love the inside scoop on what these kooks are up to now."

"Handsome?" Penny huffed incredulously. "Amelia, he's old enough to be my grandad. Yours, too!"

One of Amelia's shoulders twitched. "Eh, he's a silver fox. No one brings up Richard Gere's age, and he's, like, a thousand years old!"

Penny had no choice but to follow. Abandoning her friend as she headed into a wild goose chase simply wasn't an option.

"Hi!" Amelia walked straight up to the group of girls with a sunny grin. "What are you guys selling? Is it Mary Kaye? I *desperately* need some new makeup!"

Penny cringed. *Anyone could see through that!*

To her surprise, the other women clustered around Amelia excitedly. "We're here to spread the word!" One stuck her hand out and clasped Amelia's delicately. "Have you seen the events taking place?"

A redhead swooped in. "Magical beings, miracles...the world is changing!"

"So, you're a religious group?" Amelia asked. She sounded curious, but not over-eager.

The first girl nodded. "We're hosting a gathering. Kind of a party, really. Here." She held out a flyer.

Amelia pursed her lips. "You're not gonna sacrifice a goat or anything, are you?"

The girl giggled disarmingly. "*Nooo*! Of *course* not! We just want to introduce you to our leader, Mark. He'll explain why all this is happening, and how we can help it."

"Help it?" Penny asked, alarm bells ringing.

The girl nodded enthusiastically. "Yes! It's our mission to usher in a new age, one where the common man isn't beholden to material goods, but the old gods, and power is given through worship and sacrifice." She glanced at Amelia. "*Personal* sacrifice. Not the goat kind." She giggled again.

"Please say you'll come?" A younger woman leaned in, blue eyes wide and vacant. "If you don't like it, you don't have to stay."

"Uhh...sure." Penny was sure—that she wanted to be done with this conversation.

Amelia snatched the leaflet away. "Sure. We'll be there!" Her voice rang with false cheer, and she hustled Penny inside the coffee shop as the women turned to accost the next passerby. "They're *weeeiiirrrrdd!*"

"What did you expect, investment bankers?" Penny walked straight over to the barista. "I'd like a double-shot flat white with caramel, please." It wasn't quite her usual order of a regular latte with no extras.

"Uh, Penny? That's a lot of coffee for you. And a lot of sugar!" Amelia said.

"Desperate times call for...well, caffeine and sugar." Penny gestured for Amelia to place her order.

"What the hell. Make that two, please!"

When they'd both collected their coffees, Amelia took a sip of hers. "Woah. It's not going to put hair on my chest, is it?"

"Depends," Penny asked. "Have you kissed any were-wolves lately?"

Amelia sighed. "No, just my little leprechaun. And even *he* hasn't been around lately."

Red had spent the last weekend of break with family, leaving Amelia to pine for him. It had honestly surprised Penny. She hadn't thought of Amelia as the type to fall so deeply for a guy.

"You haven't seen him yet? He got back yesterday."

"Only in the halls. I mean, hugs are nice, but...you know." Amelia wiggled her eyebrows.

"I don't want to know." Penny had no idea how the two managed to hook up at the Academy without being caught, but she was grateful it hadn't happened in their room. Not that she knew of, anyway.

"How are we gonna get out of here, Penny?" Amelia eyed the group still hovering outside the coffee shop. "We have to get back in time for Folklore. Assuming it's still on, anyway."

"Do you really want to risk missing it just in case?" Penny asked.

The barista leaned over. "You need to sneak out the back way?" he asked.

Both girls nodded eagerly.

"Those weirdos have been scaring my customers off all day." He opened a small swinging gate that blocked off the kitchen from the shop and pointed to a door. "That way."

Penny caught sight of his name tag as she passed him on the way to freedom. "You're a legend, Tony."

"Anytime!" Tony called after them as he closed the door. "Just don't be strangers, ok! These people are killing my business!"

Penny and Amelia debated what to do with the leaflet on their way home.

"We should totally crash their party," Amelia insisted. "Get the down-low. The four-one-one. The—"

"You sounds like a 90s teen movie," Penny said. "We *can't* go, Amelia. This is way above our pay grade."

"We can't just ignore it!" Amelia hissed.

"Why are you whispering?" Penny asked in hushed tones. They rounded the corner, and the Academy came into view.

"Oh." Amelia's voice had returned to normal. "They're gone."

Penny didn't have to ask who. The corner was vacant, the only sign anyone had been there a big white bit of cardboard face-down on the pavement.

Amelia hesitated, then angled toward it.

"Mate? The Academy is this way." Penny pointed at the gate leading into the grounds.

Amelia ignored her, jogging over to the discarded sign with a nervous glance around before she picked it up. She lifted it, her face falling as she read it.

"Amelia?" Penny tried to keep the concern out of her voice but quickly ran to her friend's side.

Witch! Witch! Kill the —Itch!

The words were painted beside a crude drawing of a stick figure tied over an orange fire.

"Religious scum," Amelia said in a hoarse voice.

"Why religious?" Penny asked.

Amelia pointed to the incomplete word. "Too stodgy to swear." She laughed, but it was hollow and devoid of mirth. "We can give the leaflet to the dean. She'll know what to do."

Penny nodded, taking no satisfaction in her win. Her friend was scared, and she was, too.

A few minutes after she knocked, the dean's heavy oak door swung open. Penny was surprised to see Agent Crenel standing in the office.

"Can I help you, girls?" The dean ignored her guest, motioning for Penny and Amelia to come in.

Amelia walked forward and placed the leaflet on her desk. Then she held up the sign.

The dean's face tightened. "I'm sorry you had to see that. I was under the impression that particular issue had been taken care of." Dean March's eyes slid to Agent Crenel, who rubbed one hand through his graying hair. "Where did you find it?"

Amelia gave a terse explanation of the people they had seen loitering at the corner, followed by the details of their encounter with the cultists.

Agent Crenel's eyebrows shot up. "And they just *handed* you an invitation?"

"The guy at the coffee shop said they've been there all day, recruiting people," Penny explained. "We thought you should know."

"I must say, I'm surprised." The dean pulled the leaflet toward her and quickly scanned it. "I won't ask if you considered going alone. It might destroy my very high opinion of your intelligence."

Penny and Amelia exchanged guilty looks but said nothing.

Crenel heaved a deep and weary sigh. "I wish I could say we have the manpower to investigate this," he said. He looked at the girls, then flicked a glance at the dean.

She gave a minute shake of her head.

"But we don't—" Crenel began.

"Absolutely not! These are *my students*, Stuart. *Not* your agents. Not yet." The dean glared at him as if daring him to correct her.

Penny's heart fluttered, and she stepped forward. "If there's anything we can do to help, we'll do it. Honestly."

Amelia quickly stepped up beside her. "It's not like we'd be going in alone," she pointed out, with a beatific grin at the dean. "We'd bring Cisco and Red. Besides, from what I can tell, it's just an informational session. They're not going to scare off their new recruits, are they?"

"We could find out what they're planning next. Undercover, you know?" Penny added. Somehow the words kept flowing, even though she was mentally kicking herself. *What am I getting myself into?*

Crenel turned pleading eyes on the dean. "The event's not for two more weeks. With a bit of luck, we can squash this other issue by then."

"And if you can't?" Dean March raised a sculpted eyebrow.

Crenel seemed to be at a loss for words. He stepped back and shrugged.

A crafty grin spread over Amelia's face. "Are you saying you *forbid* us to attend, Dean March?"

The dean regarded her for a moment, then gave a tired sigh. "You know very well I possess no such authority. You are both adults, and although I would strongly advise against it, it wouldn't technically be against the Academy's Code of Conduct. Which reminds me, I probably should rewrite that." The dean turned a scathing look on Agent Crenel. "Tread carefully, Stuart. If any of my students are injured on this adventure —"

Crenel waved off her concerns, grinning. "It'll be fine, Jessica. I promise. Have I ever let you down before?"

The door swung shut behind him as the dean muttered, "Numerous times, Stuart. Numerous times."

"Dean, who are the people outside the Academy?" Penny asked, as much to divert the dean's attention as to settle the nerves in her gut.

Dean March pursed her lips and shook her head sadly. "It seems as if word of our curriculum has made it into the public eye. There are those who disbelieve the mythological invasion is occurring, there are those who seem hell-bent on encouraging it, and," she waved her hand at the poster, "there are those who claim it as evidence that their god is angry, or that they are privileged, or whatever ideological insanity they're sprouting this particular week."

"Are they targeting the Academy?" Amelia asked incredulously.

The dean hesitated, then nodded. "Please don't concern yourself too much. Agent Crenel is a very capable man, and he has the best interests of the Academy at heart. He will ensure that the students here are safe, although I would suggest you follow his directions." March pointedly glanced at her watch. "If I'm not mistaken, your next class is starting at about now. Agent Crenel will attend, to disseminate information on the protesters you saw today. I suggest you listen closely."

Both girls nodded and scurried out of the room. Penny paused to pull the heavy door closed behind her.

Amelia slapped Penny's shoulder. "I told you they were religious nutters."

"Are we really going to that cult party?" Penny asked. "With everything that's going on, you don't think we're getting ourselves in too deep?"

Amelia shook her head. "Honestly? I think we'll be safer with that brand of crazy than the ones camped outside of the Academy."

Soon after they arrived at folklore class, Professor Craster launched into a lecture about the need for safety. "There'll be no more gallivanting around or leaving after dark, you hear me? Those people are crazy, and I won't have them putting my students at risk."

There was a murmur amongst the students, and Penny heard the word "Sasquatch" mentioned more than once. Professor Craster scowled, then stepped back to let Agent Crenel speak.

"At this stage, what we're dealing with looks to be nonviolent protesters. We managed to shut down the event planned for today, but we can't make any promises for future events. For now, the FBI and the Academy are advising students to travel in groups. Don't leave unless it's absolutely necessary, and if you must go somewhere, let the faculty know where you're headed."

Groans ran through the students.

"It's not ideal," Agent Crenel admitted. "But the last thing we want is for this to escalate. Right now, it's signs and placards. If we can continue to shut them down effectively, we hope they lose interest or move on to another target. Until then, we don't want anything that may blow this up into a more serious situation."

He went on to inform the class that he would be taking the defense lesson Friday morning and detailing methods that could be used in self-defense against humans rather than Mythers. "Don't take this as a sign of alarm. It was always going to be part of your curriculum since out in the field, you'll encounter people who want to stand in your way. Most of them will need to be disabled through non-lethal means. We just decided to move the class up by a few weeks, that's all."

Once Agent Crenel had wrapped up the discussion he left, his polished shoes clicking on the old wooden floorboards.

He paused at the door and looked back to meet Penny's eyes. "I'll be around here for the next few days if anybody needs me." The door swung slowly closed behind him.

CHAPTER SIXTEEN

Penny's eyes shot open as her alarm blared. "Do we have class this morning?"

Amelia groaned from across the room. "That sound is so obnoxious. Can't you set it to tinkling wind chimes or something?"

"I tried music," Penny reminded her. "And we both slept through it every day for a week." She slammed the alarm, silencing it.

Amelia grabbed her phone and squinted into the dim glow. "Defense is, unfortunately, as scheduled."

"Ugh." Penny nudged Boots with her toe. "Get me clothes?"

Boots yawned, then coiled back up to hide her head.

Classes that week had been a scattered mess of cancellations and reschedules, thanks to the threat of protesters. True to Agent Crenel's word, though, no one had appeared to harass the students.

The official recommendations for curfew and group travel had been lifted the day before, though March had insisted the students stay vigilant and avoid drawing notice to themselves where possible.

Penny dressed, eager now that she remembered the FBI Agent would be teaching the class.

"Hurrying off to meet Mr. Hot Pants?" Amelia asked.

Penny eyed the low-cut top Amelia had picked out. "You're wearing *that*?"

"Red said he'd have lunch with me." Amelia grinned, then pouted. "But you're right. If we're going to be wrestling with Jason and Corey, I'd better pick something more appropriate."

"Like plate mail?" Penny asked. The two boys hadn't even taken the chance to grope anyone during defense training, but the sly comments they'd made didn't make the idea of tackling them appealing. Well, not unless she got a well-placed knee in.

"This will have to do." Amelia selected a high-necked leotard top. It would be impossible to pull it up or down in a simple demonstration.

"Nice choice," Penny said. Her own attire—her normal uniform of a t-shirt and jeans, topped off with her aging work boots—would have to do. "Let's go."

Penny paused as she descended the stairs to the ground level of the Academy, hearing the muffled sounds of raised voices filtering through the thick walls.

She held a hand out to halt Amelia. "Wait."

"What's that noise?" Amelia pushed past Penny and headed for the foyer.

"Amelia, that's not what 'wait' means!" Penny hurried to catch up.

They pushed the door, only to have it pushed back.

A moment later, Professor Craster poked his head out. "Get to class," he growled. "Nothing to see here."

He slammed the door closed, and Penny heard the lock click.

She exchanged a glance with Amelia. "We'd better go. At any rate, Cisco will know what's happening."

"Wait." Amelia glanced at the stairs. "Follow me."

She ran back up to the girls' dorm, turning away from their own corridor and racing past a row of closed doors to the end of the hallway, where Mara, Kathleen, and another student were clustered around the window.

"Coming through." Amelia nudged them aside to squeeze in.

Mara stepped back, pale-faced. "I'm going to class," she mumbled. "Kath?"

Kathleen withdrew to join her, wearing the same wide-eyed look of fear as her friend. When Penny reached the window, she saw why.

A cluster of people—maybe two dozen, Penny guessed—had gathered at the main entrance gate to the Academy. Through the pitted glass in the window, Penny could make out some of the signs they held.

Witch.

Evil.

Doom-bringers.

Penny shuddered. "Is it the same people?" she whispered.

The girl beside Amelia glanced back. "I saw them here earlier in the week. They brought some signs, but the police came and chased them away pretty quick." She turned back to the window. "Guess I know why my class was canceled this morning."

"Who'd you have?" Penny asked.

"Craster. Now that Jones is gone, he's taken over as the security manager for the Academy." The girl took a shuddering breath and turned away from the sight. "I'm going back to my room."

"Wait. Jones really is gone for good? It's not just a suspension?" Amelia tugged her arm. "When did *that* happen?"

The girl shrugged. "We were told Monday. They said they were going to replace him soon, but no word who they'll get yet." She shrugged off any more attempts to converse, folding her arms tightly across her chest and disappearing into one of the nearby rooms.

When they got to the defense training room, Agent Crenel was waiting. He glanced at his watch as the girls entered, but didn't say anything, and Penny was relieved to see three other students were still missing.

Clive, Heddy, and Kathy arrived barely a minute later, collectively red-faced and out of breath.

"Sorry, Professor," Heddy gasped. "I mean—wait, what do we call you?"

Crenel waited a beat before answering. "Agent Crenel is fine."

"What's going on outside?" Kathy demanded. "Why are they protesting against us?"

Looking as if he'd rather answer any other question in the world, Agent Crenel sighed. His eyes darted to the window, then back to the class. "I'm afraid word of the curriculum here has spread. The bureau is working toward an agreement that will give this Academy added protections—both under the law, and physically—but until then, we must tread carefully."

"The law?" A chill ran over Penny's arms. "What the hell?"

Crenel met her gaze, then glanced at the bag by her feet. "Of course, any harm the protestors do to a person would be covered by existing laws. However, if any unsanctioned mythological beings get injured... Well, let's just say the trial cases have been less than promising."

He quickly changed tack, moving onto the topic of vampiric defense.

Penny's mind lingered. *That agreement can protect Boots,* she realized. *But back home, would she need protection in the first place?*

CHAPTER SEVENTEEN

The venue for the cult meeting was a tiny red-brick house nestled in the outer suburbs of Portland, lit by cheery LED lanterns strung from the eaves at the front.

It wasn't exactly what Penny had expected.

Amelia shivered. "This just gets weirder by the minute."

"What did you expect?" Cisco stepped in front of them, walking to knock on the door. "A ruined castle decorated with gargoyles?"

Penny shrugged, not letting on that that was much closer to her expectations, than this, well, very normal house. "Are we sure it's the right place?"

Red thrust his hands in his pockets, shuffling nervously. "Well, the black balloons tied to the letterbox suggests that it is."

"It's more like a birthday party for an emo eleven-year-old than the meeting of a highly organized cult." Regardless, Penny joined Cisco at the door.

Cisco knocked again, and this time, it opened.

The fresh-faced young woman who stared up at him

was the one that had given Amelia the pamphlet. "Hi! I'm Felicity. You're here for the meeting?"

She stepped back to let them in when they nodded. "Just take a seat wherever you can find one. There are chips and dip on the coffee table. Um, the beer is coming, but we had to wait for Mark." She closed the door as she babbled and led them into a sunken living room with a beige shag-pile carpet. "He and Tobias are the only ones old enough to buy it," she admitted with a giggle.

Penny couldn't help but cringe at Felicity's overeager attempts to win them over. She shuffled into the living room and perched on the edge of a threadbare couch, carefully avoiding some of the nastier stains.

Four girls and two boys—definitely too young to buy booze in the States, Penny assumed—had squeezed onto the longer of the three couches. All were dressed in black, the girls sporting dark lipstick, charcoal eyeshadow, and foundation that was clearly a few shades too pale for their natural coloring.

Penny glanced around to see her friends still hovering in the doorway. She grunted and jerked her head, motioning for them to sit down.

Amelia stepped down into the circle of chairs, slotting herself next to Penny. Cisco perched on the arm next to her, and Red squeezed in at the end. It was squashed, but they fit.

"I'm Amelia, and this is Penny." Amelia introduced the boys as well, then waited expectantly.

"I'm Paige," one of the girls mumbled. She didn't lift her eyes, and none of the others spoke.

Felicity reappeared, holding a bowl of Doritos. "Forgot

to put the snacks out," she explained breezily. "So, where are you all from?" She clasped her hands, waiting expectantly.

"Oh, around." Amelia waved off the question. "Penny here is visiting from Australia. She's...staying with me."

There was a knock at the door and with a look of relief, Felicity ran off again, leaving the room in silence.

Penny hesitantly leaned forward and picked up a handful of Doritos. Amelia made a face at her—eyes wide, mouth tight. Penny shrugged and put it in her mouth. *If they want to poison us, they probably could have done it at the coffee shop,* she reasoned.

"Dude, they're nacho-style," Amelia told her.

Penny frowned, no idea what Amelia was trying to convey with the cryptic message. Moments later, trying to choke down the burning sensation, she decided that next time she'd listen to Amelia.

She heard voices at the door and turned to see two men and three more girls walk inside.

Clearly, these guys had gotten the invitation that listed the dress code. Of the men, one looked a little older. His short, scruffy beard was still a little patchy, and his lank black hair made him look older than he otherwise would have.

The other guy with him was his polar opposite. Tan skin, white smile, and sandy blond hair combed in a way that looked like he'd just flicked a hand through it—the kind of look that probably took four hours and at least two types of styling product to attain.

"Mark, Tobias! Look, we have new guests." Felicity's voice suggested that this was the most unexpected point of all. Mark, the dark-haired guy, simply grunted and shrugged. Tobias, however, rushed forward to greet the newcomers. "I'm so glad you made it," he gushed. "Sorry for leaving you alone for so long." He turned to Felicity, his voice hardening. "You should have called."

Felicity stammered out an apology that Penny interrupted, feeling bad for the girl. "It's fine, really," she assured him. "We were just getting to know everyone."

Tobias raised a skeptical eyebrow, but a scowl from Mark made him back down.

"Well, uhh, let's get started." Still flustered, Felicity gestured toward a small alcove behind the living room. One by one, the black-clad guests filed toward it.

"Are we sure this is a good idea?" Amelia murmured.

"Too late." Penny pointed ahead. Red had, in all his innocence, struck up a conversation with a reluctant young girl and was already disappearing into the darkness.

"That boy," Amelia grumbled. "He'd follow a pretty girl into a pool full of alligators."

"Cisco has his back," Penny assured her. Indeed, Cisco was next through the door, stone-faced as he glanced over his shoulder at her.

The doorway led down a narrow flight of steps into a dingy basement. Penny wrinkled her nose, wondering if the damp smell was just old laundry or a more serious problem.

Plastic chairs lined the room in an awkward circle.

Not seeing a spot that would let her merge into the wood-paneled walls, Penny simply took the closest one, yanking Amelia down next to her.

"All right, all right." Mark stood in the center of the

chatter and hubbub, a tall, rusted pitchfork in one hand. *Or is it a trident?* Penny wondered. "Order!"

The silence that fell when he thumped the staff on the wooden floor wasn't complete but was apparently the best he would get.

Ignoring the few stray whispers and giggles, he cleared his throat and began.

"Right. This is the first meeting since the...uhh, the Baghdad event—"

"You mean the ghost-summoning," a girl called.

Mark flattened his mouth in disapproval, his eyes flicking to Amelia and Penny, then across the circle to Cisco and Red. "Yes."

"That was a total fuck-up!" This time, it was the guy beside Penny who called out. "We lost the *Book of*—"

"Dammit, Craig, I know that," Mark snapped. "We don't have to air out all our dirty laundry in one night, do we?"

"Come on, Mark," Felicity said. "We summoned ghosts! Maybe we didn't intend to get all of them, but we did it! And we still have copies of the book."

Penny's heart skipped a beat. "Book? Ghosts? Come on, guys, you gotta fill us newcomers in."

A cocky smirk crept over Mark's face. "Yeah, we summoned ghosts. At a theatre. It's what we do."

"We did it once, Mark," Craig said dryly. "And it was still a fuck-u—"

"*SHUT UP!*" Mark rounded on Craig. "Shut up, you fucking *child*. Why do you try to undermine everything I do? I had—"

"Jesus, Mark, cool down." Tobias stood and walked over

to Mark, who threw off the placating hand placed on his shoulder. "You'll scare off the new kids."

Tobias's words only seemed to make Mark angrier, and yet he stood down, wrenching his arm away before stalking back to the middle of the circle. "Next time, we're gonna summon something real. Something big. Any ideas?" He glared around the room.

"Hold up," Amelia stood, ignoring Penny's tug on her arm. "Guys, this all sounds crazy." She quickly held her hands up at Mark defensively. "I mean, good-crazy. But what are you talking about? What's the end game?" She sat again, folding her arms across her chest as if daring them to answer her.

Felicity raised her hand timidly. When Mark nodded to let her speak, Penny tried not to cringe. *I haven't had to raise my hand to speak since I was in primary school.*

Felicity stood, her hands folded in front of her, head raised like she was delivering a well-rehearsed presentation. "Our mission is to bring a new dark age to America. Not to bring about the collapse of mankind, just society. To bring us back to a time where magic ruled, where pagan gods walked the lands, where crops thrived by the will of the gods, not corporate monsters."

"Does she realize she's…" Penny's whisper drifted off as she struggled to find a word that encompassed Felicity's delusion.

"Crazy?" Amelia murmured back.

Penny shrugged. "There are more than a few 'roos loose in the top paddock over there, that's for sure."

Rather than agree, Amelia turned a stunned expression her way. "What does that even *mean?*"

Penny winked. "Just listen."

Felicity's monologue continued, about how modern society was broken, the rich had all the power, and bringing back the "dark times" would create a new playing field—one where the balance was not weighted by money.

"So, how do we do it?" Penny asked, leaning forward. *I've got to find out about that book.*

"We summon monsters," Mark said. "And hunt down artifacts of great power."

"Aye, is your stick one, then?" Red asked cheerily. "What's it do?"

Mark's jaw twitched, and someone smothered a giggle. "No. It's...a replica."

"A replica of what?" Cisco asked, his eyes too wide to be entirely innocent.

"Great Poseidon's trident," Mark growled.

He opened his mouth to say more, but Red interjected. "So you haven't found one, then? That's a shame. I found a lucky penny once, but I dropped it down a drain." His gaze unfocused as he stared into the distance. "You know, maybe it wasn't all that lucky."

Penny bit down hard on her lip as Mark's blood pressure visibly rose, his face so angry it verged on comical. His pasty face filled with blood, first his neck, then his cheeks and ears turning blotchy red. She smothered a giggle as he sucked in a trembling breath.

"What Mark means to say is," Tobias interrupted smoothly, "we've found several artifacts in the past few months, but only the initiated are allowed to access those."

"What kinds of things?" Penny pressed, desperate to

bring the conversation back around to the book. "You talked about summoning ghosts. How did you do that?"

Mark went to speak again, but again, he was interrupted.

Tobias smoothly stepped between the dark-haired man and Penny. "I'm sure you'll understand why we can't talk about specifics?" His smile didn't quite reach his eyes. "There are organizations out there doing their best to close us down. If they were to find out what we have…" He shrugged, the gesture somehow ominous. "And let's be honest—we don't know you. Not yet."

"Oh. Fair enough." Penny shrank down in her seat. Something about Tobias—his quick mood swings, his false charm—made her uneasy.

The rest of them she could write off as posers, kids with too much time and not enough sense.

Tobias, however, was dangerous.

The meeting settled down after that. The members discussed recent Myther sightings, information Penny already had through the college.

Suggestions for future summonings were brought up and shot down, mostly by Tobias. He didn't give reasons, just spat "No" at the members who offered up obscure bits of lore or rattled off a wishlist of ancient deities.

Eventually, Mark had had enough. "Did you forget who started this group?" He sneered at Tobias. "You've only been hanging around for the last two months. You waltz in here, treat my people like shit, and expect us to let you take charge?"

Tobias sat back in his chair, a slow smile spreading over

his face. "Oh, sure, Mark. How does that trident work again?"

Mark's face lost all expression, and Penny shivered. The only way a guy as angry as Mark could do that was if he was right on the edge.

"That's right. It doesn't." Tobias stood, hands wide. "It's a fake. But my book, my precious *Book of Thoth*, that was real." He advanced on Mark and jabbed one finger at his chest. "And *you* lost it. You sent it into that theatre, knowing the FBI was watching. You got Dawn arrested. *You* fucked it up." With each accusation, Tobias took another step closer.

"Watch it, Tobias," Mark growled. "Or else."

Tobias snorted at the empty threat. "Or else what? You've already lost your group. You're a poser, Mark. They'll follow me until—"

Mark threw a punch. Tobias easily dodged the wild swing, laughing as he brought two fists up like a boxer. "They'll follow me, Mark."

"Mark?" Felicity yelled. "What are you doing? Stop it, both of you!"

People scattered, two scruffy boys stepping forward timidly as if to break the fight up.

Tobias grinned. "I got us a meeting with the East Coasters, Mark. Did you manage that? You've been trying for months. They wouldn't talk to *you*, but I'm seeing them next week."

Mark swung again. This time, Tobias didn't dodge. He just punched faster. The crunch of cartilage turned Penny's stomach, and Mark's howl of pain sent her heart skidding into her throat.

Someone screamed, a high-pitched shriek of horror.

"I'm the leader this group needs, *Mark.*" Tobias's needling use of the other man's name grated on Penny's nerves.

He's manipulating him, she realized. *He's been doing it for ages.* She knew the type. Tobias was a guy who could slide a poisoned barb across a crowded table and let no one see it except the recipient. He'd probably been working on the angry, insecure Mark since they'd met, undermining him in tiny ways, hoping he would eventually snap.

"Bastard!" Mark lunged, tackling Tobias. The two men grappled, then Mark landed on his back. He gurgled and spat out a mouthful of blood, the mess hitting Penny's shoe.

Tobias leaned down, and the room fell silent. "You cross me, and you will feel the wrath of gods, Mark. Now, leave."

Mark scrambled backward, coming unsteadily to his feet. "Fuck you, Tobias. This is my group." He beat his chest, voice wobbling. "It's *my house!*"

Tobias spread his hands. "So? You think anyone cares about your dingy little cottage? They don't care about this place any more than they care about you." He smirked. "Don't believe me? Go. Take your precious followers. I'm not stopping anyone from leaving." His eyes glinted as he ran them over the room, resting briefly on Felicity. Her mouth trembled, and she looked sick.

"Come on." Mark turned to go. He looked back when nobody moved. "*COME ON!*" he screamed.

Silence answered.

Mark sniffed, wiping at the steady dribble of blood coming from his smashed nose with his sleeve. He staggered back, then whirled and slammed his fist into the wall before storming away, calling out a last "Fuck you all!" as he slammed the basement door.

Penny turned back, expecting to see Tobias chuckling as his nemesis left. Instead, he had wrapped Felicity in his arms. The girl was wooden, unwilling to fully accept the embrace.

Tobias ignored her discomfort. "I'm sorry you all had to see that." His voice was heavy, as though he hadn't been taunting Mark just moments before.

"What happens now?" The girl who spoke up flinched when Tobias looked at her, but the smile he turned her way brought a small one from her in response.

"We meet with the East Coast liaison. Just me; it's how they work, just one contact with one group. Safer that way." Tobias stroked Felicity's back. "Then...then, my friends, we begin the real work."

CHAPTER EIGHTEEN

"What do you mean, you can't *do* anything?" Amelia snapped. "We risked our lives to get you that information!"

Agent Crenel shook his head in frustration. "I know, I know!" He threw his hands up. "The only thing that might incriminate them in anything illegal is the meeting with the East Coast people. They might be connecting with a terrorist cell that's active over there, but there's no evidence of that, and honestly, your guys are small potatoes. I don't think our persons of interest task force would deal with them."

"They were talking about sending the world back to the dark ages," Penny pointed out.

"Did they offer any concrete plans for doing so?" Crenel asked. When the girls both shook their heads, he shrugged. "It's not illegal to *want* the world to end, only to take steps to make it happen."

"Can't you access the email address the girls have, at

least?" Dean March steepled her fingers against her chin, lips pursed.

Crenel shook his head. "It's one thing to hack the communications of a genuine suspect, but we're talking about a seventeen-year-old girl, Jessica."

"A seventeen-year-old terrorist is still a terrorist," Amelia pointed out.

"Show me the law that says it's an act of terror to summon a ghost, and I'll make it happen," Crenel shot back. He ran a hand through his graying hair, making it stand up at odd angles. "We got lucky at the Theatre. They were in public, so we managed to make public disturbance charges stick on one of them. Other than that, we're talking about American citizens who are, for all intents and purposes, innocent."

"When will our induction take place?" March asked.

Crenel lifted his head, showing surprise at the change of topic. "Not for a few weeks. Why?"

She shrugged, ignoring Penny's curious look. "No reason."

"What are you talking about?" Penny asked.

"You'll see." Dean March stood and walked to her door. "Girls, thank you for your efforts. For now, I must speak with Agent Crenel in private." She opened the door and held it.

Penny squeezed the arms of the wooden chair she sat in, then left out a defeated sigh. "Fine. Well, try and get something more condemning next time."

"Next time?" Amelia had started to rise already but shot to her feet at Penny's words. "Are you crazy? That Tobias guy is a serial killer in the making. He's gonna have all those girls pregnant by the end of the month, ready to drink poison at his say-so."

Penny looped her arm through her friend's. "That just means it won't be boring."

They headed for the door, but Crenel grabbed Penny's free arm. "Don't go doing anything stupid. Promise me that anything you come up with, you run by me first."

Penny hesitated, then nodded. "Fine."

She left beneath the worried gaze of the FBI and the evaluating eye of the dean.

The protestors had, for the most part, been chased off or arrested for disturbing the peace and damage to private property, thanks to a well-aimed rock thrown at an Academy window. Despite that, an aura of restlessness hung over the Academy, and classes that week were subdued.

"Assignments are due by midnight on the twenty-seventh," Professor Marcus said as she handed out their tasks. "You may work in teams of any size if you wish. The grade will be based on the cumulative difficulty." Marcus gave Penny a pointed glance. "Simply taking a photograph of a friendly party god or a pet snake will not be enough to secure a passing mark."

Penny grabbed her piece of paper and scanned it. It confirmed what Professor Marcus had already said.

The task, in a nutshell, was to obtain proof of the Mythological Invasion. They had flexibility as to what that might entail—anything from a video of a Myther to an actual artifact—they had to be prepared to defend their evidence against a skeptical evaluation. They would also need to submit a five-thousand-word essay on the subject.

Movement caught Penny's eye.

She glanced at Cisco, who was gesturing for her attention.

When he saw she was looking, he displayed a string of hand movements that looked like a drunken game of charades.

Penny lifted her hands and mouthed, "What?"

Cisco pointed slowly at her, then Amelia and Red, finally bringing his finger to his chest.

He wants us to work as a team, she reasoned. *That's not a bad idea.*

Then he held up both hands and brought them together.

Um, maybe he thinks we should work closely?

He punched one hand, waved fingers at his hair, and opened both hands like a book.

He wants to summon Fabio, knock him out, and write a book about it?

Unable to come up with a reasonable translation, Penny just shrugged and tapped her watch. Class would be over in a few minutes, and they could talk then.

Indeed, Professor Marcus soon wrapped up and released the students. As they filed out, Amelia squeezed past Corey and Jason to speak to her. "So, we're all working together?" she asked, looking at Cisco.

"At least someone got it," he grumbled.

"Yeah, it was clear enough. I don't know how to find

Samson, though. Do you have any inside info on that?" Amelia waved at Red to join them.

"Samson?" Cisco looked as confused as Penny felt.

"Yes, Samson. You want to cut his hair off so we can kill him, right?" Amelia watched Cisco's face change from confused to exasperated. "Then what the hell was with all the hand waving?"

"Wait until we get to the dining room," Penny advised. "As much as I want to find out the meaning behind Cisco's mime performance, Jason is eavesdropping, and I don't want to give our ideas away."

"I am not!" Jason huffed.

"Then how did you hear that?" Penny waited until he scowled and walked off before giggling. "I swear, that guy is dumber than a box of rocks."

The group of four was soon settled at a spot in the dining room. When Penny looked up, however, they weren't alone. "Clive, whatcha doing here?" she asked, trying to sound casual.

He shrugged, eyes straying over to where Mara and Kathy sat together, their books out as they chatted closely. "I just… Can I join your group?"

"What group?" Red asked far too innocently.

Clive lifted an eyebrow. "I'm not stupid. I know you guys are going to work together. I don't know if I can do this on my own, and…"

"And?" Penny prodded.

Clive didn't answer, just lifted one shoulder.

"And he's too scared to ask Mara if he can pair up with her," Amelia said.

Clive winced, and Penny could swear that even under his dark skin, she could see a rising blush.

"Give me a minute." Amelia dropped her fork and stood. She went over to Mara's table, leaned down and said something, then returned to them.

As Amelia shoved a forkful of slaw into her mouth, Mara appeared. She grinned nervously. "Hi. Um, can I talk to Clive for a minute, please?"

Clive's eyes shot open, and he jumped up fast enough that the scrape of his chair on the floor drew every eye in the room. "Sure."

The two moved off, and Penny tried her best not to look like she was straining to hear their whispered conversation. It wasn't a long one—Mara soon left to rejoin Kathy, and Clive sat down with a thump.

"Still want to join us, Clive?" Amelia asked slyly.

He shook his head. "Uh, thanks. I'm pairing with Mara and Kathy." He stared at his plate for a minute before asking, "What did you *say* to her?"

Amelia shrugged. "I told her that if you hadn't found a group for the assignment by the end of lunch, I was going to ask you to pair up."

"Why would she care?" Red asked.

Amelia reached out and ruffled his hair. "Because she likes him, you doofus. Come on—if Cisco told you he was gonna ask me to partner with him, would you jump in first?"

"No, because we're all teaming up together." Red looked around, still confused. "Aren't we?"

Amelia dropped her head on the table. "I give up." She

lifted it, but only high enough to rest her chin on her hands. "Between you and Cisco, I give up."

"Hey, what'd I do?" Cisco asked.

"Failed mime school," Penny told him. "What *were* you trying to say in there?"

"Oh, that!" Cisco shook his head. "I can't tell you. It's...confidential." He shot Clive a pointed look.

"Oh. Right. Uh, sorry." Clive stood and picked up his plate, giving Amelia a shy grin. "Thanks for the help."

Once Clive had wandered off to sit with his new class partners, Cisco explained. "We should use Tobias to help us summon something big. We'd get huge points for that!"

Amelia and Penny just stared.

"What was the hair thing?" Amelia asked, imitating Cisco's earlier gesture.

"And this bit," Penny asked, doing the motion that looked like opening a book.

"We," Cisco pointed at the four group members, "should team up with Mark,"—the hair gesture—"and Tobias"—the punch—"And get the *Book of Thoth* or what they have of it, and summon a monster for the assignment," he finished, using book-opening hand signal for the *Book of Thoth*.

Penny shook her head in awe. "That was terrible, Cisco. Never, *ever* play charades with me. Not unless you're on the other team."

"Are you done insulting me?" he asked, clutching an imaginary wound on his chest. "I don't think I can take it anymore."

Penny tousled his messy hair the way Amelia had Red's earlier. "Poor baby. I'll stop."

Cisco bit into his burger.

Today's menu was spicy chicken filets on crusty buns with an assortment of side salads, and Penny was thoroughly enjoying it. She didn't even mind the slight bite in the chicken. Her recurring confrontations with Doritos were beginning to harden her taste buds.

"So, what's your plan?" she asked through a mouthful of food.

"My plan?" Cisco wiped a smear of mayonnaise off his face with the back of his hand, then wiped that on his shirt. "That's *your* job. You're the clever one."

"Hey, it was your idea to start with." Penny reached down to pull a small notebook from her bag. "What have we got so far?"

"I don't get the feeling we're going to be invited back anytime soon," Amelia admitted. "I mean, Tobias seemed pretty controlling of those girls. I don't think we fooled him into thinking we'd be pushovers like that."

"You've got a point," Penny agreed. "But what if we have something he wants? Information or something?"

"Or, we could just turn up." Red waved his phone at Penny. "You didn't just get that text?"

Three phones appeared on the table. "Nope, nothing." Amelia looked at Red's phone. "Who did you give your number to?"

"That Felicity girl." Red ducked the hand aimed at his head. "Hey, she said it was for meetings!"

"Maybe she forgot she added you," Penny mused. "It was just before the guys turned up, right?" She remembered the two of them talking, heads close together for a moment before they were interrupted.

Red nodded. "She jumped up so fast I thought something bit her, so she could have forgotten, I guess. Either way, we know where the next meetup is."

Next Friday, Paddy's bar downtown. $5 cover charge, don't worry, they'll accept our ID.

"A bunch of teenyboppers in a bar on a Friday Night," Cisco groaned. "What could go wrong?"

"We can go incognito," Penny said. "Stay out of sight, listen in, then figure out our plan."

"What if they're summoning something?" Amelia asked.

Penny shrugged. "We take our kits. Worst case scenario, if we blow our cover, we lose our lead. Look, at the end of this semester, we'll be a quarter of the way through our course. In two years? It'll be us against the Mythers. If we can't handle something little now, what hope do we have then?"

Red shrugged. "She argues like an Irishman."

"Is that a good thing?" Penny asked.

Red grinned. "Sure, and it is. I'm in."

CHAPTER NINETEEN

The days flew by quickly, and soon Penny was faced with the decision whether to tell Agent Crenel of their plans.

He paced the defense training room as the students watched. "This is not a game," he lectured. "The weapons we'll be training with are real. They can injure you, or even kill you if you aren't careful. All students must be fully armored, and if I see one person goofing off, you're gone. Agreed?"

A murmur of assent ran through the class, and Crenel nodded in satisfaction. "Suit up. When you're done, I want Cisco and Red to help lug this crate upstairs. We'll be outside today."

Penny pulled the heavy pants over her jeans, immediately feeling her body temperature rise. "Are all these layers really necessary?" she asked.

"I'm going to drown in a pool of my own sweat," Heddy called. "Seriously, can't we skip the vest, at least?"

"No." Crenel didn't leave himself open to any arguments. He turned to help Kathy strap her vest on instead. Once it was secure, he passed her a visor.

"No worse than home," Penny mumbled. She realized it really wasn't. She'd often trudged through swampy scrubland in heavy jeans and long sleeves. The protection was essential when the sun was hot enough to fry your skin, or when snakes were as plentiful as blades of grass.

"Boots?" The serpent gave up trying to fit into Penny's visor and lifted her head. "You might have to sit this one out."

With an irritated hiss, Boots dove back into the visor, knocking it over in her haste and spilling herself onto the floor.

"Need a hand, Penn?" Amelia grinned behind the hard plastic faceplate on her visor. She was already strapped into her armor.

Penny realized she was one of the last students to finish getting ready.

"Dammit! Yeah, help me with this strap, will you?"

Amelia happily obliged, and Penny was soon dressed and helmeted. They jogged out of the room, moving awkwardly under the weight and restrictions of the padded clothing, their vision obscured by the visors.

Penny had hoped to catch the agent on their way upstairs, but he was too far ahead of them. By the time Penny emerged from the Academy building, the students were already lined up and accepting their weapons.

"RIGHT!" Crenel bellowed. "This game has rules! You've got five minutes from my mark to scatter. Stay within the bounds of the Academy. If you get hit, you come in. If you hear the bell, you come in." He raised a hand and jangled an old bell loudly. "Don't aim for the head. Yes, we have helmets, but they're not impact-proof. You'll be marked on survival time, kills, and other criteria."

"Like what?" Jason asked.

Crenel smirked and touched a finger to the side of his nose. He handed Penny and Amelia their paint guns. "Final rule. You can use the building, but do *not* get paint on it." A hint of a smile played on his lips. "That's an automatic loss, and the dean will be on your ass for defacing Academy property—and she'll be on mine for letting it happen, which means *I'll* be making *your* life miserable too."

"Oh, shit, no!" Corey called, eliciting a smattering of laughter from the students.

"One more thing…" Agent Crenel did smile now. "Be careful."

"And…*GO!*"

Penny's heart jumped at the command and she bolted forward, figuring her best bet was to head for the wooded area. There, she could find her bearings under cover before setting out to bring down her classmates.

Her breath hissed into the visor, drowning out the sound of her feet thudding on the grass. When a shadow moved up beside her, she jerked away, then laughed.

"Dude, you scared me!"

Cisco pointed to an old garden shed. "That way."

"You trust me not to shoot you?" she asked.

"Until it's down to us." He veered off and she followed, glancing over her shoulder to check no one was behind her. She caught sight of Clive heading into the trees, Mara disappearing ahead of him.

The bell sounded; the game had begun. Penny crouched on one side of the shed door, Cisco on the other.

"I don't see anyone," she said quietly.

"Should we go for the woods?" he asked.

Penny nodded. She scurried out first, Cisco's paint gun protruding through the door as he covered her. She reached a tree, pressed her back against it, and gave a low whistle.

Cisco emerged, running in a low crouch. Behind him, a shadow crossed the grass.

Ping! Ping.

Penny shot at the edge of the shed, paint splattering forest green on the old tin wall, then on the armor of the person crouching next to it.

"Goddammit!" Heddy ripped her visor off and threw it on the ground. "You cheated! How did you see me?"

"Your shadow gave you away." Penny watched Heddy turn and start marching back to the Academy.

Thwap.

Red paint blossomed on a tree by Penny's head and she dived, landing on Cisco's already-prone body.

She hissed in annoyance. "Did it get me?"

Cisco shook his head, helmet askew. Looking down, Penny realized she was lying on his body, their hips embarrassingly pressed together.

She coughed and scrambled off, then ducked as another lash of red exploded in the grass nearby.

"Are you dead yet?" Kathy's voice rang out cheerfully.

"Not even close," Cisco called back. He pointed to Penny and drew a circle with his finger.

"No way." Penny shook her head. "We're not doing this again. Use your words, Cisco."

Cisco sighed. "I'll distract her. You get her from behind."

"Oh. Sure!" Penny dropped and waited for Cisco to run to another tree.

Kathy's aim was awful, but she was quick. Three blobs of paint hit nearby trees as Penny scurried in the opposite direction from where Cisco had gone.

Penny paused, listening for the telltale crunching of leaves.

Got her. Penny rounded the tree and fired two quick rounds. Both went wide and Kathy spun, shooting back at Penny. Penny threw herself down, the paint bullets sailing over her head.

"Oww, shit!" Kathy yelped. "That hurt!"

Penny risked raising her head. Kathy was covered in pink paint and clutched a knee.

"Sorry, Kathy!" Cisco ran over. "You ok?"

She grunted, then nodded. "No, don't touch it. You'll get paint on you."

Cisco grinned. "You shoot fast."

Kathy waited, then giggled. "I was waiting for you to add 'for a girl.' I might have shot you anyway if you had."

Penny snorted, clapping Cisco on the back. "I've trained him better than that."

"Trev is up a tree," Kathy whispered. She pointed back in the direction she had come. "I think he's trying to win by elimination. I was gonna go back for him, but…" She gestured at the pink on her armor.

"Thanks for the heads up!" Penny high-fived her, and she and Cisco waited for Kathy to leave.

"Do we go for Trevor?" he asked.

Penny nodded. "Amelia ran back toward the building, and I bet Red followed her. Clive and Mara went that way." She pointed to the far section of the wooded area. "We can get Trevor on the way."

Cisco nodded. "Split up a little, but stay in sight."

The two crept through the trees, carefully watching in all directions. Cisco hissed at Penny and she froze, then slowly turned his way.

He gestured to a branch above her.

"Don't shoot!" Trevor called. He raised both hands, gun resting on his lap as he sat cross-legged in the forked branches. His face was blotched, and his eyebrows were knitted together tightly. "I surrender."

"What?" Cisco lifted his paint gun to point it at Trevor.

Penny pushed it back down. "Cisco, he surrendered."

"It's a trick." Cisco didn't force the gun back up, though. Instead, he peered up at Trevor curiously. "Isn't it?"

Trevor shook his head, then pulled up the leg of his pants. A purple bruise swelled around his ankle. "I had an accident." Chagrined, he gave a shaky shrug, and Penny realized why he looked so upset.

"Cisco, he's been crying," she whispered, turning her head so Trevor couldn't see her. "He's injured. We can't just *leave* him there!"

Heaving a sigh, Cisco dropped his gun. "I'm coming up. I can help you down, and Penny can catch you. We'll help you back to base."

"You can't do that," Trevor hissed. "You'll lose the game.

You two are at the top of the class, if you screw this up, you'll lose your spots."

Penny drew back in surprise. "We are? How do you know?"

Trevor gave her a shaky smile. "I made a deal with the dean. I'm paying my way through with admin duties. Semester one was on scholarship, but she'll reduce my workload during finals if I store up credits now."

"Oh." She looked at Cisco. "What are you waiting for? Get up that tree, mate."

Cisco nodded and easily swung himself up to the lower branch. He soon had Trevor by one arm, lowering the boy carefully down to Penny's waiting arms. She caught him, looping one arm over her shoulders so she could support his weight as Cisco jumped to the ground.

"So," Penny asked casually once they were hobbling back toward the waiting Agent Crenel. "Where are you on the leaderboard?"

Trevor laughed. "At the bottom. Come on, you didn't see me trying to shoot that crossbow last week? I couldn't even load the damn thing." He sighed, then yelped as his bad ankle hit the uneven ground. "I'm not cut out for fieldwork."

"And I'm not cut out for the lab," Penny admitted. "But that's no reason to give up." She gave Cisco a glance over Trevor's head.

Cisco caught her look, and a corner of his mouth quirked into a smile. "I've got the kid, you shoot the bastards."

Penny gave a short nod, grinning. Ignoring Trevor's

protests, he was soon piggybacked on Cisco while Penny held both her green paint gun and Trevor's blue one.

"You know," she mused as they set off again, "the blue Power Ranger was the clever one."

Cisco sniggered. "And the pink one was the hottest."

"No way. The green ranger was smoking." Penny glanced away from her scouting duties to wink at him. "Let's head back toward the shed. We can duck inside for a quick breather."

Cisco was starting to sweat under the restrictive armor and the weight of his passenger, but it would be impolite to point that out. For all Cisco's bluster, he was still a sensitive thing.

"Good idea," Cisco panted.

He was beginning to pant more now, so Penny paused at the edge of the tree line. "Almost there," she reassured him. "Just a quick dash back to shelter. We can—*wait*. Do you hear that?"

Trevor paled. "It sounds like an animal."

The grunting noise coming from the tin shed certainly could have been mistaken for an animal, except that Penny recognized one of the voices. "Noooooo."

Cisco's shoulders shook as his hand clapped over his mouth to stifle the laughter. "That dog!" he squeaked through his fingers.

"It doesn't sound like a dog." Trevor frowned. "Wait. What's so funny?"

"It's—" Penny wheezed. She sucked in a breath and tried again, speaking too fast for the giggles to erupt again. "It'sCliveandMara!"

"What do you...oh. OH!" Trevor blushed beet-red and gave a nervous laugh. "Lucky guy, I guess."

"What do we do?" Penny hissed. Despite the hilarity of the situation, if Clive and Mara were still unpainted and emerged at the wrong time, it would lose Penny and Cisco the game. On the other hand...

"Sneak." Cisco motioned for Penny to grab Trevor's arm again.

She did so, and the two lifted his feet clear of the ground, then walked swiftly toward the shed. They crouched by the door and Penny handed Trevor his gun. She motioned for him to take the shots.

"Me?" Trevor squeaked.

"It's now or never, kid," Cisco whispered.

"We should go back out there." Mara's voice was muffled but audible. Penny heard a scuffling noise and a zipper, then the click of straps being fastened.

"Come on, no one has found us," Clive spoke quietly. "Let's just chill for a bit."

"Just don't neuter Clive," Penny whispered to Trevor. "Or go for a boob shot. That hurts."

Trevor, his face glowing bright enough that Penny wondered how it wasn't lighting the shadows, nodded. His gun nosed into the door that sat a few inches ajar. His finger pulled the trigger.

Mara screamed. So did Clive. Trevor hurled himself out of the doorway and Cisco sprang to his feet, shooting paint bullets into the small, enclosed space.

"Oh, my God. You BASTARD!" Mara yelled. Penny heard the ring of a slapped cheek.

"What did I do?" Clive asked, outraged.

Cisco ducked to the side, and the shed door slammed back. Mara stormed out, bright pink paint splattered across her midriff. Clive chased after her, his padded pants streaked in pink and blue and a red mark across his face. "Mara!"

When the ruckus died down, Penny helped Trevor to his feet. "Well, that's four down, and one hit for you. Cisco's in the lead, though."

"Thank you," Trevor said, a wide grin covering his face. "Really. I'd still be stuck up a tree if not for you guys."

"Hey, it's all down to teamwork," Penny told him. It was a line Crenel had drummed into them over the two previous defense classes.

They made it back in sight of the Academy without seeing anyone else. Crenel stood by the empty crate, Jason, Heddy, Kathy, and Red all sprawled out on the grass, armor strewn beside them. Boots was stretched out beside Amelia, who stroked her back lazily.

Mara sat with her back to the group, and Clive was next to her, neither of them speaking.

"Man down!" Cisco called. "We have an injury!"

Crenel opened his mouth to respond. Whatever words came out were drowned by the *thunk* of bullets on padded vests.

Penny looked down. Orange paint splayed across her chest and on both of her friends. "The fuck?" she wheezed. Though the vest was protective, the impact had winded her.

She soon had her answer. As Amelia and Red ran toward her, a figure stood on the balcony of the Academy behind them, arms raised.

"So long, suckers!" Corey yelled. "Last man standing! WOOHOO!"

A bright streak shot through the grass and launched itself into Corey's chest. He flew back and slammed to the ground, screaming, "HELP! Help me!"

He managed to roll to his knees, and Penny saw the glittering rainbow wrapped around his chest, squeezing it. After a moment of hesitation, she called, "Boots! Get off him. I'm ok, so you don't have to kill him."

Corey stood, and Boots fell away as he wriggled free of her grip. He picked up the paint gun and aimed the butt at her head, and Penny's heart lurched.

Boots reared and hissed angrily, and Corey flinched. By the time he recovered, she was nowhere to be seen.

"Good girl," Penny whispered. She didn't know where Boots had fled to—probably their room—but it was probably for the best anyway.

Agent Crenel was already on his way over to assist Trevor. Soon, Cisco and Penny were relieved of their burden as Trevor was carried back to the building, lifted between the special agent and the brawny Irishman.

"What an asshole," Amelia hissed. "Corey is a dick, but that was low even for him."

"Did you know he was there?" Penny asked. Her hands felt hot and her jaw was tight. Not because she'd lost—she honestly didn't give two shits about that—but because Corey had stolen any chance of Trevor climbing the ladder in Defense class. Then, as the ultimate insult, he had threatened Boots.

Amelia shook her head. "He must have been there the whole time."

"What a mongrel move," Penny seethed. "I can't believe he tried to hit Boots! And there's no way he didn't see Trevor was hurt."

Cisco shook his head. "Remind me never to group with him. He's the kind of guy who'd take a teammate down for the fun of it."

They picked up the armor and paint guns, then piled the weapons in the crate before stacking the armor on top.

Cisco eyed the sky. "Might rain. We'd better bring this in."

"I'll help." Jason sauntered over and hefted an end of the heavy box, leaving Amelia, Heddy, and Penny to bundle up the loose items.

Cisco grunted and grabbed the other crate handle. Penny clutched at a vest that slipped, then jogged to catch up,

"Your mate is a real dick," she told Jason.

"Mate?" Jason snorted. "He suggested we team up and then shot me in the back the minute we started."

"Oh." Any irritation she had for Jason slid away. "That sucks."

Once the equipment was packed away, Penny left the others to seek out Trevor. His ankle had looked pretty bad. She hadn't told him, but she had a feeling it might be more than a basic sprain.

To her surprise, Penny found him walking out of the dining room like nothing had happened.

"Uh, Trevor?" she asked. "I take it you're feeling better."

"Amazing!" he gushed. "I can't believe they used an actual relic on me!"

"The Asclepius staff?" she asked. "Yeah, it's pretty cool, hey?"

Trevor's eyes widened. "You've seen it too?"

Penny nodded. "I got pretty beat up in Defense last term, during that doll exam."

Trevor's eyes flickered away from her. "Oh. Yeah, that. Jones said my marks were too low to even let me do that exam."

Penny snorted. "You didn't miss much. I got the absolute *shit* beat out of me." She looped an arm around Trevor's shoulder. "I'm sorry we didn't win the game, kid."

Trevor looked up at her, smirking. "Who says?"

Penny pulled back. "Well, Corey was the last one standing, with a body count of four. He pasted us."

"Paste? Like, craft paste?" Trevor screwed up his face, confused.

"I mean, he annihilated us." Penny ground her teeth at the injustice. "I can't believe he'll walk away from that with top marks."

"Oh!" Understanding dawned, and Trevor grinned. "You should go have some lunch." He nodded back toward the dining room. "If you go now, you might catch the last of the fireworks."

Frowning, Penny dropped her arm. "Okay?" She headed toward the dining room, calling back over her shoulder, "Anyway, I'm glad you're feeling better, Trev."

"Thanks, Penny!"

Penny pushed open the heavy dining room door just in time to see Corey slam his fists on the table across from Agent Crenel.

"Easy now, kid," Crenel warned in a hard voice.

"This is bullshit!" Corey kicked a chair next to him, and it went flying across the dining room. Two girls from the second class stood and hurried out of the room, leaving Penny alone with Crenel and Corey.

I should leave. Penny sat down anyway, trying to seem as unobtrusive as possible. *Then again, I can't miss this.*

"I won that game, and I did it by the rules." Corey seemed to have trouble controlling his face. It twitched angrily.

"You won an *aspect* of the game, son. I was quite clear that marks would be given for more criteria than just shooting everyone." Crenel leaned back, giving Corey some space. "It just so happens that the criteria was teamwork and adaptability, not camping out like a sniper and shooting at an injured classmate."

"Fuck your criteria. It should have been accuracy or initiative, not teamwork bullshit. That's a cop-out. You just don't like me." Corey stood, punching the table again. "You'll hear from my parents about this! You can't fail me! They paid good money for me to be here."

Corey shouldered past Penny, then whirled around. "And that snake needs to be put down," he spat.

Corey stormed out, leaving Agent Crenel alone at the table. Penny waited a minute, then wandered over. "What was all that about?" she asked.

Crenel sighed. "Don't pretend you didn't figure it out. The game had a teamwork aspect; that was the 'extra criteria.' I've only been teaching you lot for a few days, but I wanted to see if my lesson was sinking in. I was hoping most of you would work in teams. Most of you did. I just didn't expect it to go so spectacularly bad."

"Do you think his parents will kick up a fuss?" Penny asked.

Crenel shrugged. "Jessica won't care if they do, and her opinion is the only one that matters—but perhaps Boots should give him some space for a few days." He flicked open a stack of papers in front of him and started jotting notes.

Penny craned her neck, but his tight scrawl was illegible to her.

Crenel moved the papers out of her eye line. "This isn't a normal college, Penny. We can't tolerate students who aren't in it for the right reasons. By the end of this year, the March-Blaisey Academy will officially be a training academy for the FBI."

"Oh." Penny waited for the words to sink in. "Wait, what?" She slid into the chair Corey had vacated. "What the hell does *that* mean?"

Crenel tapped a finger on the table absentmindedly. "I've been trying to convince Jessica to do it since she started this damn Academy. We have a training unit set up, but it's too small. We're not working fast enough, and this Mythological Invasion is overtaking our efforts to contain it."

Crenel was tired, Penny could see that. His gaze was distant, and she got the feeling he was rambling almost without realizing it. Deciding to at least try to get more information out of him, she leaned forward. "What does that mean for us?"

Crenel met her eyes. "We'll be sending you out on missions before you're ready. Giving you tasks that put you in danger. Maybe getting some of you hurt." He smiled, but it didn't reach his eyes. "But we don't have a choice. The very nature of the bureau attracts people who are set in their ways, abide by routines, and are skeptical down to our very core. It's a handy skillset, but it's not the one we need for this."

"Oh." Penny shivered. "That doesn't sound good."

"It sounds necessary." Crenel stood up. "But not for you."

"What do you mean?" Penny asked, startled.

Still watching her closely, Crenel said, "I know you haven't signed up for classes next term. That's ok; you told me from the start that I'd have to convince you." He turned to leave. "But if you're gonna change your mind, kid, make sure you're really committed. Once this starts happening for real, there's no going back."

He left, slipping out of the dining room without making a sound.

Penny sat down with a thump. She hadn't realized she'd stood up. *What the fuck am I gonna do?*

CHAPTER TWENTY

P enny nursed a warm beer, fiddling with the synthetic locks of blonde hair adorning her head.

"You're way too stressed out." Amelia slid a basket of wings over. "Eat something, and stop playing with that wig, or it'll fall off."

"I'm just nervous." Penny smiled and tried to focus on the conversation Cisco and Red—both hidden under the shadow of baseball caps—were having about sports. Three seconds later, she had tuned back out again.

They were nestled in a corner booth at Paddy's, waiting for Tobias and his crew to show up for their meeting. The team had arrived early in the hope of getting a good table where they could stay out of sight, and the plan had worked—the table for nine with a small 'reserved' plague on it just *happened* to be right near an empty booth.

Their disguises were basic—hats for the boys, Penny in a long, blonde wig and Amelia under a headscarf—but they had walked right by Heddy outside the Academy, and she hadn't blinked.

Now, they just had to wait. Penny had spent the last forty minutes dwelling on Crenel's words, wondering just how deep they were digging themselves...and whether, after everything, Penny really could just pack up and leave.

An elbow dug into Penny's side. "Is that..." Cisco pointed at a girl talking nervously to the bartender.

Penny's breath caught in her throat. "It's Felicity. Duck!" The four friends studied the grain of the table as if they had never seen wood before. Once Felicity was seated with her back to them, Penny's heart began to slow. She shrank back as two more girls joined the reserved table.

Fifteen minutes later, the new arrivals were seated and were scouring the menu.

"Neither Tobias or Mark are here," Amelia pointed out quietly.

Penny craned her head over the booth to look. "All the seats are filled. Looks like they weren't invited?"

"Maybe Tobias is at his big meeting." Cisco sucked the flesh off a chicken wing and tossed the bones in the basket before reaching for another. "Can you hear what they're saying?"

"What who's saying?"

Penny stifled a scream as she flinched away from the small green man who had appeared next to her. "Who the fuck are you?" she asked in a squeaky voice.

"Paddy." He raised an arm to gesture overhead. "This is me bar! Now, who are they?" He pointed at Felicity's group.

"No one!" Penny resisted the urge to punch his curious face, realizing the instinct was born from adrenalin, not sense. Causing a scene right now was the worst thing she could do.

"Nay, girl. They're *some*ones, or ye wouldn't be watching them, would ye?" Paddy plucked Penny's abandoned drink off the table and took a sip. He sighed happily. "Ahh! It's as warm as a blarney rock on a sunny day."

"Whoever the fuck you are, leave us alone," Cisco hissed.

Paddy turned a wide smile on him. "Or what? Ye'll make me? That might get the attention of those pretty lasses at the table, and I'm guessin' ye wouldn't want that, now, would ye?"

Red leaned over. "Listen ta me, ye wee feckin' leprechaun. Leave us alone, or I'll curse ye 'til the devil makes a ladder from yer wee back, aye?"

"Wow, Red." Amelia caressed his arm. "How very Irish of you."

Paddy climbed on the table, his buckled boots gleaming. "Get fecked." He leaned down to come nose to nose with his fiery-haired countryman. "Or buy me a drink." Paddy dropped into his seat with a grin. "It doesn't cost ye much ta be polite, now, does it?"

Cisco made eye contact with Red, who palmed his forehead, then nodded. "Aye, get the wee prick a drink. We can make him work for it."

Cisco slunk up to the bar, doing his best to avoid notice from the neighboring table.

"So, why're we eavesdropping on yon wee lassies and lads?" Paddy asked. "If ye let wee Paddy in, he might be of use...if ye keep the whiskey flowin', that is."

"What kind of use?" Penny demanded.

Paddy puffed his chest out. "I'm drippin' with Irish luck. While I'm here, you canna lose!"

"Should we tell him?" Penny asked. They'd touched on leprechauns a few times in class, usually with Professor Madera but also, surprisingly, in Craster's folklore class. The prevalence of Irish bars meant leprechauns were one of the most commonly sighted Mythers in America, he had told them.

High in self-interest, rarely malicious, treat with care, Penny remembered. *And always bribe with top-shelf whiskey, ale, or rum.* She hoped they wouldn't run out of money before the night was done.

Cisco returned, juggling five shot glasses. He put them down carefully, shielding them with his hands.

"One for the leprechaun," he said. He smacked Paddy's grasping hand away. "If he promises not to cause a fuss. If you help us out, there will be more to come—whether it's the good stuff or the bad stuff depends on how valuable your service is. All right?"

Paddy scowled, his eyes glued on the amber liquid. "If you startin' with the dregs, we're off to a bad relationship."

"Do you agree?" Cisco pressed.

Paddy nodded, and when Cisco slid the shot glass toward him, he snatched it up. The leprechaun sniffed it, inhaling deeply with his eyes closed. "Oh, laddie, this will be a very good relationship indeed."

Passing a glass to Penny, Cisco sighed. "It better be. You don't wanna know what that round cost me."

Once all four friends were in agreement, they quickly filled Paddy in on their goal. Paddy's eyes lit up, and he quickly agreed to help, reminding them of the whiskey almost as an afterthought.

He's loving this, Penny realized. The thought gave her confidence that he wouldn't betray them.

Their group fell silent when Felicity cleared her throat and tapped a glass with her fork.

"You all know why we're here today," she began.

"I don't," Paddy muttered, but he did it quietly.

"I don't," someone at the table called. It was a girl with long black hair and a pale face. She shrugged. "I missed last meetup. Where is Mark? Why are we meeting on a Friday?"

"Mark left," Felicity said quickly. "I know, it was a surprise to everyone. Tobias is stepping up to take his place, but...well, I wanted to make sure everyone is ok with that."

"Does Tobias know about this meeting?" a guy asked.

Felicity gave a small cough. "Yes. He'll be here a bit later. He had a meeting with those people from Brooklyn."

"Why do we need them?" The guy shot back. "We're doing just fine on our own. We were doing just fine before Tobias came and messed everything up, too."

"Messed it up?" a red-headed girl shot back. "Tobias is the only one who actually found something we can use. Mark is just a poser. Tobias is the real deal."

Red slipped away from the table and returned a few minutes later. The conversation fell quiet for a bit, then turned to the group from Brooklyn. At the same time, a waitress delivered another basket of chicken wings.

Penny learned that the East Coast group was trying to recruit Tobias and his people—though it turned Penny's stomach to think of those eager kids as 'belonging' to a creep like Tobias. Apparently the east coast was rife with Mythers, and nothing as benign as drunk leprechauns. Crenel had confirmed that a vampire outbreak was taking root, among other problems.

"What about the test?" The redhead asked. "Tobias said they'll want us to prove ourselves. Last time we tried doing something, Dawn ended up in the slammer, and we lost the book."

"That was just practice," Felicity assured her. She reached down and patted her oversized handbag. "Our copies aren't complete, but we have what we need."

"We need that copy," Penny hissed.

Cisco grinned. "And I know just how to get it. We'll have to leave right away, though, so let's leave that until the end."

Unable to decipher Cisco's cryptic wink, Penny let the matter drop. She trusted him to come through.

Meanwhile, Paddy was getting restless. "I can steal it for ye," he peered. "For another shot of that fine nectar."

Amelia got up to go to the bar. "I'll buy this round," she offered.

Penny watched as her friend sauntered up to the bar with a confidence that gave her a pang of jealousy. Not that she begrudged Amelia all the happiness in the world—her friend deserved it—but Penny wished she had just a smidge of Amelia's bravado.

In fact, Penny realized, simply by going to the bar, her friend had already attracted a guy. Penny's heart rose into her throat when she realized who the guy was.

Tobias approached Amelia from behind, leaning over to

sniff her hair as she ordered drinks for their table. *Ew, gross*. Out loud, Penny snapped, "That's Tobias. He's about to bust Amelia!"

Paddy jumped on the table. "Not today!" He hurried over to the bar and clambered up a stool, yelling for the bartender. As expected, Tobias turned toward him, irritated by the leprechaun's obnoxious yelling.

Amelia was trapped, waiting for the drinks she had ordered. If she simply vanished, that would attract even more attention from Tobias.

"Cisco?" Penny hissed. "Tell me you have *something*." She watched him root through the duffel bag he'd brought with him with a worried look.

His face turned to relief. "Found it." He drew out the black and withered Hand of Glory.

Back at the bar, Paddy's ruckus was drawing all the wrong attention. Tobias had already turned away and was leaning over to speak to Amelia. Then he drew back, her face locked in his grip as he forced her to look at him. "Shit. Hurry!" Penny stood, ready to go to her friend's rescue.

"Goddammit, I forgot to bring a lighter!" Cisco looked around desperately.

"Cisco. Seriously?" Penny pointed to the flickering tea light candle on the table.

Cisco smacked his forehead and dipped the hand into the flame. Penny waited for the drowsiness—nothing.

"Sorry, me friends." Paddy's face appeared at the edge of the table. "Yer friend has been made. Oh! ye got yerself a glory hand! *Handy*, those are." He burst into laughter at his joke.

Penny's mind raced. "There must be a locked door nearby."

Amelia pulled away from Tobias, her eyes darting toward Penny in terror. She took a step, but Tobias grabbed her arm tightly. A flash of silver sparkled at his other wrist as he raised it to her throat. He looked toward Penny's table with a wolfish grin.

"Aye, the top-shelf whiskey is behind lock and key." Paddy's face dropped. "Used to be easier to steal. Now it's damn near impossible!"

Red grabbed his wallet and dashed for the bar, Penny on his heels. As he stopped to call a bartender over, Penny walked straight up to Tobias. Amelia lifted her face to Penny, confusion creasing her face.

"Do we have a problem?" she asked loudly. "Let her go."

"No!" Amelia shrank closer to Tobias. "You don't have to do that, Tobias. Please...don't leave me."

Tobias dropped Amelia's arm, lifting his hands up defensively as he turned his smile on Penny. "No problem. I was just surprised to see you two here—at a *members* meeting."

"Tobias?" Amelia turned to Tobias, her eyes glazed and unfocused. She shook her head, a quick jerk as if to throw off a confusing thought. "It's ok, Penny. He won't hurt us. It's *Tobias!*" She leaned into him, and he wrapped a protective arm around her.

Penny took a shaky step back. "What did you do to her?"

Tobias shrugged. "Do to her? She's my friend. I wouldn't hurt her." He turned to Amelia, who warmed under his gaze. "Would I, babe?"

Amelia snuggled closer to him. "You're so *warm*."

"Amelia, listen to yourself," Penny pleaded. She glanced back over her shoulder—Red was fidgeting impatiently as the bartender drew out a set of jangling keys and walked to the whiskey cabinet. "Tobias is not your friend!"

Amelia pulled back, eyes dark and heavy. "He's not? Yes, he is." She blinked hard. "I...I love him."

Clenching her jaw against the nausea that roiled in her gut, Penny leaned forward. "Amelia? Listen to me. I am your friend, your *best* friend. Tobias is forcing you to do this."

Amelia tugged away, tilting her head and narrowing her eyes. "No. No, I just feel... Oh, Tobias." She sank back into him. "Mmm."

Tobias grinned at Penny and raised his right hand, wrist facing her. The tip of a silver arrow peeked out from the top of his sleeve. "Penny, listen closely. Amelia is mine now. If you come after us..." He shrugged, the grin still smeared on his cocky face. "Well, you don't want your friend to get hurt, do you?"

"You're *already* hurting her, Tobias," Penny snarled.

"No, he's not," Amelia insisted. She caught Penny's eyes. "He loves me; he'd never hurt me. Just like Corey wouldn't hurt his friends. Tobias is loyal."

Penny stumbled back a step. *Corey? Corey is a prick. He stabbed...oh!* Amelia knew what was happening and was doing her best to fight it.

"Amelia," Penny said carefully. Her heart raced and the room buzzed, and Amelia's sleepy eyes filled Penny with dread. "Tell me what to do."

"Just…" Amelia blinked hard. "Just wait and see." She smothered a yawn. "It'll all be ok."

Amelia slumped. Penny reached out, but teetered to one side and missed. She stumbled and fell. Her face smacked the floor, and darkness clouded around her. The last thing she saw was Tobias, on his knees, slowly tipping to one side.

"Penny, wake up!"

Penny's eyes jolted open, and she reflexively gripped the dry fingers that touched her hand.

"Woah, don't snap them off." Cisco leaned down and grabbed Penny's hand, hauling her to her feet while awkwardly pressing the Hand of Glory into her palm. "Let's get you out of here."

"Amelia? Amelia!" Penny almost dropped the relic. "We need to go now!" Penny glanced at the flame and it sputtered, a glowing blue nub on the tip of a finger.

"The book?" she asked. Her mouth felt like she'd been sucking on the dead hand and she screwed up her face, trying to work moisture into it.

Cisco clasped Penny's hand, the dead limb wedged between them. "Felicity will have it. Come on."

Holding tightly to each other and to the hand, the two quickly found Felicity's bag and unzipped it. Penny fished out the folder of crisp, white paper and tucked it under her free arm. "Let's go!"

They ran for the exit, ignoring the patrons slumped over drinks and the bartender draped over the bar. "Did you check that everyone was ok?" Penny asked warily as Cisco pushed the door open.

"Yeah." Cisco moved aside for her to pass . "We had to

save one guy from drowning in his soup, and I don't think we'll be welcome back there again...but hey, we did it!"

The crisp night air took care of the last of Penny's fatigue, and Cisco blew out the guttering flame. Cisco pulled Penny down the street and around a corner.

"Amelia!" She spotted her friend sitting on the sidewalk, leaning against the glass window of a tobacco shop, Red's arm around her protectively. "Are you ok?"

Amelia looked up, and Penny's heart dropped. Lines of mascara dripped down her face, and she gave a shaky smile. "Those arrows really pack a punch," Amelia admitted, sniffling.

"Oh, hell." Penny sat beside her, and Red pulled away a little so Penny could wrap her friend in a hug.

"It's ok, really." Wiping her nose on her sleeve, Amelia chuckled hollowly. "I mean, it feels like I just went through the world's worst breakup, but I know it's not real, you know?" She reached out and squeezed Red's knee. "I know I still adore this big lug, and I know Tobias is a total dick. He's like...like a boyfriend who just beat the shit out of me. I know I need to walk away, but it still hurts."

"Someone needs the shit beat outta *them*," Red muttered.

"Can I help?" Paddy sauntered around a corner. "Paddy is nothin' if not loyal to his countrymen. Even the big'uns like yerself." He gave Red an appreciative grin.

"Paddy, you knew about the hand of glory." Penny felt hope catch in her chest. "What about Cupid arrows? Will it just keep wearing off until it's gone?"

Paddy sucked his lip, then pulled out a fat cigar—where from, Penny had no idea since the little leprechaun had no pockets. "Nope, can't say I know fer sure." When Penny's face fell, he rushed to reassure her. "I'm sure it'll be fine, me dear. Just wait out the worst of it, and don't be getting prodded with it again."

Penny leaned back against the glass, relief flooding her bones. Red wrapped Amelia in his arms again, holding her tightly.

"Just don't say I never took one for the team," Amelia said quietly. "Next time, Cisco gets to fall for Mr. Tall, Dark, and Deadly."

Cisco laughed. "Ok, it's a deal."

CHAPTER TWENTY-ONE

A gent Crenel tapped the paper in front of him. "So let me get this straight. You stole Academy property, almost lost a student to a Cupid spell, gave away your only lead into an organization working against all of society, and let them leave not only with unknown numbers of *Book of Thoth* copies, but also a Cupid's arrow in the hands of a cult leader?"

Penny shrank down in her seat even farther, face burning. "Not how I'd sell it, but yeah. That."

Though Cisco, Amelia, and Red were all crammed onto seats next to her, Crenel's tirade was addressed directly to her.

"Now, Stuart." Dean March looked at Agent Crenel over her glasses. "I wouldn't call neglecting to fill out requisition paperwork *stealing*. And you yourself said these children haven't yet been proven to be a credible threat. Surely if they were that dangerous, your operatives would have been able to move on them by now?"

Crenel's jaw pulsed. "We got word yesterday—yes,

while you were in there putting lives at risk—that your group of 'children' has been in contact with a terrorist organization." Crenel threw his hands up. "So, yes, I would say my organization is about ready to move in."

"No!" Penny sat bolt upright, blood draining from her face. "You can't! That bastard Tobias has those girls under a spell, and they don't know what they're doing!"

Crenel took a slow, painful breath and let it out the same way. He ran a hand through his hair, something he seemed to do a lot in Penny's presence. "This group they've made contact with...they're no amateurs." He avoided Penny's eyes. "We may have no choice."

"Oh, bullshit," Penny spat. "First you said you couldn't go in because they might be innocent. Now that you know they probably are, you're gonna lock them up? *Shoot* them?"

Crenel lifted his hands in defeat. "What would you have me do? Let them summon Dracula and set him loose on the people of Portland? Let hundreds of innocent people die instead?"

"No!" Penny clenched her fists and slammed them on the dean's desk. The dean raised an eyebrow but didn't otherwise comment. "I don't know! You're the professional —you figure it out."

"I thought I *had* figured out something," Crenel snapped. "I thought I'd figured out I could trust you to come to me first."

Suddenly realizing the source of his ire, Penny deflated. "Oh. That. Sorry."

"Sorry?" Incredulous, Crenel turned to Dean March. "She's sorry?"

"She did say that she was," the dean replied smoothly.

Penny swore she saw a hint of laughter in the dean's eyes. *Surely not.*

"I really am," she said, injecting a note of sincerity into her words. She did mean it. "I just got caught up with everything. I forgot."

Slack-jawed, Crenel stared at her for a minute. "That's it. It's official. I'm too old for this!" He stood and walked out of the room.

Penny dropped her head into her hands. "I really screwed this up, didn't I?"

"Hey, it wasn't just you," Cisco pointed out.

Penny shook her head. "It was. I promised him I'd keep him in the loop. And…" She didn't want to say the rest. "And I think I disappointed him."

"What, because you didn't ask his permission to go to dinner?" Amelia asked, skeptical.

"No." Penny looked down at her hands. "Because he knows I'm leaving."

"*What?*" Amelia screeched. "You're leaving?"

"Come on, Penny. You can't still be planning to quit! Not now." Cisco looked as surprised as Amelia. "Not after all we've been through."

Amelia turned on Cisco. "You *knew?*" She turned toward Penny, eyes glittering. "I can't believe you didn't tell me. I thought we were friends."

Penny reached out and tried to say something, but Amelia was gone.

"Fuck." Penny realized the dean was still watching them. "Uh, I mean fudge. Sorry."

"Boys, I think Penny and I need to have a little chat."

The dean shot a daggered glance at Cisco and Red, who quickly excused themselves.

"Do you think Agent Crenel will ever forgive me?" Penny asked in a small voice.

The dean smiled. "What for? You made your plans clear from the beginning. Stuart just...well, sometimes his expectations exceed reality."

"He plucked me from my home," Penny said, urgency tightening her voice. She had to make someone understood. "I never asked for that scholarship. I was happy in Larrabee, just me and Boots."

"You were happy, but were you content?" The dean watched Penny. Once sure she wouldn't get an answer from the girl, she sighed. "It's nobody's decision but yours, Penny. We can't force you to stay."

"I know." Of course, Penny knew. *So why does it feel like I'm betraying my friends?*

The dean slid a drawer open and plucked a sheet of paper off the top. She slid it across to Penny without speaking.

Penny scanned it quickly. *Please be aware that after the agreement is in effect, all students will need to re-sign admittance paperwork and accept the new terms.* "I don't understand." She handed the paper back. "What is this for?"

"Something I have been working against for some time, but I'm beginning to realize is necessary for the Academy and for the country." Dean March carefully put it away. "Mr. Blaisey and I have signed a formal agreement to become an official FBI training organization. I'm sure it won't change your mind, but I wanted to tell you just in case. Have a nice day, Penny."

Penny stood, taking the dismissal for what it was. "Thank you, Dean March."

———

Three weeks passed. Penny had repaired her friendship with Amelia by.... Well, by covering the elephant in the room with an invisibility cloak and feeding it cookies until it dropped into a food coma, too tired to knock anything over.

Both girls stepped carefully around the subject of the end of the semester. They discussed exams, but not vacation plans; they talked about the change of seasons, but not the return to the Academy.

Despite the fragile truce, a pit of sadness had opened inside of Penny. She would miss Amelia, and that didn't *begin* to describe how she felt about leaving Cisco behind.

Cisco wasn't as willing to let the matter drop as Amelia was. Every time he managed to corner Penny, he peppered her with questions. What would she do back in Australia? What would Boots do if Mythers were outlawed? As more people gained the ability to see the supernatural, how would she keep the serpent safe?

Penny responded by shutting down and refusing to answer. *I have a plan*, she told herself over and over.

But did she?

Of course, I bloody do, she reassured herself. *Take Boots home, move out to the bush, and turn into a miserly old spinster, alone in my misery.* Penny groaned and pulled the blanket over her head. "Amelia?" she called.

Instead of answering, Amelia yanked Penny's blanket away. "You aren't ready? Penny, we'll be late!"

Penny took in Amelia's padded coat and knitted scarf. "Oh, hell. Tell me it's not Thursday?"

"It's Thursday." Amelia turned and grabbed a pile of clothes off the floor. She tossed them on the bed. "You dress, I'll go sneak some breakfast out of the dining hall. Hurry!"

Penny leaped up and quickly threw on a shirt and jeans. She tossed on her leather jacket and snatched a scarf from Amelia's bed.

The door opened just as she was sliding on her good boots.

"Coffee and a croissant." Amelia held out a coffee thermos and a wrapped parcel. "You done?"

Penny nodded, stamping her second boot on before taking the proffered gifts. She flicked the paper napkin to one side and sank her teeth into the pastry.

"Mmm, yum!" She looked back at the lumpy bedspread. "You coming, Boots, or are you sleeping in?"

The lump wriggled, and Boots peeked out of a fold in the blanket. She tasted the air, then quickly slithered into the knapsack she had claimed as her own. Penny laughed and hefted it over her shoulder.

The two girls trotted downstairs. Instead of turning toward the classrooms, they headed toward the back of the school. Professor Marcus was already waiting, and most of the class was with her, hands shoved in pockets as they breathed mist into the air.

"Everyone here?" Professor Marcus called.

"Still waiting for Red," Cisco said. "He overslept."

"And Clive." Mara shook her head. "That boy would sleep through an earthquake. I bet his alarm is screaming in his ear, and he's totally oblivious."

"I'm not going to ask you how you know about his sleeping habits, Mara," Marcus gently admonished. "But I will remind you that the campus sickbay has contraceptive products free of charge for the safety of our students."

Mara mumbled something, her face red.

"I see those two made up after that paintball debacle," Penny murmured. Just then, the two missing boys appeared on the verandah.

"We're here!" Red grinned and tried to smooth down the hair that he clearly hadn't combed before leaving his room. "Sorry I was late. I had to drag old Clive here out of his bed. He sleeps like a dead horse!"

"Mmph." Clive was dressed, but only just. His belt hung loose, and the buttons on his shirt were crooked. He rubbed his eyes, then breathed on his hand and sniffed it. "Close enough."

"Ew." Mara turned her back on him, shuffling closer to Kathy.

"Ahem." Professor Marcus turned and gestured to the students. "Come on, before we miss it."

"Miss what?" Kathy asked. "Breakfast?"

The professor hushed her, and they walked silently down the length of the Academy lawn. When they reached the pine trees, she held up a hand.

"We must be quiet and move carefully, or we will scare them off." Ignoring the whispered questions, she moved farther into the dappled shadows.

Not long after, she stopped again, dropping to a kneel

and waving at the students to gather around. She pointed into a tiny clearing, where sunlight streamed through a break in the trees and sparkled on dewy cobwebs.

Penny crept closer, heart in her mouth. She put her bag down, and as if understanding the need for subtlety, Boots carefully nosed her way out. She could see the circle of tiny red mushrooms that enclosed the surreal sunbeam.

"Softly, now," the professor whispered.

Penny glanced over to her. The childlike wonder on the young teacher's face was touching. When Penny looked back, she realized why Katie Marcus was so enamored.

Two feet off the ground, flitting amongst the light and shadows, three fairies danced. Their tiny feet moved as though they stood on clouds while their wings fluttered in a quick blur. One held a yellow feather the same color as her dress and twirled it like a parasol.

As Penny's breath caught in her throat, Boots silently made her way to the middle of the circle. The fairies swooped down, seemingly delighted by their visitor. One alighted on Boot's head, twirling a pirouette, while another sat on her tail, clinging to it as it undulated through the grass. Their dresses sparkled, their colors softly echoing Boots' rainbow patterns.

The third fairy—the one with the feather—fluttered over to a spiderweb. She looped the web around and fastened it into a circle, then attached the feather. Wings slowing, she drifted down to drop the makeshift necklace around Boots' head.

"That's so beautiful." Kathy's voice broke the spell, and Penny looked at her. When she looked back the fairies were gone, the only evidence a satisfied snake wearing a feather necklace.

"Aww, Kathy!" Heddy admonished.

"It's ok," Professor Marcus said softly. "They only ever stay for a few moments."

"How did you find them?" Penny asked. She kept her voice hushed. Something about the atmosphere in the familiar Academy grounds had changed.

Marcus smiled. "I called them." She pointed to the ring of toadstools. "Some spores were shipped to me by a friend. I sprinkled them here last week, and they grew in a day. The fairies appeared in three. If you come down before the dew evaporates, you can see them; but never for long. They will give you a glimpse and then disappear."

The professor pointed to a branch overhead. Squinting up, Penny saw a camera nestled in a fork. "The cameras show they only reveal themselves if someone is watching."

"The Cottingley fairies only showed up when no one was looking," Jason said.

"What, you're a fairy expert?" Corey snorted.

Jason didn't rise to the bait. "You slept through Craster's class again?"

Professor Marcus stood. "It's true, the girls claimed that. But how would they have seen them? And why did their fairies never appear without them?"

"Because they were a hoax." Kathy brushed off her dress. "They admitted it."

"Ah, but it was a *successful* hoax." Marcus helped Heddy to her feet. "Real or not, people believed those photographs for years, which is why they exist today. Our task is to

AMY HOPKINS & MICHAEL ANDERLE

discover how their reality matches the beliefs and how it contradicts the perceptions at the time."

The class trudged back to the Academy, and Professor Marcus dismissed them. "Go and eat some breakfast. We will start class half an hour late to allow for that. Our topic will be classic fairies versus the Cottingley hoax, and comparing both to what we saw today."

Once in the dining room, Penny shed her coat and scarf, handing the latter to Amelia. "Thanks for the loaner. It was glass-cutting weather out there!"

Amelia waved it away. "Keep it. It looks way better on you."

Penny hesitated, then bundled the scarf up with her coat. She'd get Amelia a new one for Christmas. *Except I won't be here to give it to her.*

She hadn't booked a flight home yet, but school would break up just a few days before Christmas. As an un-enrolled student, Penny would no longer be welcome to stay in the Academy dorms.

Guilt tickled her, but she shook it off.

"You're thinking too hard," Amelia said. "I smell hot chocolate. You want one?"

"Oh, perfect. You sit, I'll grab it." Penny headed over to the counter.

"Still hungry?" Cook grabbed two plates. "I'll dish plates up for both of you."

Penny grinned. "Thanks, Cook. And two hot choco-lates, please?"

Balancing the hot, marshmallow-laden drinks and four pastries on a tray, Penny turned to head back to her table.

Agent Crenel was in her seat, blithely ignoring Amelia's

262

angry scowl. Boots curled on the table between them, her tail twitching nervously as her head swung between the two of them.

Penny sighed. *What now?* She looked around for Cisco and found him chatting with Jason and Heddy.

She detoured to their table. "There's a fox in the henhouse," she muttered to Cisco.

He looked up, confused. "A what in the who?"

Penny rolled her eyes. "A dingo in the chook house? There's a special-bloody-agent at our table, you dork."

Cisco flicked his eyes toward their usual spot in the dining hall. "Oh! Right." He tossed a quick apology at Heddy and Jason and followed Penny over to the FBI agent and his surly observer.

"Hey, Agent Crenel." Cisco threw himself into a chair next to Amelia, folding his arms. "'Sup?"

"Cisco. Penny." Crenel nodded at each of them.

"Agent Crenel." Penny greeted the agent cautiously, eyeing her friends.

Boots, unsure of the student tension in the air, gave a low hiss.

Silence dropped over the group. Penny tried to wait it out, carefully sipping her chocolate but leaving the pastries untouched. She soon broke, the scent of flaky pastry forcing her to surrender.

"All right. What the hell, you guys?" She eyeballed Cisco and Amelia.

Amelia turned her head just slightly so that she didn't have to meet Penny's eyes. "*He* should have told us you weren't staying."

"What? That was none of his business to start with."

Penny held up a warning finger. "And if *anyone* should have told you, it was me." She dropped the hand and pushed her plate away, her appetite suddenly gone.

"Yeah." Amelia kept her stony glare on the table. "You should have."

"Look, guys, I'm sorry." Penny met Amelia's eyes. "I should have come clean from the beginning. It's just...I've never had a friend like you. You took me under your wing so quickly. I didn't want you to start pulling away."

Amelia's mouth twitched downward and her chin trembled. "Oh, you big goose." She threw her arms around Penny. "I wouldn't have, you know that!"

Blinking away the burn in her eyes, Penny hugged her back, then extricated herself, reluctantly meeting Cisco's eyes. "Can we talk later?" She silently begged him to say yes, knowing that if she had to, she would pour her heart out while Crenel, Amelia, and half the bloody dining room watched.

"Sure." Cisco coughed to clear the sudden huskiness in his voice. "But we still don't know why he's here." He jabbed a thumb at the agent.

Crenel cleared his throat, looking awfully uncomfortable. "Right. Well, something has come up. It's...not pretty."

Penny leaned over to look at the folder he slapped on the table. Crenel glanced around to make sure no one was close. He tapped it and leaned closer, keeping his voice low.

"Your kids are wrapped up in something too big for them to handle," he said. "And it's about to blow up in their faces.

"What do you mean?" Penny eyed the folder, but it stayed closed.

"That East Coast group? Contact with them has made them persons of interest." Crenel pressed his lips together. "I shouldn't even be telling you this. They'll rake my ass over the coals, and Jessica... Well."

"You came to us for a reason," Amelia reminded him gently. "We can help, Agent Crenel. Just tell us what to do."

Crenel's eyes darted around the room again. "They're planning to summon a vampire. If they pull it off?" He lifted his hand and clicked his fingers. "Boom. They're done. Domestic terrorism charges, conspiracy, you name it."

"Well, shit." Cisco leaned back, gently thumping the table. "I'm assuming you think we can prevent that?"

Crenel shrugged. "Maybe. Either talk them down or kill whatever they summon before it can do any damage." Crenel's eyes dropped. "I don't know how much good it'll do, but it might gain them some leeway."

"How do we find them?" Penny asked. "I'm guessing they won't be meeting at Mark's any time soon."

Crenel appraised her. "So that's it? You'll do it, no hesitation?"

Bewildered, Penny looked at Cisco and Amelia. "Well, duh! These kids are under a freaking Cupid spell! We're not going to say no." The other two responded with silence, and Penny's resolve faltered. "Are we?"

"What?" Amelia jumped. "No! I was just wondering if a crossbow is better for vampire-slaying, or hand stakes. I mean, you can't sneak a crossbow into a nightclub."

Cisco shook his head. "Look, I really won't feel

comfortable unless we take even the smallest sized flamethrower the Academy has. You know, the little ones that fit in your hand?" He chewed his lip. "Stakes, holy-water bombs, and maybe some general weapons, just in case they pull something else at the last minute."

Their matter-of-fact acceptance of the situation brought the sting back to Penny's eyes. *These are good people,* she realized. *Really, honestly, good people. They'd go anywhere for me. Can I truly throw that away?*

Aloud, she asked, "What about Red?"

"Oh, he'll love this!" Amelia clapped her hands. "You know, every time we do something dangerous together, when we get back to the dorms, he—"

"Stop!" Cisco clapped his hands over his ears. "He's my roommate. I already hear too much."

"Wow, Amelia, that boy of yours is toe-ier than a Roman sandal." Penny ignored the puzzlement that crossed Crenel's face. "So? Where are they?"

Crenel laughed, shaking his head. "I'll be in touch as soon as we know, kid." He stood but paused before leaving. "You know, you folks have a good thing going here. It'll be a real shame to see it end."

Just like that, Penny's mood popped like a balloon.

Amelia reached out and rubbed her arm. "It's ok, hon. We'll make the best of it while we can, right?"

Penny had to clear her throat before answering. "Yeah. While we can."

Penny didn't catch up with Cisco until after their afternoon class. She chased after him in the hall, grabbing his elbow just before he disappeared around a corner. "Can we talk?"

He nodded. "Library?"

They walked there together, Penny itching with impatience under the silence. They found the library deserted, much to her relief.

Cisco sank back into a plush corner chair and gestured to the leather bench next to it.

Penny sat, leaving room for Boots to pull herself up onto the chair beside her a moment later.

Penny took a deep breath. "Cisco, I'm sorry I—"

Cisco spoke at the same time. "Penny, you know you don't owe me an—"

Penny laughed self-consciously. "Look, I'm sorry." She held up a hand to forestall his objection. "I know you don't need me to say it, but I'm going to anyway. I'm sorry." She looked down into her lap and fondled Boots' head, waiting for his response.

Cisco leaned forward and took her hand. "Penny, I know Boots has to come first. Those protestors? They scared me as much as they did you. I don't blame you for not wanting to stay."

Boots raised her head. Her beady black eyes stared right into Penny's soul. A forked tongue flicked out and Boots reached her head up to nudge Penny's cheek, pushing her head up so that Penny faced Cisco.

Cheeky shit. Penny gave the serpent one last daggered glance before reluctantly raising her eyes to meet Cisco's.

"I don't want to leave," she admitted. "But I don't know how to make it work if I stay."

"Maybe *you* don't." Cisco pulled back, dropping her hand. He smiled, though, a kind grin that made his eyes sparkle. "But with me, Amelia and Red on the case? We can totally figure this out!"

"It's not that easy. There's so much *stuff*, Cisco." Penny's face dropped. "The laws here are changing so much faster than back home. That law that passed? It means Boots is at risk. I wouldn't be able to live with myself if something happened to her here."

Boots roiled, raising her head to hiss angrily. Startled, Penny jerked back. "Woah, buddy. What's up your nose?"

Boots responded by rolling herself off the leather bench seat and up onto Cisco's lap. She nuzzled his chin, one sly eye on Penny as she did so.

Penny scowled. "Hey, it's you I'm trying to protect, fang-face. Behave, or I'll change my mind and make a nice pair of shoes out of you instead."

Cisco barked a laugh, quickly masked by a cough when Boots pulled back to glare at him. "That was how she got her name?"

Penny nodded warily. "She's a pain in the ass, really. Obstinate, foolhardy, and downright mean sometimes." She reached over to tweak the scaled tail still draped over the edge of her chair. Boots flicked it away hurriedly, burying her head in Cisco's neck in an all-too-obvious sign of manipulative affection. "But I still love her, even when she's acting like a complete drongo."

"Ah." Cisco carefully dislodged Boots from his neck, where she'd pushed all the way around to give Penny a haughty glare from his other shoulder. "Far be it from me to come between a girl and her snake. I don't want to get bitten—by either of you."

I'd only bite if you asked. Penny snapped her jaw shut, thankful the errant thought hadn't slipped out. *Where the hell did that come from?*

She stood with a nervous laugh. "I really have to go. I haven't finished my Folklore homework, and Craster's insisting it be done by tomorrow. See you around?"

Cisco leaned back and flashed her an easy grin. "Sure. See you around."

CHAPTER TWENTY-TWO

Days passed. The end of the first semester drew closer with each passing moment, as did the end of the year. Knots of anxiety clenched in Penny's gut each time she thought of Felicity and her friends.

She checked in with Agent Crenel daily. "They've gone underground," was all he could tell her. "As soon as I know something, I'll tell you." Still, he never disclosed even a hint of weariness at her questions; rather, his face etched deeper with worry with each passing day.

Penny blinked and shook her head, trying to bring her focus back to the fat textbook before her. The freshly-printed anthology of American Modern Myths had only arrived the week before, and Craster had allowed them this lesson to study for the upcoming exam.

The Mothman is, rather than a malicious entity in itself, a harbinger of news. It appears only when—

A rustle nearby pulled her attention away again, and she looked up to see Cisco thrusting a thin stack of papers at her.

"You forgot to pick yours up this morning," he explained sheepishly.

Penny scowled. The dean had called a meeting before classes to explain the new merger with the FBI. "It won't mean a great deal of difference for you yet," she explained. "But the paperwork you all signed on enrollment is unfortunately now void. Please return the new forms by the end of this semester." Her eyes had brushed over Penny as she spoke.

Penny hadn't grabbed a copy, and apparently, Cisco had noticed. *Of course, he had.* She shook her head, refusing, but Boots coolly slid up to gently take them in her mouth, then dropped them on the textbook.

Penny bared her teeth at the serpent and stuffed the papers in the back of her folder, ignoring Cisco's victorious smirk.

"Remember, students, chapters twelve through twenty-five will be our focus for the exam." A chorus of groans met Professor Craster's announcement. "The book is fascinating and thus easy to read for pure enjoyment, but I would advise you to pay particular attention to read those sections before the end of term."

"*So* enjoyable," Kathy groused. She flipped a page with an exaggerated sigh.

Heddy raised her hand. "Professor, is the exam content focused more on the evolution of the older myths, or the discovery and interpretations of—"

A knock at the door cut Heddy off as the professor hurried to open it.

Crenel stepped inside, eyes quickly alighting on Penny.

"Morning, Jim. I'm afraid I need to borrow Penny for a moment."

Craster nodded at Penny, who had already shoved her book and notebook into her bag. Rather than wait for Boots to make her way into her knapsack, she gestured for the snake to follow as she trotted to the door. It was only ten minutes until the end of class. Crenel would have waited if his summons wasn't time-sensitive.

Crenel led her to an office on the lower floor, a tiny study tucked away from the main passages of the school. Penny perched on the desk, Boots wrapped protectively over her shoulders while Crenel paced. The snake could taste Penny's anxiety.

"I haven't been entirely honest with you," Crenel started. He stopped and looked at her, then glanced away and started pacing again. "We've had an agent on the kids' tail for the last two weeks. She was trying to infiltrate the organization and get some information on what the East Coast team was planning."

"And?" Penny didn't chastise him for his silence. She knew that no matter how much she cared, he would always put his country first.

"She's gone silent." Crenel turned back to her, his eyes bright with worry. "We haven't heard from her in three days."

"Why are you pulling me in now?" Penny gripped Boots' tail, squeezing it. The snake didn't mind. She flicked her tongue at Penny's neck and squeezed tighter, the sensation a steady grip in a tumultuous sea of emotion. *He must know something, or I wouldn't be here now.*

Crenel dug in his pocket and took out his phone. He

tapped the screen, the glow reflecting on his face as he opened a new, darker screen. He passed it to Penny.

It was a text, an unsaved number with no prior history. It showed the current date at the top and a timestamp of only a half-hour earlier.

An image of a satellite shot was attached. It looked like an industrial park. Below it, a message read, **Red door 3 from end. send the kids, not the guns**.

Penny handed the phone back. "Your missing agent?" she guessed.

Crenel nodded. "No one else knows. I wanted to let you in first."

"So, where is it?" Penny asked impatiently. "Let's go!"

Crenel shook his head. "Kid, number one rule: never rush into a situation unprepared."

Penny frowned. "I thought the number one rule was 'always trust your team?'"

Crenel smirked. "I'm glad you're paying attention to my lessons."

Penny slid off the desk. "Your advice has been noted. I'll assemble my team, and we'll prepare."

For the first time in weeks, a genuine smile creased the face of the aging agent. "Your briefing is in twenty minutes."

"I don't understand why we can't tell the dean," Amelia said for the third time as she pulled her belt tight. "I mean, maybe she can help?"

Penny shook her head. "Crenel is already treading the

line between right and 'sanctioned.' He'd get his ass kicked if he brought her in." She blew out an anxious breath. "Where the hell are the boys?"

Right on cue, the dorm room door flew open. Cisco shuffled in dragging a duffle bag, Red behind him.

"I told you, get another bag," Red insisted. "That big lump of weaponry will have every damn eye in the city on us if you insist on dragging it with us."

"Red's right." Amelia hustled the boys inside and closed the door behind her. "What do you have in there?"

Cisco grinned, sheepishly. "Everything. Damn near it, anyway."

He hefted the bag onto Penny's bed and tipped it over. Out spilled two crossbows, a sword, three rolls of vampire stakes, two small flamethrowers, the hand of glory, a gold pocket watch, and an assortment of blades and guns.

"You're kidding, right?" Penny perched on the edge of the bed. "We can't carry all that!"

Cisco raised his hands in defeat. "Fine! Who cares that I spent all afternoon signing this stuff out?"

With some arguing—Red insisted on taking the sword despite the others voting against it three to one—they soon had the weapons pared down to what they could hide on their bodies, one crossbow, and the vampire kits.

The staff was a sticking point. "We can't hide it," Penny pointed out. "It's big and awkward, and a pain in the ass to carry. If we lose it…"

Cisco groaned. "You're right." He moved it to one side. "It's too big. And so is that sword, Red. I really don't see why we need it."

Red tossed the Arthurian legend on the bed in disgust.

"And what if it's not vampires, hey? Those eejits could be bringing all kinds of Mythers over!"

"Fine!" Penny threw her hands up in defeat. "Take the damn sword, but don't let anyone see it, and *don't* stab yourself!"

Red grinned and quickly belted on the leather sheath. "Aye, that's what a real man feels like." He swaggered across the room, almost clipping Boots on the head with the wrapped blade.

"Kill me now," Amelia moaned. "You know he thinks he's actually King Arthur when he's wearing that thing?"

"Are we ready?" Cisco asked.

"Just one more thing." Penny reached under her pillow and drew out the gift Crenel had left with her at the briefing. The lead arrow looked plain compared to its silver counterpart, but in her opinion, it was even more valuable. It was Felicity's ticket to freedom.

Amelia shook her head in wonder. "Who knew Cupid had two arrows?"

"Wikipedia," Red shot back. He grinned. "I looked it up earlier. It makes sense, though. What if he stuck himself with that silver one and fell in love with a hairy linebacker? He'd want a way to reverse the spell, wouldn't he?"

The four students filed out, Cisco carrying the bag over his shoulder, Penny with the arrow tucked in her belt. She turned to say farewell to Boots.

"I'm sorry we can't take you, dear." Boots hissed angrily and jabbed her tail toward the backpack Penny used to carry her around.

Penny shook her head. "Not this time. It's too dangerous."

Boots hissed again, then yanked the bag down.

"No!" Penny stood back, hands on hips. "Absolutely not."

Boots tightened her grip on the bag and awkwardly made her way to the door. She gave a sideways hiss at Penny on her way past.

"Boots!" Penny grabbed at the serpent's tail, only to be rewarded with an angry snap.

"She's as stubborn as you are, Penn." Amelia squatted to take the bag from Boots, then held it open for her to climb in. "Either she comes with us and we keep an eye on her, or she sneaks after us and gets into trouble on her own." With Boots safely inside, Amelia hoisted the bag over her shoulder. "Which would you prefer?"

"Remind me never to let you babysit my kids." Penny didn't offer to take the bag. *Let Amelia deal with a sore back for a change, you heavy beast of a snake.*

The team made their way downstairs, only for Cisco to freeze at the bottom. Penny pushed forward to see Dean March standing at the door. She gave a tight smile and opened it for them.

"Out for a stroll?" she asked primly.

"Uhh, yeah." Red tipped an imaginary hat. "Some fresh air, you know?"

"We're working on our Items Acquisitions assessment," Cisco added. "I've got permits for everything, I swear."

The dean nodded her head. "I know."

The four students exited the door under her piercing gaze. Penny stepped through last and looked up to see the dean's hand outstretched toward her. Dean March faltered.

"Good luck, Penny." She smiled, this time something real and heartfelt, if small. "I hope you can save her."

"You knew?" Penny asked in disbelief.

Dean March nodded. "My husband is a good man—and a good agent. He's terrible at keeping secrets, though."

The door shut before Penny had time to pick her jaw up off the ground.

"Husband?" Penny whispered. "Well, stone the flaming crows."

CHAPTER TWENTY-THREE

R ed crouched by the warehouse door. "Got it yet?"

"Shh!" Amelia twisted the lock pick one last time. "Got it."

"How do you know how to do that, anyway?" Penny asked.

Amelia winked but didn't answer. Instead, she turned to glare at Cisco. "I told you the Hand of Glory would be useless. There are probably a million locked doors in this place!"

Cisco pulled a face, then quietly slipped inside the building. Penny followed, blinking as her eyes adjusted to the low light.

Amelia waited for Red to pass, then let the door shut behind her.

The dim light was extinguished, leaving them in darkness.

"You were saying?" Cisco murmured.

Penny snapped her flashlight on. "Come on."

The narrow shaft of light illuminated an empty warehouse. Penny's stomach sank as she looked around.

"There!" Cisco nudged her, his own light pointing toward a door at the back.

Penny adjusted the backpack. She hadn't been able to resist Boots' apologetic head-butt as they'd climbed out of the car. Now, Boots watched over Penny's shoulder as they advanced toward the door.

Red pressed his back next to it, a stun gun clutched to his chest. Penny reached for the arrow, heart pounding. Amelia carefully tried the door handle. It turned, and the door swung smoothly open.

Opaque plastic sheets hung across a room, a flickering light behind them. A figure paced across the light, throwing shadows that writhed and twisted.

"This isn't you, Felicity. You're not a bad person! Tobias has done something to you."

The figure turned, one hand raised in a fist. "Not me? Then who is it?" This voice was guttural and angry. "Tobias has done nothing except show me the truth."

She turned on a heel again to pace to the other side of the room. "The truth? Is the truth that you're a monster?"

"Two people," Cisco said.

"Sounds like someone is on our side in there," Amelia said. "Was Crenel's agent a woman?"

"He didn't say." Penny strained to hear better. Something about both voices...she shook off her unease.

"Let's go." Red stepped forward, crouching. He pointed to Penny and Cisco, motioning for them to go around to the left.

Penny sidled to the edge of the curtain. The figure

paced away from her, the brown hair in a tight braid easily recognizable as Felicity's. Across from her, on the other side of the lantern, a woman sat on a chair, hands bound behind her back.

"YOU!" Felicity whirled and raised a hand toward Penny. "He said you'd come." Her hand shook, finger twitching on the trigger of a small handgun.

Oh, shit! Penny's breath caught in her throat.

"Easy, now." Cisco held out his own weapon—a small knife. He dropped it to the ground and held his palms up. "We're here to help you, Felicity."

Felicity backed up, eyes wide and frantic. "Lies. It's all lies. I don't need any help!" She whirled toward the bound figure. "I keep telling you, I'm fine!" she screeched.

"I know you love him, Felicity." Amelia's voice drew Felicity's attention, and the girl spun unsteadily toward her. "I know you do. I did, too. But it's a trick, Felicity." Amelia kept her voice low and soothing. "Tobias used it on me, too. He used a cupid's arrow, Felicity. Those feelings, that love you have for him? It feels so real…"

Penny crept forward, drawing the lead arrow from her belt and gripping it in her hand.

"So…real," Felicity murmured. She lowered the gun. "Feels so real."

"It's not real," Amelia crooned. "None of it's real. Felicity, you're a good person. You are. Tobias made you do those things. He tricked you with magic."

"Magic." Felicity took another step, foot dragging.

"You feeling a bit sleepy, lass?" Red asked cheerfully.

With that, Felicity collapsed. Red stepped up behind her, flicking a golden pocket watch in his hand.

Penny had to wrench her eyes away before she, too, was lost. "Where the hell did that come from?"

"It was in my pocket!" Red cracked up at his own joke. "But seriously, I saw it sitting next to the Hand and thought it might be just what we needed. Was I wrong?"

"Enough chatter," Cisco said. He nudged Felicity's unconscious form with his foot. "Let's do it."

Penny knelt and took Felicity's arm. She used the arrowhead to scratch it, drawing a thin line of blood to the surface of her pale skin. "Let's hope that works." She lowered Felicity to the ground. "Red, take her."

Penny stood and hurried over to Felicity's hostage. Boots was already tugging at the ropes, using her long fangs to loosen the bindings tying her hands together. Penny tugged them free and leaned around.

"You're gagged?" Penny watched, stunned, as Special Agent Karen Delouise undid the cloth tied around her mouth.

"Blech. It wasn't even clean." Delouise looked around. "Is she ok?"

Penny ignored the question, looking around the sparsely furnished room. "Where is the other woman?"

"It's just us." The agent stretched her arms out. "Everyone else has already gone."

"But she was talking to—"

"Herself." Delouise stood and walked over to the girl, crouching beside her unconscious form. "She knew something wasn't right. She was trying to fight it."

"I swear, that arrow had better work," Amelia growled. Her eyes were suspiciously bright.

"Aye, and if not?" Red leaned over. "Felicity, lass, it's

almost time to wake up. When you do, ye'll have a mighty craving for Twinkies, and ye'll have a healthy dose of disgust every time you think of that gobshite, Tobias. Now…" He snapped his fingers. "Wake up!"

Felicity's eyes fluttered open, lashes dark on her white face. "What...what happened?"

"How do you feel?" Penny asked.

The younger girl sat, shaking her head slowly. "I feel...like I've been in a dream. Like…" She looked around, and what little color left in her cheeks vanished. "Oh, God. What have I done?"

"You kept me alive, for a start." Agent Delouise helped Felicity to her feet. "I know you're hurting, kid, but we don't have time to deal with that now."

Felicity's eyes widened, and she gasped. "The summoning!" Her stomach growled loudly to punctuate her words, and she blushed. "Sorry. I'd *kill* for a Twinkie right now."

CHAPTER TWENTY-FOUR

They took Agent Delouise's car, although Penny regretted letting her drive. She clung to the door handle of the tiny vehicle, Cisco practically sitting on her lap next to Amelia and Red.

"They're doing it at the waterfront," Delouise explained as they screamed down Main Street. "At dusk."

Penny eyed the orange sky. "That doesn't leave us much time," she called.

The car screeched to a stop, and Penny peered out anxiously. They were still on Main, the traffic backed up three streets behind the edge of the Willamette River.

"Oh, no." Amelia pounded on the door. "We have to stop here. The bridge party will have traffic stopped for miles!"

"Bridge party?" Agent Delouise snapped. "That's today?"

"What the hell is a bridge party?" Penny demanded.

Delouise quickly explained that after a six-month upgrade, the Hawthorne Bridge was open to foot traffic for only a single night. The city had organized food trucks and street performers in celebration of the upgrade and expected thousands of locals to attend the event.

"That's why he chose here," Felicity admitted quietly. She twisted around in the front seat to look back at Penny. "He wants to set the vampire loose here, during the festival."

Delouise leaned on the horn. Then, seeing no break in the traffic, she slammed the car into reverse.

She maneuvered out of her spot in traffic, heedless of the horns blasting around her, and drove into a side street, then up onto a sidewalk.

"You can't park here!" Cisco opened the door and tumbled out. He pointed at the towering building next to them. "You've just illegally parked at a courthouse."

"It's an immigration court. They don't deal with traffic offenses." Agent Delouise winked, then popped the trunk of her car. She started tossing things to Cisco to hand out.

"Holy-water grenades. Even if it's not a vamp, it'll do damage. Bullets… Oh, wait, I'm not giving you a gun." She ignored Red's disappointed grunt. "Solar flares, stakes and —you've got stakes? Give those back, then."

Penny rolled her shoulders under the weight of the added weapons. "I can't carry all this," she admitted.

"What's in the bag?" Agent Delouise frowned. "What-ever it is, princess, you don't need it."

Penny lifted an eyebrow. "Boots?" she called.

Agent Delouise started when the bag wriggled and Boots raised her head. The serpent gave her a toothy smile.

"Oh. Sorry, I didn't know. Can she help?"

Penny nodded. She didn't know what Boots was

capable of but she knew her friend would have her back, no matter what.

"Let's do this."

As they ran toward the bridge, the crowd grew. Penny desperately searched for any hint of danger, but her senses were flooded by the bright lights and loud music, mingled with the dull roar of traffic and the honking of boats below.

Behind her, the raucous call of bagpipes grew until the musician whizzed past, balancing on a unicycle as he played.

"Where are they?" she yelled, struggling to make herself heard over the cacophony. Cisco looked as frustrated as she felt.

"Tobias said the waterfront," Felicity pointed to the edge of the bridge. "He'll need a quiet spot to cast the spell."

Penny tugged on Cisco's arm, and he hollered for the others. They backed away from the crowd, clustered together so they didn't get separated. Spying a narrow flight of steps to the street below the bridge, Penny darted down and looked around. "Nothing!" She cursed, turning to Felicity in desperation. "He didn't say where?"

Felicity's big eyes filled. "I swear, he didn't. I don't think he even knew. He was just going to find a quiet spot on the waterfront to summon the vampire. That was all he told us."

"Why does he need to be on the waterfront?" Penny asked. That didn't make sense. Vampires didn't need water.

Boots jostled in the bag, and Penny slid it off her shoulder. She set it down, allowing Boots to get out and stretch.

"Look, I think we should split up. We can go in groups of three—one upriver, one down."

"That's good in theory." Cisco ran his eyes over the water. "But what if he's on the other side of the river? We could be miles off course."

Boots nudged Penny's foot. "Not now, Boots. Look, I know it's not a perfect plan, but it's all we've got. We can do this, or we can stick together and only cover half the ground."

A sharp tug on the cuff of Penny's pants made her look down. Boots pulled harder, undulating her body backward as she yanked at Penny's leg. "Or we could follow the snake."

"Anybody got a better idea?" Delouise asked. Without waiting for an answer, she headed off. "Let's hope the rainbow here leads us to our pot of gold."

Penny spotted a tall figure through the trees. He pushed back his hood and looked out at the small group before him. "Tonight is a momentous occasion!"

Tobias's voice rang out clear in the night. Penny couldn't resist a glance at Felicity. The girl's eyes burned with hatred.

Guess the arrow did its job, then. She turned her attention back to Tobias.

"The world will know who we are. They will know—"

A flash at the corner of her eye distracted Penny for the briefest of moments. She didn't see Tobias fall. Agent Delouise stepped out of the trees, looking down on the convulsing pile. The dozen watchers scrambled to their feet and she raised a second hand, this one pointing a gun at them.

"Steady, kids." Delouise fished a silver arrow from Tobias's sleeve and held it up. Then she snapped it in half.

As one, the small crowd stepped back. Girls clutched their heads, shaking them in bewilderment. The boys blinked, confused. None rushed to the rescue of their leader.

Penny rushed forward as Agent Delouise flipped the limp Tobias onto his stomach. She snapped a cuff around his wrist as he stirred and began to laugh.

"You're too late," he gasped. He lifted his eyes to Penny, a brightly rigid grin shining out below manic eyes. "Too late!"

"You set a vampire loose on those people?" Penny hissed. "How could you, you piece of shit?"

Tobias laughed even harder. "No! Are you daft?" He suddenly sobered, though the grin didn't fade. "That spell they gave me had so much more power than that? Why vampires? Did they think I was too weak for anything bigger? That I couldn't do it?" Tobias's eyes rolled back as he dissolved into laughter again.

"Agent Delouise?" Penny stepped back as the ground beneath her trembled. "What's going on?"

"I don't know." That admission sent a chill into Penny's bones.

Boots slithered carefully toward the water's edge, her tongue flickering in and out as she tasted the air. Then, with a sudden, coiling spring too fast to comprehend, she shot through the air, slamming into Penny's chest and sending her sprawling on the ground. "Boots? What the—"

Something rose, blocking the lights from the other side of the water. Penny felt it more than saw it—a creature so immense that when it moved, the world moved with it. Someone screamed.

An inhuman screech bellowed through the air, and a long, black limb slammed into the ground, leaving a gash in the grass bigger than a man. It hit right where Penny had been standing a moment earlier.

The limb rose again to reveal lines of suckers attached to the bottom. The tentacle wrapped around a tree, pulling it free from the ground and then letting it fall.

The beast rose, and its bulbous head and sharp beak flopped onto the riverbank.

Tobias's laughter rang out again. "It's a Kraken," he wheezed. "I summoned a goddamn Kraken. Take *that*, bitches!"

Penny dove to one side as another attack came. Nearby, the revelers on the bridge had begun to notice. Screams rang out, pulling the Kraken's attention.

Penny watched the beast turn, heart in her mouth. "We can't let it go!"

"It doesn't have a bloody steering wheel!" Red yelled. "What do you want us to do?"

Penny grabbed at her belt. *Holy water. Stakes. Crosses. Ah! Gotcha!* She drew out a silver throwing dagger and hurled it at the Kraken. It bounced off the rubbery skin harmlessly. "Dammit!"

Agent Delouise lifted her gun and fired three rounds at

the beast. It stopped and swung its head slowly back. "Shit. Maybe shouldn't have done that."

"Cisco!" Penny yelled. "Amelia, Red!" She waved an arm, and with worried glances behind them, her friends ran to her. To her relief, Boots also appeared. She'd lost sight of the snake in the chaos.

"This is out of control," Cisco gasped. The monster flailed and smashed down another tentacle, tearing the branches off one side of a pine tree.

Still lying prone, Tobias yelled. "It's over, suckers! The End Times are here, and they will destroy you!"

"We brought half the goddamn weapons room with us," Penny reminded them. "And we've been training for this." She grabbed Cisco's backpack and held it upside down, shaking it. Weapons scattered on the ground as she looked for anything that might help.

"Solar flares. That'll distract it, maybe blind it. Grenades—I'll take one. Cisco, crossbow?"

Cisco passed her the weapon. Penny pulled it out and grabbed a bolt, then tossed the bow aside and darted back into the bag.

"Duct tape?" Amelia asked incredulously when Penny resurfaced. "What, are you gonna tie the Kraken up and stick it in the trunk?"

Penny ignored her. She used the tape to bind the grenade to the bolt. It would no longer fit in the crossbow, but it would suit her purpose perfectly. She thrust it through her belt.

"Red, you were the best in sword practice. You think you can lower our threat from an eight to a seven?"

Red lifted the sword in a white-knuckled grip. "This

seemed like a good idea back at the Academy, Penny, but I don't think I can cut through that." He jerked his head at the Kraken.

"Of course, you can. Just get me close." Penny palmed a wooden stake in one hand, a holy water grenade in the other. "Boots? Stay." She dropped to a knee. "I mean it. I might need you to come rescue me."

The snake hissed gently and slowly dipped her head in agreement. Penny patted her briskly, then stood. She looked at Red. "Do your best to take off a limb or two."

"What do we do?" Amelia asked.

Penny grinned. "Flambé that sucker." She unclipped the small flamethrower from her belt and threw it to Cisco. "See you soon!"

"This isn't how you trust a team, you know!" Cisco yelled.

Penny yelled back, "Yes, it is! I'm trusting you to have my back!" To Agent Delouise, she yelled, "Shoot it again!"

Two more shots rang out. Whatever Delouise said in response was drowned out by another almighty screech as two tentacles rose, then slammed down. Penny dove to the left, Delouise to the right. As the slimy limb began to pull back, Penny slipped a dagger from her vampire kit and plunged it into the rubbery flesh.

The creature shrieked again.

The tentacle jerked and writhed for a moment before slipping back into the river but another whipped out, wrapping around Penny's waist and yanking her into the air.

She sucked in a breath a moment before icy water closed around her, bubbles rushing past as the beast shook her. Penny's stomach lurched and she was in the air again, the rubbery suckers against her skin pressing tighter by the second.

Penny plunged the knife into the thick muscles around her waist and the Kraken flinched. Toward the shore, flames glowed and the Kraken screamed, its grip loosening on Penny as it turned to the new threat.

Penny held on, wrapping her arms around the tentacle as it rose higher. Securing her legs, she loosened her grip a little and began to slide.

It was a slow process. Twice, the Kraken dumped her in the water before lifting the limb again, but even in the midst of almost drowning, falling, and being crushed against the riverbank, Penny knew the creature wasn't paying attention to her.

Flares went off, making the Kraken reel and screech. The smell of burnt oil permeated the air, and once Penny saw a tentacle swing past missing its tip. "Go, Red!"

It was crunch time. Water lapped at her waist, and the limb she grabbed had grown too wide to wrap her arms around securely. Twisting, Penny saw the black orbs and gaping beak of the creature.

"Steady," she said, mostly to herself. She twisted her body, holding on with one arm and yanking the grenade-stake from her weapons belt. She held it up, wavering as the Kraken twitched and screamed.

The limb beneath her tensed. *No! Don't move yet!* It was now or never. Ripping the pin out with her teeth, Penny hissed out a fast breath, then threw. Her feet lost purchase as the beast flung the tentacle she stood on toward the shore.

Her hands slipped, unable to grip the smooth, rubbery flesh. She plunged into the water, struggled to the surface under the weight of her wet clothes, then sank again.

Her arms flailed, pushing her back up to the roiling surface to gasp for air.

A shadow crossed over Penny, blocking the light. An explosion of bubbles threw her back down before an enormous, writhing weight slammed into her, trapping her under the water.

It had worked, she realized, even as a mess of suckers and limbs closed around her. The Kraken fell. *It worked!*

Penny's lungs strained. Her ears buzzed as her body screamed and finally let out the last of her precious air in a rush of bubbles.

The darkness closed around her as a final thought drifted through her mind. *I don't want to go home.*

CHAPTER TWENTY-FIVE

Penny came to, coughing dank water into a puddle on the sand. The pulsing in her head took up a rhythmic beat.

"Pull us up!" The scream beside her seemed distant, then she rose into the air.

Penny wondered if she had died and this was her passage into the afterlife.

Does it have to be so noisy? The crisp, pulsing beat grew louder and made Penny think of that movie, the one where everyone was at war, and a chopper had come to collect the injured.

"Let's go!"

Movement clutched at her gut.

Wait. That is *a chopper.* She tried to ask what was going on, but the words came out as a garbled moan.

"Kid?" She opened her eyes to find a helmeted face peering into hers. "She's alive!" The face disappeared, and darkness fluttered back in. As she drifted off, she imagined the voice again. "Does anyone know how to get the snake to fill up the river again?"

Penny missed final exam week and had to request extensions on all her assignments, all of which were approved without question.

Her recovery from near-drowning came at a miraculous rate, but the buzz around the mission had rocked her mind and scattered her concentration for weeks.

None of it, though, came close to the shock and awe she felt when viewing the news footage.

A journalist en route to film some feel-good shots of the bridge festival from overhead had covered it all from a helicopter—the giant squid breaking the water's surface, Penny's capture and eventual attack, and the unbelievable act that had saved her life.

Boots had swallowed the river.

More than the epic battle against a mythological horror, the city of Portland had been awed and enamored with the video of the rainbow-colored serpent lying along the now-dry Willamette River, swollen to the size of the channel and bloated with water as it sucked away the deadly river that threatened to drown Penny.

When the journalist had seen a dim circle of light peeking out from between two limp tentacles, he'd thought it was nothing. The trio on the riverbank waving their arms and pointing at it? Probably just excited about the giant squid.

However, the call over the chopper radio had given that

tiny light all new significance. "There's a girl down there," said the voice, apparently someone from the FBI.

Sensing the scoop of the century, the journalist and his pilot had landed in the middle of the Willamette. If *that* didn't get them a Pulitzer, then the rescue of the woman who had saved Portland certainly would.

When she'd finished watching the footage on her phone for about the ninetieth time, Penny reached out to scratch Boots' back. "I'm glad they didn't see you leave," Penny mused.

After the chopper had left, Boots had opened her giant mouth. The footage showed the river swelling as the serpent shrank.

As far as the people of Portland knew, Boots had swum off to some magical land.

Penny tapped the completed assignment in front of her. It was titled *The Kraken* and detailed the history of the monster, and contained a log of events related to her acquisition of one of its suckers, harvested and given to her by Cisco from the limb Red had sliced off during the fight.

The library door swung open, and Cisco, Red, and Amelia piled in. "Are you done?" Amelia asked. "I know you said you needed this week to finish your assignments, but come on! We haven't celebrated yet!"

"You look pretty done to me, Penny." Red picked up the assignment and flicked through the pages. "Is that your last one?"

Penny lifted her hand and waggled it. "Just one more thing to do," she explained.

The door opened again and Dean March strode in, two

sheets of paper in her hand. "On my desk by five p.m., please."

Penny took the papers, grinning. "Of course, Dean March."

"What's that?" Cisco leaned over to peek at the paperwork. His eyes widened, and his smile grew. "Penny, are you..."

"What is it?" Red asked, stepping back as Amelia slid past him.

"Enrollment forms!" Amelia screeched. She threw her arms around Penny. "You're staying!"

Penny hugged her back, meeting Cisco's eyes over her friend's shoulder. "Yeah. I'm staying."

THE END

Book two in the series, Werewolves and Wendigo is now available as a pre-order at Amazon.com.

Does a werewolf's fur match his natural hair color?

I think I'm about to find out. Boots and I are back at the Academy, with a few changes — we're now officially in training to be Special Agents, and that means we get to go on super secret missions.

Something is on the hunt. I can feel it in my bones. Except, the evidence doesn't add up.

It's not like I don't have enough to do. I need a job —

someone has to pay for Boots's newfound love of lattes and pastries. And of course, classes are even more grueling than ever. And then there's Red's weird behavior…

With Boots at my side I'm ready to plunge into a new semester. Let's just hope we make it out alive.

Pre-order Now at Amazon

AUTHOR NOTES - AMY HOPKINS

OCTOBER 19, 2019

If you read the dedication (everyone reads that, right?), you'll know where Penny came from.

As authors, we're always told no to self-insert, that writing your own ass into a book is the height of egotism, that books based on the people who wrote them are pretentious.

Fuck those people.

Except... Penny isn't really based on me. She's kind of an amalgamation of all the Aussie women I know. All the friends I've had, all the women I've looked up to. She is born of the white sand of Airlie, the dripping leaves in Paluma, the slick stones of Paronella, the long, winding mindfuck of the Bruce when you left at 4am, the sun is setting right in your eyes, and home is still a few hours away.

None of those are the globally known places of Australia. They're not Bondi or the Opera House, Uluru or sexy Melbourne. They're the places I remember from years ago, places that will probably look a lot smaller when I finally go back.

Mike told me to stop pretending. Stop pretending I'm not an Aussie girl, that I don't live in a small town, that I know how to walk in stilettos and rock a miniskirt. I don't. I wear jeans and t-shirts, my hairdresser knows the drill (I don't care as long as I can put it in a ponytail), my only shoes are sneakers, gumboots, work boots and a single pair of sandals for 'going out'. My friends are all the same. We're practical, sensible, and our adventures are on beaches and mountains, not nightclubs and fashion strips. I love reading about those things, but they're not *me*.

I was scared to do that. MY life? It's pretty chill, and I love it, but it doesn't make for riveting reading. Michael assured me otherwise. With the right setting, the right cast, my small town Aussie girl would shine.

I think she did. Penny isn't a character in a book. Not anymore. By about the second page, she was *real*, living, breathing, and sassing me right from the page.

(That's my recollection of events, anyway. Michael's version *might* be more along the lines of "I dunno, I said some stuff, she said some stuff, I said try write an Aussie character." I may have read a little more into it, but you get the idea.)

- A. H.

P.S. Screw Dora. I got all the way to final edits before someone pointed out that Boots, Diego (Cisco's original name) and Backpack are all Dora the Explorer characters. For the sake of my readers and to save them from the relentless torture of having the backpack song stuck in their head, I changed Diego to Cisco.

I'm still salty.

AUTHOR NOTES - MICHAEL ANDERLE

OCTOBER 24, 2019

Thank you for reading this book and following Amy and Jace on these crazy adventures when the Veil is torn asunder!

A very short bit about me. I'm just under four years old as a releasing author. My first book (*Death Becomes Her – The Kurtherian Gambit* 01) was released on November 2, 2015. Since then, I've written dozens of books and been a collaborator on dozens of series. Along the way, I built a fairly large Indie Publishing company.

To that end, I met Amy Hopkins when she worked on the Age of Magic with CM Raymond and LE Barbant. I'm not sure how the three of them met, but they have a great relationship. Fast forward, and I was minding my own damned business when Amy and Jace interrupted my very important meeting (read this as "I was probably tacking a nap because of jetlag.")

The one important aspect of Amy I knew about was her biting Aussie humor. I never know what might come out of her mouth (or fingers since we communicate via ZOOM or Slack messaging mostly), and I felt she should let loose and be her in these books.

I thought, if there is someone who is scathingly truthful and funny, it's her.

(CM Simpson as well, but she is also an Australian. So it makes total sense that Amy and co. are cornering the market on this type of writing and humor.)

So, when I was talking with her, I was encouraging Amy to allow her inner snark to reign supreme. Then I realized exactly who I was talking to.

Perhaps, I thought, I should suggest a bit of restraint.

So, it's my fault if you are easily offended. Nothing I can do about it at this point, but I hope you aren't ;-)

So, sit back, grab your e-reader of choice, and enjoy these stories. Amy and Jace are sure to entertain ;-)

Ad Aeternitatem,

Michael Anderle

CONNECT WITH THE AUTHORS

Amy Hopkins Social
Website:
https://amyhopkinsauthor.com

Facebook:
https://www.facebook.com/thespellscribe

Michael Anderle Social
Website:
http://www.lmbpn.com

Email List:
http://lmbpn.com/email/

Facebook:
www.facebook.com/TheKurtherianGambitBooks/

www.ingramcontent.com/pod-product-compliance
Lightning Source LLC
Chambersburg PA
CBHW031622100726
47898CB00006B/1911